The Dark Journey

OTHER BOOKS BY

Julian Green

∽

THE CLOSED GARDEN

AVARICE HOUSE

THE PILGRIM ON THE EARTH

SUITE ANGLAISE

∽

THE
DARK
JOURNEY

By Julian Green

Translated from the French by
Vyvyan Holland

Harper & Brothers Publishers
New York *and* London
MCMXXIX

c 19

The Dark Journey

Copyright, 1929, by Harper & Brothers

Printed in the U. S. A.

FIRST PRINTING, AUGUST, 1929
SECOND PRINTING, AUGUST, 1929
THIRD PRINTING, AUGUST, 1929
FOURTH PRINTING, AUGUST, 1929
FIFTH PRINTING, AUGUST, 1929
SIXTH PRINTING, AUGUST, 1929
SEVENTH PRINTING, AUGUST, 1929
EIGHTH PRINTING, AUGUST, 1929
NINTH PRINTING, AUGUST, 1929

H-D

Part One

Chapter One

ON REACHING the railway footbridge he paused and reflected: "Why should I hurry? I shall be too early in any case. It can't be more than half past five. I think I'll go to the café and wait for half an hour. And then what?"

He uttered the last words aloud, and then shook his head in a gesture of negation, as though he did not want to hear the answer to the question he asked himself. He stood for a moment without moving, his head bowed and his hand on the iron hand-rail, then he slowly mounted the steps and leaned his elbows on the parapet of the bridge. From this position he could see the station, three hundred yards down the line, a dull little brick building, beyond which ran a long avenue of plane trees leading from the station to the town. Here and there stood middle-class slate-roofed villas, each with its garden packed with lawns and shrubbery. Two endless rows of lime trees rose to the left and right of the railway track, as though mounting guard over it.

He cast his eyes over the various features of this landscape and, pulling out his watch, he stared at it for a long time with the rapt air of a man who does one thing while thinking of another. He was still young, but there was about him something of that blighted and bitter look that one so often sees in those whose early years have been a perpetual struggle. His face was full and sallow, with the flaccid skin that foreshadows hanging cheeks later on, and those deep lines that trace a kind of perpetual grin around the mouth at the age of forty. His light-gray eyes had a trick of staring fixedly at whatever they were observing. His large fleshy nose and thick lips gave the impression of a man of not much will-power, but one who clung tenaciously to his comfort and his habits and was capable of considerable firm-ness when they were threatened. He was very care-fully shaved, very sprucely clad in dark gray with a black tie and, as a touch of frivolity, a mauve silk handkerchief which stuck half out of the upper pocket of his jacket.

For some moments he remained motionless, anxious not to break the deep silence reigning around him. The short autumn afternoon was drawing to its close and a red glow began to appear in the sky.

At length he straightened himself and struck the parapet with his fist, as one whose meditation is ended, and continuing on his way he went down the steps and reached the road on the other side of the railway. Though tall and sturdy, he walked with his head bowed and his shoulders slightly bent as if ashamed of his height and strength. He rubbed his hands together and walked with the quick, precise step which sometimes denotes an absorbing train of thought, as though something of the soul's preoccupations pass into the body and impart their rhythm to it.

Proceeding thus, he arrived at the gate of a large property surrounded by majestic trees. A wide oval lawn, intersected by winding pathways, stretched to the foot of a kind of small manor-house conceived in the wretched style of forty years ago. Fountains, rockeries, and heraldic flower-beds succeeded in conveying an impression of great wealth at the disposal of great pretensions. A little enameled plate fixed to the gate bore in slanting capitals the two words, *"MON IDÉE."*

Such as it was, this house held his attention for a moment and wrung a sigh from him. Then he turned reluctantly and retraced his steps towards the foot-bridge. Once more he consulted his watch and, the problem of what to do to pass the time suddenly changing to panic lest he should be late, he began to run.

The lamps were lighting up one by one as he entered the main street of the town. He was panting a little from his exertions, and in spite of the cool breeze he carried his hat in his hand. When he was level with the church he took a little side-turning to the right and entered a café from which a yellow light shone upon the pavement before it. His gaze wandered round the room and he noted with satisfaction that he was alone; there was not even a waiter there. He strode quickly toward a table which filled half of one of the windows, and sat down. His entry had been so unobtrusive that it had passed unnoticed

and he had to rap on the white marble with his
knuckles to draw attention to himself.

Seated before a glass of black coffee, the smell and
taste of which were mingled in his mind with, among
many other things, the sad and commonplace adventure which he pursued from week to week, he gazed
out of the window with an eagerness which constant
habit had been unable to allay. Across the road two
shops faced the café. One of them, a baker's shop,
held no interest for him and he only gave it a very
casual glance; its window contained nothing but two
long quartern loaves, standing on end against a
copper rail in such a manner as to attract the attention of any stray customers, though it seemed as if
no more customers were expected at that hour, for
the gas-jet hanging from the ceiling was turned
down to a faint blue flame. The other shop, painted
almond-green, flared out into the night with a hard
strong light that seemed to envelop the whole street.
On the glass door appeared a diagonal inscription in
large letters informing all and sundry that the
Widow Ernest Brod, laundress (rough or fine work
undertaken), was the proprietress of the establish-
ment; and, in confirmation, five or six dress shirts
arranged in the window caught the attention of the
passer-by with their dazzling surface of newly-
starched linen. A heavy curtain hanging from a rod
surrounded this display with its white folds and hid
the interior of the shop, but a continuous murmur
bore witness to the activity within. From time to
time a head appeared abruptly above the curtain and

glanced rapidly up and down the street. Then the man started, as though some one had called him by name. Once the laundry door opened suddenly and he heard a shrill voice scream something out, and an answering laugh. The sound of this coming unexpectedly to his ears made him start; the blood mounted to his cheeks and he pressed his forehead against the window in his eagerness to see into the back of the shop, but everything became blurred before his eyes. He saw nothing but a sheet hanging from a line, which irritated him, and then a woman's arm, bare from elbow to wrist, came out and shut the door again.

He stopped looking at the shop and bowed his head. All the tension in his face gave way to a great bitterness which seemed to age it. With a weary sigh he rapped on the table, placed a few coins by his half-empty glass, and rose. The black clock hanging on the wall struck six. At the same moment the waiter appeared. He was an anæmic young man with shifty eyes. He looked at the clock and smiled knowingly when he recognized the customer striding up and down the café.

"They won't be long now," he said, as he swept the money into his pocket. "After six, or ten past, there's no holding them."

The man turned toward him and leaned against a table.

"You think so?" he asked.

And in a slightly hoarse, strained voice he added: "Perhaps you know them?"

"A bit," replied the waiter, with a smile and a shrug of his shoulders. "Monsieur has obviously not been long in these parts."

"Why do you say that?" returned the man, fretfully.

"Because here we all think that the best of them wouldn't be worth the trouble of drowning."

He began to giggle slyly, but, seeing that his jest fell flat, he stopped and went on in a serious, confidential voice, while wiping the table with his duster:

"It's a pity monsieur is in such a hurry. I might have told him a thing or two."

The man made a visible effort and drew a little nearer.

"Eh? What could you have told me?"

The waiter half sat on the edge of the table.

"If you're interested in the elder one," he began, with a kind of forced jollity, "the dark one, who delivers the washing in the town, I advise you to look out for yourself. You couldn't have a worse woman, or a more dishonest."

"And the others?" demanded the man, impatiently.

"The others? But there's only one other besides the proprietress and the little girl who helps to deliver the washing. It's not the little girl by any chance?" he asked, ready to burst out laughing.

"The little girl? Who said anything about the little girl? How do I know how many there are in there?"

The tone in which these words were uttered must

have surprised the waiter, for his eyes opened wide and for a moment he said nothing.

"If it's the other," he replied at last, "it's Angèle. Her mother died last year."

Any further confidences were interrupted by the man's departure on seeing some one leave the laundry.

Chapter Two

HE WAS once more in the street leading to the footbridge. The moon had not yet risen and it was very dark, but his eyes could trace the pale pattern made on the night by the girl's white blouse. He quickened his step and was soon so close to her that he could distinguish her bare neck and arms. She became aware of his nearness and stopped; he did likewise.

"You're walking too fast," she told him, crossly. "If anyone passed by now, tomorrow everyone would know that you had followed me. Let me go on ahead."

She waited for a short moment, doubtless waiting for a reply, but he said nothing, torn between the desire to approach her and the fear of annoying her. He heard her steps move off, but he did not follow her at once, letting the distance that separated them increase from moment to moment. It was difficult for him to give this proof of obedience. He told himself that he would count up to thirty before starting after her; then the sound of her footsteps began to diminish so rapidly that, seized with sudden anxiety, he asked himself whether she was not trying to run away or to hide herself, so as to make a fool of him. Yet still he did not move, and in the bitterness

10

of that moment he suddenly experienced the strange and unexpected pleasure that one sometimes finds in mastering one's impulses.

A strange thought came to him. What was to prevent him from turning back to the town and going home? By a whim of fancy not uncommon in melancholy people he saw himself doing the exact opposite of what he wanted to do, turning his back on this girl whose steps were at present dying away into the silence, and he imagined himself regaining his room whence sorrow and desire had driven him since morning. In the succession of these pictures there was something so imperative that they disconcerted him. Could he really abandon this adventure even if he wished to do so? But what made him think of anything so absurd? What a time for introspection when the girl was probably wondering why on earth he didn't come! It seemed to him as though his reason had left him for a moment and that it had returned abruptly; and he began to run, his heart tense with the fear that he had waited too long and that he would find her gone.

The sound of his feet striking the ground reverberated painfully through his head. He began to quicken his stride, and caught the girl up almost at once. She seemed angry with him.

"You deserve that I should have gone away," she said. "I told you the footbridge."

He was panting, his face close to hers. His searching gaze made out her white cheeks and her eyes in the gloom. His relief was so great that he laughed.

"I thought you *had* gone away," he explained in a breathless voice. "So I ran."

She shrugged her shoulders.

"You're so keen on meeting me, then?"

"Don't you know I am?" he pleaded, taking her fingers in his hand. "Won't you ever believe me?"

She freed her hand hastily and walked on a few steps.

"Don't let's stay here," she said. "I told you it was dangerous."

He followed her at once, and they both walked on in silence. When they were within sight of the footbridge he took her firmly by the hand again and said to her:

"What can I do to please you, to make you nice to me?"

Her voice was softer as she answered him:

"I don't know. It's for you to find that out."

The man fell silent. Suddenly he gripped her wrist a little harder.

"Tell me, why are you afraid of people in the street seeing you?"

"Good Lord! I don't want everyone to know that I meet men like this," she returned, swiftly.

"Meet me like this, you mean?" he asked, furiously.

"Yes, you."

"Other men don't matter, do they? I suppose you are ashamed of me."

The girl's eyes as she lifted them to him were full of amazement and anger. They had come to a street lamp and stopped abruptly, as though the great splash of light held them there.

"Other men?" she asked. "What do you mean?"

His self-assurance ebbed beneath the look she gave him, and he flushed.

"I mean that you don't want people to know that you see me."

"Why not?"

"That isn't for me to say. You know better than I do."

"How do I know what you've got in your head? Tell me why you're asking me all these questions or I'll go away now. I didn't come here to bicker with you."

He sighed, exasperated at his own tactlessness.

"Don't go away. I was in the wrong."

"So I should think," she observed, contemptuously. "If you brought me here only to make a scene, I promise you it will be the last time."

He bowed his head and said, gently:

"As you don't want anyone to see you, you mustn't stop here. Let's cross the bridge."

"And then where can we go?" she asked, not moving.

The man looked at her for a moment without answering, trying to guess how she would take his next words; a diffident smile hovered on his lips.

"I was going to suggest that you should dine with me," he said.

"Dine with you? Where?"

He waved his arm, indicating the country at the other side of the railroad.

"At Lorges."

"Certainly not. It's too far."

"We could take the train. It passes in five minutes."

But she shook her head.

"I tell you I won't dine with you."

"Why not?"

"That's my business."

"You're in a hurry to get back? You're going out this evening?"

"I'm not going to answer you," she replied in a temper. "A little while ago you said you wanted to speak to me. Say what you have to say and let me go."

"I can't talk to you here, under this lamp. Do let's cross the footbridge," he begged.

She let him take her hand, sighing to indicate that she was conferring an exceptional favor on him. Neither of them uttered a word until they were over the bridge.

"At any rate, you're not frightened of me?" he asked with forced joviality.

"No. You do ask funny questions."

"But even if you're not frightened, that doesn't mean that you like being with me, does it?"

In a lucid interval he realized that he was talking like this because he did not know what to say, and that the very stupidity of his words would make the

girl think him a fool. Why should he give her a
chance of saying: "No, I don't like being with
you"? He went on, quickly:

"Anyway, that doesn't matter. All I want is
that you should be pleased and happy, do you see?"

She made no reply.

"Look," he said, fumbling in his waistcoat pocket.
"I've brought you a present. I meant to give it to
you later, but since you are in such a hurry. . . .
It's a ring. See."

"A ring," she repeated, curiously. "Oh! isn't it
pretty!"

She tried to snatch it, but he had foreseen this
and held it firmly between his thumb and first finger.
It was a silver ring containing a minute sapphire.

"At least let me put it on for you," he said.

She made a little impatient grimace.

"All right. If you like."

He came closer and seized her hand, but he was
trembling so much that he could not manage to put
the ring on.

"I should have taken her arm and pressed her
against me," he told himself, horrified at his own
clumsiness. "Perhaps she would let me do it now.
Later she won't." And in sudden despair he said
to her:

"Take the ring and put it on, yourself."

Noting the sudden change in his voice, she raised
her eyes. No doubt she was moved to pity by the
distress in his face, which was no longer animated

even by desire and held nothing but misery and weariness.

"You're a funny man," she said, putting the ring on her little finger. "You behave as though it bored you to be with me."

He shrugged his shoulders despairingly.

"I see quite well that you will never love me," he said, at length.

She did not answer this. He was grateful to her for her silence, cruel perhaps, but less heart-breaking than words would have been. They recrossed the bridge and reached the outskirts of the town without exchanging another word. But as she was leaving him she smiled and said, "Tomorrow, then?"

A violent emotion, in which joy and sadness both took part, prevented him from thanking her, but his eyes followed her until she disappeared from view.

Chapter Three

Abоut half a mile away and at the very moment when this conversation was taking place, Madame George Londe was seated deep in thought before her mirror, waiting until it was time to go into the dining-room. Her entry was a ceremony which could not be performed without certain preparations, for Madame Londe, although no longer young, had lost none of the coquetry of twenty-five, and she would never have dreamt of appearing before her customers without lavishing the allurements of paint and powder upon her waning beauty.

She was sitting in a little room, tucked away between two doors, which seemed to serve as both a pantry and a dressing-room. Against the wall stood a white wood dresser, and beneath a gasolier hanging from the ceiling was a dressing-table painted bright pink. The last piece of furniture was provided with an oval mirror which for the last two or three minutes had reflected a face which was expressionless save for two watchful eyes.

What were this woman's thoughts? She seemed to be neither happy nor unhappy. Leaning slightly forward, her hands resting loosely on her hips, her attitude was that of a person watching a performance. Her tense gaze traveled from the narrow fore-

head framed in brown curls to the arrogant mouth
which was beginning to sag at the corners; a carefully studied smile corrected this fault in public.
Then, having finished with the face, the eyes fixed
themselves upon the eyes; it was as though they
were trying to probe deep into those black pupils
into which the gas cast two yellow points, so insistent and almost wicked was their examination.
From time to time the lids closed, heavy lids darkened by late nights, to open again inevitably on the
same gloomy and disapproving stare.

She was clad in black taffeta, her bust being com-
pressed into a bodice which left her neck and her
plump white forearms bare. A violet silk ribbon
tied in a bow round her neck contrived to conceal
her double chin. A ruby on her right hand and a
scrap of lace at her bosom gave a note of elegance to
her attire, but there were four or five ugly darns
in her dress that spoke of hard times and ill-dis-
guised penury. The pink of the dressing-table was
in strong contrast to all the melancholy poverty of
her worn-out clothes and her hard face; it was like
an over-bright passage of color in a somber painting
flung in, as it were, in derision, or to accentuate the
hardness of the rest of the picture or the brutal
energy of the composition.

A clock struck and roused Madame Londe from
her revery. She sat up and waited until seven
chimes had echoed in the silence of the little room
before rising. Then a smile lit up her features and
put sudden animation into her eyes. It was as

though the woman had been released from a spell
and, waking from a magic sleep, began to live again.
She smoothed her hair rapidly and, after a last
glance at the mirror, she made for the dining-room
door.

However, before going right in she bent down
before a screen near the door and applied an eye to
a spot where the red plush that covered it had been
torn away. In that way she could see who was in
the restaurant, as the stage-manager of the theater
studies the composition of the house through the hole
in the curtain. She remained thus for an appreci-
able time, her shoulders bowed, her legs slightly
bent, motionless as an animal about to spring. Now
and then, stifling a sigh, she put her head on one
side and then, not satisfied with what the left eye
saw, made her right eye also help in the examination by bringing it into line with the rent which she
widened by poking the end of her finger through it.

At length she left her post and entered the room.
Three strides separated her from a sort of cashier's
desk on a raised platform, behind which she sat every
evening. From this elevated position she dominated
a large room, long and narrow, in which two rows
of six tables stood against the walls. In the midst
of the space that lay between them there rose a fair-
sized oval table at which about a dozen customers
could sit, and beyond this table and the huge bunch
of autumn flowers that decorated it, Madame Londe
could see the street through the glass door on which
her name appeared, the wrong way round.

She folded her hands on the marble of the desk. For the moment the room was empty, but it was only seven o'clock and Madame Londe was there merely to give, in some sort, an example of punctuality to her customers. She knew too well that after a quarter past seven the meat and vegetables would be overdone. It is true that a notice on the wall gave the hours of meals, but that did not prevent people from arriving late. She heaved a deep sigh of impatience and murmured, "Why don't they come?" with the weary voice of the spectator who groans, "Why don't they begin?" before the lowered curtain. Yet she knew quite well that the same thing happened every evening. Every evening a few minutes past seven found her at her observation post behind the screen, a superstitious habit which she had formed one day that two customers had arrived without her knowledge, before she had made her entry. And now she had to while away the time for a quarter of an hour, a long quarter of an hour during which her idle hands kept shifting the little vase of flowers which stood on her desk and the big black book which she opened and shut with ever-increasing violence. She did not know how to wait. But since no one ever arrived less than a quarter of an hour late, why did she not alter the time of the evening meal?

Perhaps it was in answer to some such question that she kept slamming her account book on the marble. Was it necessary to add a quarter of an hour to a day which was already interminable? No!

She had declared that the restaurant would be open at midday and at seven, and at midday and at seven she was there, behind her cash desk.

At last she turned in exasperation toward the little room where she had finished her toilet, and called, "Grégoire!" A far-away voice answered, "Coming!" and there was the sound of a door opening somewhere.

"Bring up the soup!" ordered Madame Londe without waiting for the person she had called to come into the room. Having the soup brought up was the last resort, the method she employed when she felt that despair was getting the better of her. She imagined that that "brought the custom in," as she put it. For she had often noticed that the arrival of the waiter bearing the soup-tureen coincided with that of Monsieur Goncelin, the corn-chandler, who took all his meals there and who, as a rule, was the first to enter the restaurant. But she lived in terror that one day this magic rite would lose its efficacy, that her corn-chandler would arrive late, like all the others, and that she would have to abandon her faith in it. So she only had recourse to this measure when her patience was completely at an end.

She hid her face in her hands and, with her elbows on the desk, listened to the sound of footsteps moving to and fro in the kitchen. It was as though she were offering to Heaven the mortification of that last cruel moment of waiting. It was no good telling the waiter to hurry; the man asked nothing better

than to have done, so as to be able to get out into the
streets as quickly as possible. On the other hand,
Monsieur Goncelin would or would not be punctual,
and Madame Londe could do nothing about it. There
was nothing to do but to let things take their course.

Suddenly she pulled aside her hands and looked
up. The door had opened and some one had come
in. It was not the corn-chandler, it was a man she
had never seen before in her life and who had already removed his hat and was sitting down. She
could hardly believe her eyes, so certain was she
that Monsieur Goncelin would be the first to cross
the threshold of her restaurant, and, shaking with
surprise, she examined the stranger with such in-
tentness that he, in his turn, raised his eyes and
stared at Madame Londe as though he expected her
to address him. But she only flushed and remained
silent, and he lowered his head and unfolded his
napkin.

Madame Londe experienced some confusion at
having betrayed astonishment and she told herself
that this gentleman must think her very foolish, but
her discomposure had not been too great for her to
note a dozen details in the clothes and appearance
of the stranger, and her practiced provincial eye
had seen enough of him to furnish her with all sorts
of reflections. To retrieve her blunder she now
affected an air of indifference and changed the black
book and the flower-vase about. The man was well
enough turned out. Where did he come from? He
could not be a commercial traveler; she knew the

members of that profession too well to make any mistake about that. And then he had neither overcoat nor bag, yet he was certainly no one from the neighborhood, unless, and her heart gave a bound at the thought, unless he were a newcomer to Lorges or Chanteilles. Four years before, two gentlemen had come to settle down in this way at Chanteilles from Orléans, and she remembered that the first time she saw them in the restaurant she experienced the same emotion as this evening, for, by a strange accident, she had had no wind of their arrival, she who usually knew everything before anyone else. It is just as humiliating for women like Madame Londe, who are dominated by curiosity, to allow themselves to be taken unawares by any incident as for a lighthouse keeper to miss the passing of a ship.

At length, after some moments of vexed irritation which manifested itself by the movement of the little flower-vase from one side to the other, she gradually reverted to indignation against herself, and, folding her hands once more on the marble desk, she raised her head and gave the stranger a long stare. He was dressed in gray; a mauve handkerchief hung from the upper pocket of his jacket. From time to time he lowered his eyes and absently put little pieces of bread into his mouth. But in Madame Londe's eyes this man was not the dull traveler who comes and sits for half an hour at a restaurant table; he was some one about whom she knew nothing and who, consequently, was an object of exceptional interest. She looked upon him al-

most as an enemy, for the sole reason that he knew
a thousand things which she did not even suspect—
his name, his profession, his life, so many secrets
which she would have liked to have wrested from
him. His melancholy air and his disdainful silence
were a direct challenge to her curiosity. Many customers had, naturally, seated themselves at that
table at one time or another, and all of them, yes,
nearly all, had greeted her on entering with a smile
or a friendly word, even those that did not know
her. This had made it so much easier for her to
insinuate her questions in the course of any conversation that might take place between herself and the
customer when he came to the cash-desk to pay his
bill.

For that was the custom at the Restaurant Londe.
Although the waiter handed you your bill at the
end of your meal, as usual, you paid the amount
into the hands of the proprietress herself. This
custom possessed many advantages. Seated on high
on a sort of throne, Madame Londe found it easier
to smile, question, and, when there seemed to be
any chance of it, to beguile. She adopted a manner
that was both dignified and hypocritical, flung a
gracious word here and there as a queen might do,
and gave change with an air of bestowing charity.
All these spurious acts of generosity were seldom
without effect, for this woman, who was consumed
with the desire to please so as to acquire knowledge,
had marvelous intuition where human nature was
concerned. Without possessing the subtlety ordi-

narily attributed to her sex, she knew, nevertheless, what to say and what to do to procure the good graces of a customer and to extract from him a promise to come back. She directed all her efforts to securing this as soon as a newcomer made his appearance. She relied on moderate prices and certain treacherous facilities for payment to accomplish the rest. This was another difference, indeed, between her house and, for instance, Paris restaurants; one could open an account here, as at the grocer's or the chemist's; and Madame Londe knew, by twelve years of experience, that a man who owed her for ten, five, or even three meals was a lost man, that is to say a customer definitely acquired for the restaurant.

But how can you attract some one who does not even look at you and for whom, apparently, you seem not to exist? How dared he eat his bread without waiting for his soup? Idiot! What could he be thinking about? Didn't he see her? Or was he pretending not to see her? Couldn't he feel her eyes burning into his forehead and his shoulders? She had now recovered her presence of mind and tried to put into her face and into her eyes all the authority of which she was capable; but what was the use? This man's thoughts were clearly far away from the Restaurant Londe and were concerned with something entirely different. She clenched her fist on her book. Would he talk at the end of dinner? When he had eaten all his bread, would he ask for more?

In the meantime the stranger appeared to be quite unaware of the impatience which was gnawing at the proprietress's heart. In the bitterness of her defeat Madame Londe almost missed the arrival of the corn-chandler, who greeted her with one of those grand hat flourishes in two movements that survive only in the provinces. She bowed and said in a voice which trembled a little with vexation:

"Good evening, Monsieur Goncelin." And to the waiter who came at that moment, bearing the soup, she said, tartly:

"Go and serve the gentleman in the corner there!"

What would she not have given to have known his name and to have been able to say:

"Take the soup to Monsieur So-and-so! He has a train to catch at such-and-such an hour."

Instead of which she added, angrily, exasperated by her own ignorance and by the look of amazement on the waiter's face:

"Heavens, man! Hurry up, will you! Can't you see he's eating all his bread?"

The customers began to arrive in a continuous stream, the door being opened again as soon as it shut. All these greeted the proprietress with heartiness tinged with respect, and she distributed her own greetings right and left, like a sovereign from her carriage, flattered by the attentions of which she was the object, and gradually growing calmer.

With much scraping of chairs the ten or twelve people who had come in took their places. All of

them, to judge by the promptness with which they
reached their places, were regular customers of the
restaurant, and conversation was already filling the
room with the deep, persistent rumble of a beehive.
Two waiters in white aprons went round the *table
d'hôte* in opposite directions, dispensing soup.

Before the babble of conversation and the clatter
of dishes, Madame Londe's heart swelled. This was
the moment for which she lived, to see those backs
bent and those heads bowed before her and, in a
sort of way, at her feet. She seemed to see a sign
of obedience and submission in their attitudes.
She counted the customers half aloud: Ten at the
table d'hôte and one by himself at the little table
near the door. Ah! How insignificant he appeared
now! A short while ago she had been annoyed because there was something provocative about his
presence in the empty room, but now that the *table
d'hôte* was full, he shrank into nothingness in his
corner.

She half closed her eyes better to enjoy the hum
which rose up to her. In the joyful hubbub of dinner she picked out the thick accent of Monsieur
Goncelin boasting of a good stroke of business, the
sharp voice of little Pariset discussing politics, and
the spluttering voice of Monsieur Léon answering
him. Monsieur Morestel was arguing again with
the younger Pinsot, and Monsieur Trept, who was
such a good talker, was telling a long story involv-
ing his landlady, Mademoiselle Clarafond. Then
she tossed her head in a gesture of tolerance and

knowledge; she knew all about these people, their
occupations, their little love-affairs, their troubles,
their debts, their possessions. Not a moment of
their lives seemed to have escaped her, for she knew
what questions to put to them when they paid their
bills, and they all gave her information about one
another. A great deal of her prestige, indeed, depended on the information she possessed. No one
remembered more scandals, more misfortunes. Her
memory never let anything escape it and every one
of the hundred petty details that she gleaned right
and left each day were, to her, precious knowledge
that might some day be turned to account.

After a moment she reopened her eyes and pulled
herself together. She had an idea. She remembered
something she had been told that very morning
about a visit of one of her customers to a neighboring town, and to show that she *knew*, she suddenly
observed in a loud voice that could be heard above
the murmur of the table:

"I bet Monsieur Trept went to Champricourt
yesterday morning, to buy himself a new hat."

There was a short silence and every head turned
toward her; then fat Monsieur Trept, recovering
from his first surprise, cried:

"It's quite true, Madame Londe. It would be hard
to conceal anything from you."

The gentlemen began to laugh, and with one
accord looked toward the hatstand where, among
the weary-looking and faded bowlers, there hung a
darker bowler which seemed to be ashamed of its

brethren. For a minute she felt almost as happy as she had ever been, and she responded to the sound of this flattering hilarity like a flower to sunlight. She half opened her black book and pretended to look for something in it, indifferently, but her heart was thumping with joy in her bosom. He had seen, that time, and heard, that prig at the end of the room! She had caught his puzzled glance. Maybe he knew who the proprietress was now—a woman of authority who knew how to speak firmly to these men, and who, besides, had her wits about her! And in her satisfaction she slid her flower-vase a little more to the right, with the triumphant gesture of a chess-player who, by moving a piece, lessens his opponent's chance of victory.

No doubt she could not yet pride herself upon having won the game, but it was clear that her remark had struck home. The man seemed suddenly to come to himself, and stared at Madame Londe with the anxious, surprised look of a sleeper who is waked too abruptly from his sleep. She exulted in this stupefaction which seemed to avenge her for the embarrassment into which she herself had been thrown such a short time before. The moment had arrived for her to attack; the enemy must not be given time to recover. As one of the waiters was passing by her she leaned a little to one side and said, quickly:

"Put down that soup and go and ask the gentleman at the end if he wants his place and his napkin kept for him. And mind you are polite about it."

But the moment the waiter turned his back she felt that she had made a tactical error and was on the point of calling him back. That lout Grégoire would probably bungle the whole thing. Perhaps she ought to have waited until the Unknown came to pay his bill. She did not feel at all sure of him. Yet something prevented her from interfering; she wanted to see what would happen, she wanted to know at once. A fierce and ever-increasing curiosity attracted her to this man, and for a moment she saw nothing but him, seated well apart, as though to distinguish himself from the rest of the customers and to rivet her attention. Why had he taken a place apart from all the others, unless it was to defy her?

It seemed to her that the waiter was being deliberately slow, positively crawling round the center table. She craned forward to follow his interminable journey and then sat up again, unable to control her impatience. When Grégoire reached the table near the door, she strained her ears to catch what he said, but in vain; however, she was far from reassured by the bewildered expression that appeared on the stranger's face, and kept muttering beneath her breath in a voice of rage: "Idiot! Idiot!" without giving any clearer indication as to which of the two men she was apostrophizing. She gathered that the stranger was having her questions repeated to him and then saw him shrug his shoulders as though he did not know what to answer.

She closed her eyes in shame, and opened them again only when Grégoire stood before her.

"Well, what did he say?"

"He said he would let me know at the end of the dinner."

"Of course, my lad," cried Madame Londe, in a voice loud enough for the stranger to hear, "the gentleman can't form an opinion of the food before he's eaten it. Did I tell you to go and ask him about it now?" And then she added, menacingly, in a lower voice:

"Not a word! Get out! Go back to the kitchen, you fool!"

Only the last part of this little scene had been followed by the other diners, who stopped talking and stared at the proprietress in mute amazement. She withered them with a look.

"Is there anything you want?" she asked, brightly. "Bread? Water?"

And, selecting one of them at random to vent her fury upon, as a schoolmistress comes down upon a bad pupil, she burst out:

"Do you want anything, Monsieur Pinsot? Isn't the soup all right? Do you know any place where it's better?"

She folded her hands in a pretense of calm, but she had lost her head and her voice was trembling.

"Any place," she went on—"any place where the prices are fairer than ours or better facilities are given for payment, eh? You owe me for six meals,

Monsieur Pinsot. Have I ever once asked you to
settle up?"

Monsieur Pinsot, a poorly-dressed, anæmic young
man, passed his finger over the lenses of his pince-
nez, which the steam from the soup had fogged; he
then made a movement as though to get up, thought
better of it, and remained seated.

"No," he muttered.

"No!" repeated Madame Londe. "You are
right, Monsieur Pinsot, I have never dunned a customer in my life."

These words fell upon a solemn silence; not a
murmur rose from the table swept by the dominat-
ing glare of the proprietress. By what power did
she terrorize the eleven diners who sat there before
her with eyes like those of schoolboys discovered in
some mischief? What was the game of cat and
mouse that she played with them that prevented them
from daring to protest against her reprimands? By
what process of overdue accounts had she reduced
them to this abject state of submission?

For a moment she enjoyed the consternation she
had caused, her nostrils dilating with pleasure.
Then she saw that the stranger was looking at her,
and she guessed that he was thinking of the scene
he had just witnessed. This delighted her; she
closed her eyes as though to impress upon her mind
and to contemplate the spectacle of her triumph,
and she experienced the voluptuous sensation of being rocked.

After a few seconds' hesitation the diners began

to steal furtive glances at one another, nodding
their heads as though they were fellow-conspirators;
and an interval followed during which the only
sound was the one they made in swallowing the last
spoonfuls of their soup.

The remainder of dinner was eaten in gloom.
Anxiety prevented the diners from resuming the
conversation on the same plane as before and the
remarks they interchanged in low voices now had
something timid and constrained about them. Their
evening was ruined. It was obvious that by mutual
consent they were trying to shorten a meal which
could henceforth afford them no pleasure.

From the eminence of her throne, the proprietress
let her eyes wander over the abashed faces of her
customers, and examined, as they passed, the courses
that were being brought in silence. Her expressionless face was like that of a tyrant contemplating the
desolation he has caused. Yet her eyes darkened.
Of course she had won the game now; her instinct
had stood her in good stead; she had guessed the
stranger dining at the end of the room to be a feeble,
unhappy creature, fleeing from some one or something, and by the power of her authority alone she
was going to compel him to come to her. Perhaps
he did not know it yet, but she was quite confident
about it.

She was so confident about it that she began to
lose interest in it; this, of itself, assured her of her
victory, for by a strange freak of her nature, as
soon as she felt herself to have overcome her quarry,

that quarry ceased for the time being to be at all desirable. In order that her pleasure should be renewed it was necessary for her calm to be disturbed again and that in the subsequent struggle she should again enjoy the taste of triumph; in a word, the quarry had to rebel and try to free itself. Hence the contempt in which Madame Londe held her customers. She had no use for their submission, and only prized their obedience according to the extent to which she had to fight to get it and to keep it.

These men had been coming to feed at her feet for many years; she treated them like children, scolding them perpetually, but, if she could not bear not to see them in this state of moral bondage, her unsatisfied soul found emptiness even in the hour of her triumph. Actually, she possessed what takes the place of intelligence among uncivilized people, namely, a deep insight into human beings and things. Although this prevented her from being happy, she had not the strength of mind to suppress it, and she had relapsed into the melancholy by which her whole life was consumed. And was this stranger, now lingering over his fruit, worthy of the trouble she had taken to enslave him? Was her life to be nothing but spying on the men who came to her and preventing them from going elsewhere? And a voice within her which refused to be hushed answered: "Yes, that's it, to order about men who are too weak to resist you, to speak harshly to them like a sergeant to the soldiers under him. From time to time death and the hazards of life will take one or two away from you, until the day when death will take you, too. Then your restaurant will be closed, your possessions will be scattered, people will talk about Madame Londe whose prices were so fair, then you in your turn will fade from everyone's memory and you might just as well never have lived at all."

She had a revulsion of feeling. Why did she suddenly feel sad? Was she not respected throughout the whole locality, honored, even powerful? What more did she want? She was brought back from her reflections by the diners, who rose one by one and made their way to her desk, either to pay their bills or to ask her to put them down. She became herself again and her features hardened; her profession took entire possession of her again. Wasn't Monsieur Goncelin going to pay yet? Why was he so keen on running up petty debts? A slight puckering of the brow, to indicate the degree of gravity of the situation; a moment to enter Monsieur Goncelin in her big book. Wasn't Monsieur Pinsot going to pay, either? Very well, Monsieur Pinsot, but be careful! A moment for Monsieur Pinsot. Monsieur Léon came next, and paid. A smile for Monsieur Léon. Monsieur Gorche, too? Good! That made four meals without wine, didn't it? (Without wine because of Monsieur Gorche's well-known malady. Madame Londe knew all about it.) A smile for Monsieur Gorche.

"Monsieur?" The new customer stood there. He handed her his bill. She took the paper with an imperceptible movement of her hand, and raised her head without raising her eyes.

"Did the waiter explain to you?" she asked, softly.

"Yes, madame. I want to pay."

"Since you are coming back, I will put your account down."

"But I don't know whether I shall come back."

These words pierced the proprietress's heart like a dagger. She raised her eyes and stared at the stranger, incapable of speech. Could she have been mistaken, and was this little man going to escape her, after all? He looked so shy, and a moment ago she had been so sure of him! It was all that Grégoire's fault; he had probably been rude to him. She herself should have explained the customs of the house to this gentleman (he became a gentleman again by the mere fact of his resistance). And the shame of having to sustain a rebuff in front of all her customers sent the blood rushing to Madame Londe's face. If only he had had a bag, then everyone would have understood, confound it, that he was a traveler and was merely passing through Lorges, but it was obvious that he was living in the neighborhood, since he had not even an overcoat with him.

The outraged vanity of the woman made her suffer dreadfully, and for a second she thought of giving her vexation full play, when a sudden inspiration gave her back her courage. She cast her eyes slowly over the customers who were listening to this conversation, and, reassured by the cowardice she read in their faces, she took the bill that the stranger had handed to her and tore it into four pieces. Then she proclaimed in a loud, high voice:

"The rule here is that a regular customer does not pay for his first meal."

She glared at her customers again, as though to defy them to utter a protest. Not one of them stirred; they were all perfectly certain that they had paid for their first meal at Madame Londe's, but amazement, and the fear of displeasing this woman, kept them silent. Instinctively they drew closer to one another, hemming in the stranger, who said nothing. The proprietress turned her attention to him again.

"I imagine," she pursued in an uncompromising voice, "that monsieur will not refuse me the pleasure of offering him this first meal?"

Then, taking advantage of the stranger's confusion and of the tacit acquiescence which she read in his eyes, she mastered her emotion (what would she do if, after all, he declined her offer?) and, abruptly opening her book, she put it in front of him, her finger pointing to the top of a blank page. By this means she would avoid having to ask him his name and confessing before everyone to an ignorance from which she had already suffered enough.

"Will monsieur please be good enough to sign here," she said in a voice which she strove unsuccessfully to keep steady. Her throat was dry. He had taken up the pencil. Why didn't he sign? Was he going to insult her in front of the whole *clientèle* of the restaurant? Really she had had enough of this little fellow's defiance. If he didn't sign she would slap his face.

After a moment's hesitation he declared:

"But I don't know when I shall be able to come back."

Then he raised his eyes and seemed to be trying to find a solution to his difficulty in the proprietress's face. For some seconds they looked at one another in silence. The man's face was emaciated with sorrow and weariness. What did all these people around him want, and that woman who seemed to be gloating over him? He felt like a criminal in the dock, dragged to the judge's feet by a crowd of witnesses.

"It is enough that I know monsieur will return some day or other," replied Madame Londe between her teeth.

Perhaps he was intimidated by the voice in which she said this, for he bent his head and signed. The proprietress turned the book round at once and cast an eager glance at the signature.

"Good evening, Monsieur Guéret," she said, with a nod. "I hope we shall be seeing you again soon."

And, recovering all her strength of mind and her insolence, she said in a sharp voice, as much for the pleasure of bullying her old customers as to give her new customer an idea of her power:

"Come, gentlemen, don't dawdle! The room must be empty in five minutes. I have no time to waste here. Out you go!"

She puffed herself out on her daïs, and in a gesture of triumph moved the little flower-vase toward the left. She had won the game.

Chapter Four

As he shut the restaurant door behind him a thought struck him, the same thought that had always struck him for some years past in times of great stress—"It is destiny, my destiny." And this conviction reassured him, as feeble creatures are reassured when their fate is placed into the hands of a superior being, even if they have to suffer for it, even if it costs them their lives. Henceforward he would not have to decide anything for himself; events, whether good or bad, would happen of their own accord. Since this woman insisted on his returning to her, he would return, and in this he saw a sign, the mark of a mysterious will that presided over his destiny.

That very morning he had been seized with a sudden foolish joy as he felt in his pocket the ring he intended to give Angèle. Why should he not succeed, after all? Until that moment he had not thought it possible; indeed, he always felt quite sure of not getting anything he desired too keenly; life had taught him that; but during a brief moment, without any reason, he had believed in his success and had said to himself, "Even if she does not love me she will understand that my sufferings are too great for me to bear." And the long days of anxiety that he had passed seemed to him to be a small price to pay for that instant when happiness seemed to be drawing near him.

He recalled this morning illusion, now that night had come and he was alone and discouraged, and he shook his head. At the end of a day like that, he had the impression that years had passed in the space of a few hours and that he had suddenly become old. Then tears came into his eyes and he dreamt of the youth of which time had robbed him. All the sordid love-affairs he had had before took on in his eyes the same aspect of dreary monotony. By a process natural to him he saw himself again as he was once, ten or twelve years earlier, his heart laden with desires, lifted out of himself by the promise of a world which was being slowly revealed to him. And what, after all, was this world which he had half seen as in a delightful dream? To what did the magic of adolescence reduce itself? In the memories which came back to him now, he could see nothing but the bitterness of his early disappointments, the wretchedness and sordidness of realization, the horror of words, of gestures, of money given and received in silence; the pangs and recriminations of marriage; the patience one had to learn to live perpetually with a person of whom one had been tired for years; the gradual poisoning of his entire life.

He stopped, and leaned against the wall of a house. Since the past had assured him of so much misfortune later on, what good could he expect of the future? What was the use of telling himself that in a year's time, in two years, he would perhaps be happy? Was he not just as foolish as in days gone by when he used to wait for a generous fate to lavish happiness upon him? And in ten years, fifteen years, when he was old and disappointed, would he not still be sighing, as he was doing now, in the same credulous way?

In the street with its unlit windows the wind whistled mournfully, with a soughing that was like a human voice; then it ceased suddenly like a person who forgets where he has got to in telling a story. It could not be later than nine o'clock, but in remote little towns like Lorges, night does not suffer that kind of desecration which capitals inflict upon it by dazzling it with lights, and it was in darkness that Paul Guéret regained the highroad that took him back to Chanteilles.

He could not avoid sighing as he reached the railway footbridge. He had only been settled in the neighborhood a month, and he was already bored with everything there. In these new surroundings he had thought to forget his boredom, at any rate for a short time; and yet a few days had been enough for him to become his old self again. And he put his hand on the hand-rail where he had seen Angèle put hers. What a depressing fate, what a cruel jest to be made to suffer for a creature whom he would one day forget as he had forgotten so many others, and to have to leave that creature to carry his desires elsewhere! He tried to recall her individual

features; that very evening he had examined them
with a certain ardent curiosity, as though to compensate for the bashfulness of his hands and of his
lips with the boldness of his eyes, and yet he could
not call them to mind now; he tried closing his eyes,
but her features eluded him or, if not her features,
at any rate something in their character, that element which makes one recognize a person at first
glance. For on reflection he could recall the shape
of her nose and of her lips and even the expression of
her eyes, but there was no life in the portrait which
he traced from memory, and the face escaped him
even while being near him, exactly as a name on the
tip of the tongue continues to elude the memory.

"I know her so little," he confessed to himself.
"How, then, can I say that I love her so much?"
Tomorrow, if he saw her again, he would at first
only recognize her with difficulty and then she would
gradually resume her real appearance in his eyes,
and it was by these freaks of memory, by this game
in which her face appeared and disappeared by
turns, that, from life-long habit of mind, he judged
of the profundity of his desire.

When he reached his own street he looked up, and
frowned on seeing a light in his bedroom window.
He had hoped to be able to go to bed at once and
sleep, instead of which a woman whom he did not
love was going to ask him awkward questions, questions which she thought she had a right to put to
him because she was his wife. For a moment he
thought of staying out and walking about in the

country until that light which was lying in wait for him went out; but the need of sleep in which to forget his troubles soon put this out of his head. He opened the door and went upstairs.

She was tidying the room and pushing the chairs against the wall when he entered. A tall woman, still young, but rather ugly in spite of an appearance of health and strength that was not unattractive. She reminded one of a peasant girl whom town life has taught to despise her head-dress, her kerchief, and her velvet skirt, and who wants to dress like a lady, without succeeding in ridding herself of her taste for black. Her hat, which she had not yet taken off, threw a shadow across her face. The sturdy contour of her bust was accentuated by the shiny material of her taut bodice, tucked into a serge skirt which molded her hips and thighs and did not relax its hold until it reached her knees.

"There you are," she said, turning round.

He hung his hat on a peg and sat down at the round table in the middle of the room.

"Yes," he replied, without looking at her. He opened a newspaper lying close to his hand, but his eyes wandered from paragraph to paragraph and he seemed to take no interest in the news. How he hated that moment; how it weighed upon him! Something compelled him to study his wife's attitude, and in spite of himself he tried to guess what she was going to say. He saw her hesitate a moment with her hands on a chair back, obviously about to ask a question; then she removed her hat and placed it on the table.

"You don't ask me what I've being doing or where I've been," she remarked, sitting down opposite her husband.

He pretended he had been absorbed in his newspaper.

"Well?" he said.

"Aren't you interested to hear that I've been to the shop?"

"Did they pay you?" he asked.

She nodded. Her large features, set too close together, gave her a somewhat foolish appearance which the dreariness of her expression could hardly counteract. He could not help mentally comparing this face with Angèle's, and he asked himself what force, what convention, prevented him from rising there and then and telling this woman the truth, namely that though he was talking to her he was thinking of another woman and that his whole heart and mind shunned her and shrank from her.

"Not too soon, either," he observed, mechanically.

She tossed her head again and asked:

"And you?"

Her blue eyes rested on him with a persistence that made him feel uncomfortable; it seemed to him as though she were doing this to force him to answer. Years ago he had liked her eyes; he used to admire their delicate color, their almond shape, and the kind of glint of gayety that always shone in them, but now the eyes remaining young in an ageing face seemed a mockery to him. "Her good points merely accentuate her bad ones," he thought.

And aloud he answered:

"I got paid for my lessons, as usual."

"When are you going to ask for a rise?"

"A rise?" he repeated, lowering his newspaper completely. "It's the only thing you ever talk about. Do you think one asks for a rise at the end of three weeks?"

"It's more than three weeks, Paul. We came here in August."

He shrugged his shoulders.

"You're childish. I shall not ask for anything before April or May."

"We won't have enough to live on this winter, then," she replied, calmly. "Have you thought of the expenses of our move?"

He looked at her squarely and asked:

"What are you driving at, Marie? Is it my fault that we aren't rich? Perhaps you think I don't work hard enough?"

"I think you work hard enough, but that these people, who are rich, don't pay you as they should."

"Don't you understand me when I explain to you that I cannot ask for a rise after a few weeks. A rise isn't a gift. One has to wait six months at least."

"You ought to have asked for more to start with."

"Let's presume that I made a mistake, then. Will that satisfy you? In any case, it's too late to ask for more. Too late and too soon."

"Have it your own way."

She took her hat, rose from her chair, and left the room. A few minutes passed. He blessed that moment of solitude which allowed him to take up the thread of his revery and to imagine a hundred impossible things, a different life, all the happiness which had been denied him. He had been lacking in spirit with Angèle; he should have offered her money in the first place, instead of letting himself become sentimental and arriving at a point when he dared not even speak to her or touch her. She might perhaps have refused, but then he would at least have known where he was. The uncertainty of his present position exasperated him. What was more ridiculous than making love, real love, to a girl who was perhaps only after his money? Perhaps? Of course she was! He suddenly became certain that she would have accepted money. What girl in her straits would not? That explained why she consented to meet him in the street, but always kept him at a distance. She was waiting to be offered that money, to be bought. And he had given her a ring, a ridiculous childish ring stolen from his wife. It was the only thing he could find in the way of a present. Fool! He had been afraid of hurting her feelings when he ought to have taken out his pocketbook and counted out the notes. And she had taken the ring indifferently and had left him almost at once, no doubt despising him and quite rightly.

"I don't want you to be upset," said Marie, returning to the room. "I dare say we shall pull through even if it means borrowing."

He turned sharply at the sound of his wife's voice, and looked at her dully. The simplicity of the creature surprised him. She had lived with him for years without having the least idea of his thoughts. She had seen nothing, guessed nothing; no one had ever told her anything. She sewed from morning till night, and once a week she went to the shop which bought her work. He knew that that was her whole life. Not a single desire, not a moment's uneasiness ever came to trouble the serenity of this tranquil soul during her hours of work. From time to time, it is true, she worried as to how certain financial problems were to be solved, but her natural placidity soon regained the upper hand. Her contentment was largely due to the poverty in which she had been brought up, but it was a form of monotonous and spiritless happiness the sight of which irritated her husband because he knew what credulity lay at the bottom of it. He sometimes thought that he would prefer the bitterness of a jealous woman to Marie's eternal good-nature, and he despised her for the meekness with which she accepted his bullying, her obedience, her kindness, yes, even her kindness, which he seemed to see in everything she did.

"I'm not upset," he said, wearily. "You imagine all sorts of things. Have you closed the shutters?"

She looked at him for an instant, her hands resting on the table, as though trying to understand the things he would not tell her. Her gaze irritated him.

"Leave me alone, do!" he went on, with a tired sigh. "I've been working very hard today and I want to go to bed. Don't ask me any more questions, Marie. Just go and fasten the shutters."

She turned without a word and went toward the window, which she opened wide. The sky suddenly appeared as part of the room, filling it with its stars and shadows. In spite of his melancholy the man turned his head and looked at it; all at once something made his heart beat quicker, a confused yearning toward that silent immensity which seemed to beckon to him. What peace lay in the depths of that black sky after the babble of human speech!

"Oh, to be happy!" he thought, as though until then he had never realized the force of those words.

One by one the shutters closed in upon the room.

Chapter Five

IT SEEMED to him that he had known this garish
room with its velvet curtains and thick pile carpet
all his life, for certain hours of boredom seem to last
a lifetime, and it was there that he was most painfully bored. Sometimes, when it became intolerable,
his gaze would wander from the lesson book and
travel along the picture-laden walls. He examined
them carefully, noting all the details which he knew
by heart but in which he kept trying to discover
something new. The child's voice grew blurred and
distant as in a dream; sleep gradually mastered his
heavy eyelids and his head began to nod on his chest;
then fear would rouse him, the fear of hearing his
pupil cry suddenly: "He's asleep! Monsieur
Guéret's asleep!" And if that were to happen
Madame Grosgeorge, who was never far away and
who, he was sure, spied upon him, would come in
with her usual abruptness and discharge him.

That morning it was pouring with rain, and gusts
of wind were stripping leaves from trees in the
Grosgeorge garden with a kind of frenzied joy, con-
vulsing the shrubs and mowing down the flowers,
those wretched begonias in which the owners' mono-
grams were traced at the corners of the lawn. Rills
of water ran through the gravel. Above all this

carnage the limes waved their branches impotently. He cast furtive glances out of the window. This violence of nature was in such sharp contrast with all the heavy mediocrity of the room in which he was shut. A thin sheet of glass was all that separated him from the keen fresh air and the screaming of the wind in the trees; a pane of glass was enough for him to feel himself a prisoner. Anyway, what would he do with his liberty if it were suddenly given to him? The answer to the question was easy; he would hasten to the Rue des Teinturiers, where Angèle was working at that hour. Naturally. And how would he manage to see her, to talk to her? He reflected for a moment, but could think of no way. From the café where he sometimes sat, opposite the laundry, it was impossible for him to see the girl except as she was leaving; and it was precisely at that moment that he became distracted, and lost his head, his fear of not seeing Angèle being so great that he was unable to distinguish her from her companions around her. In a confused way he would see three laughing girls passing the café, and in less than two seconds they were gone. What odious conventions ruled the world! Somewhere, surely, on this earth there were green fields, forests in which he could hide or lose himself, young and beautiful women who might perhaps have loved him; but dire necessity kept human beings apart from each other, kept every door shut and took a delight in dumping into one street people who would have found happiness in the next one; happiness existed for him somewhere in the world, and he was distracted because he could not find it. When he ran after women it was this that he was pursuing. He was like a silly fool whose eyes have been blindfolded to play blind man's buff and in whose ears people shout: "Here! There! Farther on!" And he was running around in circles, going to right and to left, a wild and ludicrous spectacle, growing daily older and more disappointed. Other men had hundreds of love-affairs which came to them of their own accord, apparently, simply because they did not look for them. Perhaps this child droning out his page of history would be one of them, some day, especially as he was rich.

This last thought roused him to sudden fury. He leaned over the boy's fair head until he could smell his skin and his close-cropped hair. A mad impulse came to him to smack the little boy's head and to enjoy his subsequent surprise and fear. The child was rich and he was poor, and because he was poor he had to listen to his mumbling voice and correct him gently each time he made a mistake, instead of hurrying off to that woman and giving her money, money to slake the passion that was burning his heart out. What savage deity had put gold on one side and desire upon the other? Was it a game, a bad joke?

He had reached this point in his reflections when the door suddenly opened, making way for Madame Grosgeorge. She came in with a swift, silent step and came up to the table at which the child was working. It was impossible to guess her age. Her impassive face was quite unlined; this surprised people, probably because of the extreme hardness of her expression; her suspicious black eyes with their almost metallic glint were, indeed, those of an old woman, but she had a straight slender nose, a small and pretty though somewhat thin-lipped mouth, high cheek-bones and, stretched over these delicate features an extremely white skin the velvety softness of which could bear the scrutiny of even a practiced enemy eye. It was easy to see that Madame Grosgeorge possessed a kind of willful obstructiveness which betrayed itself not only in her speech and in her movements, but also in her manner and even in the restrained way she had of breathing; it was as though she bore her lungs a grudge for what they compelled her to do. She was tall and thin, but strongly built, and was clad in a blouse of yellow lace and a brown cloth skirt. Her black hair was going gray at the temples; she did not trouble to dye it, but it was dressed with meticulous care.

"The hour is not quite over, Monsieur Guéret," she said in a dull voice. "During the last few minutes I should like to form an idea of the way in which you make my son work. Of course you will both behave just as though I were not there."

She sank down into a Louis XIV armchair at the end of the room in an attitude of expectancy, one foot crossed over the other and both her hands clasped on one of the arms of the chair. The child cast a terrified glance at his tutor, who, after looking from his pupil to Madame Grosgeorge and back, sat down again.

"What have I got to do?" whispered the child; he knew his mother well enough to realize that this visit boded no good.

"Now, my boy," said Guéret in a voice which he tried to make sound authoritative and kindly, "finish reading your page of history."

"There are only three more lines, monsieur."

"Never mind; finish them."

The child bent over the book as though he were about to lick it and mumbled a sentence of which not a single syllable was audible.

"Shut the book," ordered Guéret, when this test was over, "and tell me what you have retained of your lesson."

"Retained of your lesson," repeated the child. He was a fair, sickly boy, the pallor of whose face was heightened by the ever-present fear of a possible slap; his small nose was strewn with countless freckles. He remained open-mouthed for a moment; his confusion communicated itself to his tutor, who flushed and adopted that patient and at the same time irritated voice which children fear so much.

"I am asking you what you remember of what you have read, what impression it has made on you, on your mind, on . . ."

No reply. Guéret stole a glance at Madame Grosgeorge, but she seemed turned to stone. The woman's immobility seemed to him more alarming

than her anger, and drops of sweat began to trickle
slowly down his forehead.

"Tell me, my boy," he went on in a forced voice
the sound of which disgusted him, "what was the
story all about?"

"What? Oh! The king."

"Good. Very good. And what king? Louis XI,
Louis XII?"

"Louis XI."

Without taking his eyes from Guéret, he reached
beneath the table and scratched his calf.

"Very good indeed! And . . . what did they do
to him?" asked the tutor, thoughtlessly.

"They put him in a cage."

There was a moment's consternation during which
Guéret could think of nothing to say. No doubt his
question had been badly put, but why was it enough
for Madame Grosgeorge to appear, for everything
to go wrong? From the beginning of this scene she
had not made the slightest movement, but sat listening with a kind of polite ferocity, waiting to see
what was going to happen.

"Think of what you are saying," said Guéret, with
a gruffness induced by fear. "You know quite well
that no one put Louis XI into a cage; on the contrary, it was he who . . . Go on. It was Louis XI
who . . ."

"I don't know!" cried the child, frantically. And
he began to sob, looking at his mother over the back
of the chair. Madame Grosgeorge started. Guéret
made a half-hearted movement in the boy's direction

and stood up. To add to the general confusion, the clock struck eleven.

"André," said Madame Grosgeorge, "I warn you that you deserve to be slapped for making such a noise. You had better stop at once or you'll see if I am joking."

The child put his hands to his mouth to stifle the sobs which he could not keep back and looked beseechingly at his tutor; but Guéret was at a loss to know how to deal with the situation. He stood with his back to the window and remained there for some moments with his hand on his heart, like a man who is about to justify his actions; but, the attitude suddenly striking him as being absurd, he flushed and let his hand fall.

"I am extremely sorry, madame," he stammered.

"I intend, Monsieur Guéret," said Madame Grosgeorge, without appearing to have heard his apology, "to send my son to school next year. Do you think he could pass the entrance examination? Think it over. Don't say yes merely to please me. Take your time."

Her voice was strangely gentle, but a threat was concealed behind it, and Guéret had to strain his ears a little to catch her words, for her lips hardly moved as she uttered them. It was impossible to read anything in her features, which seemed incapable of expressing any human emotion; yet her eyes fixed themselves on people and on things with a force and intensity which lent a sort of ardor to their glance. She considered the tutor without taking her eyes from his face, into which uneasiness and shame sent the blood rushing; it was as though she were trying to fathom the confused manner in which the answer to her question was taking shape in the brain of this humiliated man, behind that forehead glistening with sweat. She enjoyed this spectacle for a moment, breathing it in like a lascivious animal, then she drew herself up a little and rubbed her hands noiselessly together.

"I think, madame," said Guéret, who imagined that he detected impatience in this gesture of hers, "that with some months of sustained effort your son will be able to pass the entrance examination."

"I see that we are of the same opinion, Monsieur Guéret," she resumed, turning her head slightly with a trace of coquetry. "You mean, I take it, four or five months of diligent study?"

"Precisely, madame; about four or five months."

"Four or five months of diligent study," she repeated with the smooth accents of a well-bred woman, "under the direction of an able, hard-working tutor. . . . Are we still of the same opinion, Monsieur Guéret?"

"Yes, madame . . . of course."

"A tutor who takes an interest in his pupil, who sees to it that he understands what he is studying . . . Do we still think the same?"

"Certainly, madame."

"A tutor, in fact, who does not confuse his pupil by asking absurd questions, but who carefully prepares at home the lesson for the morrow; in short,

Monsieur Guéret, what I call a conscientious man who understands his duty and does it. Have you anything to add?"

He shook his head. Even had he wanted to say anything his embarrassment would have prevented it.

"Good," she said. "You may expect my visits to be more frequent in future. André!"

The boy turned toward his mother.

"Come here when I call you," said Madame Grosgeorge in the same smooth voice. "Will you never learn to obey promptly?"

With an obvious effort André got down from his chair and made his way to the corner of the room in which his mother was waiting for him, motionless as a statue. He was a small boy, dressed in a dark blue jersey that fitted closely to his narrow chest and puny arms. His bare legs protruded from a pair of serge knickers that were much too large for him. As he walked he dragged his feet as though he were trying to kick up the red and violet wool of the carpet.

"How often have I told you not to drag your feet?" asked Madame Grosgeorge when he stopped in front of her. "Come closer."

She had replaced her two hands on the arm of the chair and looked at the child, who bit his lip and tried to avoid her eyes.

"Before punishing you," she said, softly, "it is right that I should explain why I am compelled to do so. In the first place, you read your page of history extremely badly. You mumble your words, and you do not attempt to understand and retain what you read. Consequently, you are just as ignorant afterward as before, and waste your time and your father's money. Again, you refuse to cure yourself of your habit of kicking up the carpet as you walk. It's no use crying. Raise your head and look at me."

As she said this she clenched her teeth a little and fixed her eyes on those of her son. Then, keeping her elbows close to her sides, she lifted her right forearm, drawing it back as far as it would go. She remained poised for a moment without moving a muscle of her body and then suddenly, after a slight turn to the right to gather impetus, she struck the child across the face with the force and brutality of a machine. He quivered, panting with terror, and began to scream. Meanwhile his mother kept her eyes upon him; she seemed not to hear his cries and gazed at the cheek from which the red mark made by her hand was slowly fading. Something strange had crept into the woman's black eyes, an expression of greedy pleasure which transfigured her handsome face and momentarily brought back its youth. At that moment her mind was completely taken up with the fact that nothing existed for her except the mark made by her hand. Had anyone shouted "Fire" behind her, she would probably not have looked round.

Guéret gazed at this scene with a horror that

rooted him to the spot. He had a wild desire to seize the child in his arms, but the very thought of such a daring move seemed awful to him. The whole of Madame Grosgeorge's personality radiated such force and vitality, and viciousness endowed her with such terrific authority at the moment, that he was no more capable of openly defying her than he would have dared to deprive a wild animal of its prey. He kept silence, involuntarily following with his eyes the child who was retreating uncertainly, with bowed head, before the horrible look with which his mother followed him.

A few seconds passed in silence, broken only by the little boy's sobs, and then, abruptly, as though a spell had been broken and liberty of action restored to her, Madame Grosgeorge shuddered and raised her eyes to the tutor.

"Well," she said, crisply, "it is after eleven, Monsieur Guéret. I don't know what you are waiting for."

As she said this she rose and walked toward the door. He was still standing in the same place, and as she passed before him he noticed the fineness of her clear-cut and graceful profile; her cheeks were flushed with an emotion of which this flush was the only sign; behind her ear, just below a strand of gray hair, one of the pieces of whalebone that held up her high collar pressed lightly into the white flesh and made a dimple. A sudden confused feeling came over him, in which admiration was mingled with disgust, and, seizing his book and his papers, he followed Madame Grosgeorge into the hall.

When he reached the garden, a moment later, he remembered that in his agitation he had forgotten to bid her good-bye.

Chapter Six

THE four cardinal points of his new life were his low-ceilinged room with its narrow window, Madame Londe's restaurant, the little deserted café, and the Grosgeorge villa. There were also streets and highways—streets through which he timidly followed the woman, and highways where he talked to her or pleaded with her, at night. They were the means by which he traveled from one corner of his prison to another.

There were also the two rivers which enfolded in a similar embrace the two neighboring towns of Lorges and Chanteilles. They bore names such as are sometimes hit upon by the genius of the people with a felicity of expression that is perhaps its most precious quality. One of them flowed languidly through its reeds, and dawdled beneath the ancient ramparts of Lorges, and you had to study the waters of the Sommeillante very closely to see them move. The other, that came from higher ground, hustled its joyous bubbling stream through Chanteilles; it was called the Preste, and gave its name to a short avenue which ran five or six yards above the level of the river. To walk along the Boulevard de la Preste was the chief Sunday afternoon occupation at Chanteilles, and the weather had to be pretty bad for the inhabitants to forego it. Even people from Lorges used sometimes to come and mingle with the groups that strolled along with the slow step so favorable to conversation, and they would lean jealously over the parapet with a sham air of indifference. But on weekdays this part of the town was not much frequented, as all the activity of Chanteilles was centered around the market place. So that on a fine October afternoon, if the wind were not too high, it was very pleasant to sit beneath the limes on the promenade and to meditate to the sound of the riotous and ceaseless murmur of the river as it hurried by.

That day he sat down on a seat not far from the parapet. A gentle breeze rustled the branches above his head and he could feel the frail caress of the autumn sun on his hands. The birds in the pallid sky seemed to be bidding farewell to summer. One could see a great distance without effort through the clear air. Beyond the houses on the further bank of the river ran a highway bordered with black fields and bare orchards, and beyond these again the gray and blue roofs of Lorges, grouped along the streets of the town around the half-ruined spire of Saint-Jude. One could not see the Sommeillante, which lurked behind the ramparts, but a line of willows marked the lazy line of its course. And, further on still, spread more fields and wide lush meadows, and low hills, whose crests caught the sun, basked in the light, and shone white as chalk cliffs.

For a few moments he studied this calm, smiling

countryside, so out of harmony with the grief and anxiety gnawing at his heart. He was becoming too old to lull his sorrows with false hopes, and he was too weary, also. After years and years of love-affairs, disillusionment, and mortification, there comes a moment when the soul can bear no more and refuses to obey the body and follow it in its shame. Though the girl had written to him and made an appointment to meet him at this place, he had only come out of cowardice and weakness and so as to have no regrets for neglecting an opportunity offered to him; for he knew quite well that she did not want him, and he despised himself for being there, seated on the seat she had indicated. And yet it would have been impossible for him to go away now. He knew that, too.

Once again he unfolded the note which he held clutched in his hand, and read it.

Don't you want to see me any more? she wrote. *What have I done to you? When I take the washing to the Villa Mon Idée tomorrow I shall go round by the Boulevard. Be at the first seat at two o'clock. Angèle.*

The impertinence of it! Giving orders like that. "Be at . . . " indeed! And there he was. He pressed the note to his lips. "At any rate," he thought, furiously, "I will take her by the arms." Her firm round arms, her arms which were too white and let him, nay, commanded him to, imagine the rest of her body. A wave of heat rose to his face and he shut his eyes, seized with a kind of giddiness.

The rippling of the river mingled with the buzzing that filled his head.

"Always," the river seemed to murmur, "always, all through life, the same, all through life."

He had not seen her for three days, since the day on which he had spoken to her on the highway. What had he done since then? He didn't know. Does one know how one spends the time when one suffers so deeply?

A quarter of an hour later she appeared, carrying on her arm a basket which she bore without an effort. A triumphant carriage is natural to beauty. There is something solemn and regal in all its movements; at its approach something is stilled in the heart of man. When he saw this woman coming toward him he forgot all that he was going to say to her. Her perfect face and the splendid movements of her body annihilated the universe about them. He stared at her hungrily. She was wearing a white blouse which left her arms and neck bare. A white apron covered her skirt. The marvelous play of shadow in the folds of her dress seemed to mold the material to the lines of her body and her limbs. And suddenly joy entered Guéret's heart with a greater tumult than the river made in its headlong race to the sea. He forgot everything, his sufferings, his rancor, and he saw her for the first time, white and swathed in light; and he shuddered at the thought that he might not have come.

She smiled. "Don't stand there like a dummy,"

she said, coming nearer to him. "People will notice us. Let's go down to the river."

Together they made their way toward the flight of narrow stone steps that went down to the Preste. When they were on the river bank she cast her eyes around to make sure that they were alone. He looked at her without speaking.

"How funny you are!" she said, with a smothered laugh. "I thought you would be glad to see me."

Her words, spoken in a low voice, were almost drowned by the sound of the water. Then she asked, a little louder, "Haven't you anything to say to me?"

Nothing to say to her! She stood there before Guéret, younger and fresher than he had ever dared to imagine her in the dark dreams of his solitude. Once or twice she pressed her hand across her forehead to brush aside a strand of brown hair which the wind kept blowing there. He wanted to laugh and to seize her hand, but his naturally distrustful nature curbed this impulse. He thought of this girl's indifference and cruelty toward him. Perhaps she had come there only to laugh at his glumness and his love-making.

"Why did you come?" he asked her.

Before replying, she studied his face, to which suspicion and dreary meditation had given a look of hardness. The brilliance of the sunlight obliged Guéret to bend his head, but his eyes never left the girl. She was struck by the change in his features and the bitterness she saw there.

"What a question to ask!" she said at last, reproachfully. "Do you want me to go away?"

He was on the point of answering, "Yes." He was suddenly struck with the uselessness of this interview, the uselessness of his whole life; despair took possession of him and he sighed. He raised his arms slightly and then let them fall back to his sides.

"I shall be so unhappy in a few minutes when I have left you," he said. "And yet what have I to regret? Nothing; you don't give me anything."

"You once told me that all you wanted was to see me," she replied, with childish vanity.

He turned his head away.

"Perhaps I have become more exacting," he muttered, without looking at her.

As soon as he had uttered these words he felt that they were unwise and silly, and he was afraid she would misunderstand, but she took his hand and said to him with a kind of forced gayety:

"You must be reasonable, you know."

The contact of her hand made him feel awkward, was almost repulsive to him. For this girl to give him her hand like this was so different from anything he had imagined, so much too simple. Besides, her skin was not so warm as he expected and this both disappointed and delighted him. It struck him that this was probably as far as he would ever get with her.

"It would be much kinder of you not to hold my

hand if you don't mean anything by it," he said, harshly.

"What!" she cried, letting his hand fall. "I am kind enough to meet you here, and yet you speak to me like this!"

He was suddenly overcome by uncontrollable rage.

"To meet me!" he repeated. "You call this a meeting, a quarter of an hour's conversation in the middle of the road or on the banks of the river? And other men! What do you give them? Are they all as easily satisfied, I wonder!"

The color left her cheeks.

"Other men?" she muttered. "What other men?"

He did not catch her words, but he saw her lips move. Then the shame of having offended this woman sent the blood to his face, and he tried to appear self-confident, thrusting his hands into his coat pockets. He felt so ugly in the light that shone on his face that he wanted to run up the stone steps and away. And yet something prevented him.

"Other men . . . " he stammered, without realizing what he was saying, " . . . richer than me."

At the bottom of one of his pockets he was fingering a banknote which he had placed there a little time before, in obedience to an obsession that it would be better to offer Angèle money than to bore her with his entreaties. Now something urged him to make this gesture, not the desire to buy the girl's surrender, but a base longing to insult this creature whose favors he despaired of getting. As though to defy him she seemed more lovely than ever, standing there on the banks of the river whose noisy babbling filled the silence. He looked spitefully at her face which his memory found it so difficult to retain; even the reflection of beauty that exists in memory, even that eluded him and refused to stay with him.

Before he could take his hand out of his pocket she found her voice:

"If that is what you think," she exclaimed, her eyes blazing with anger, "I had better go."

"Where to?" he asked, taking a step toward her.

She hitched her basket up on her arm and, turning her back on Guéret, left him without another word. He made no effort to try to stop her, but watched her following the river bank below the avenue wall as far as a flight of steps that led up to the bridge, a couple of hundred yards away. He felt as though each step that widened the distance between them lifted some of the load of sorrow from his mind. He became calm again, almost gay. He sat down on one of the steps they had gone down together.

"It's better so," he observed, aloud.

As he said this he clawed at his chest as though he wanted to tear off his waistcoat and shirt. A dreadful anxiety began to get hold of him again. He knew all the symptoms of approaching sorrow as well as a sailor knows from the look of the sky that a storm is brewing. He knew exactly what was meant by the sudden oppression that doubled him up and the difficulty he found in breathing. How could he ever have dreamt for a moment that he was going to be delivered from his sufferings, from himself? All at once he got up and ran to the spot where he had been standing when Angèle left him. His eyes followed the river bank as far as the bridge. She was no longer in sight. She had had time to cross the bridge and disappear while he was rejoicing, seated on the steps, that she was no longer there. Was he mad? What was the good of tearing at his chest, now, and walking in this woman's footsteps, moaning her name? There was probably not another man in the world who would have acted with so little self-control and common sense. He seemed to combine all the follies of youth with the disadvantages of old age, and aspired, with an infantile brain behind a wrinkled face, to conquer a girl in all the freshness of her beauty. And, in spite of the tears of mortification that flowed down his cheeks, the futility of the whole affair made him laugh.

Chapter Seven

ILL. Yes. Good Lord! my boy, don't try to tell me you are sorry. It's no good putting on airs with me. I know my wife is a nuisance and a prig. You must hate her being here. She's a bit difficult, eh? Go on! Don't pretend! I shan't repeat our conversation."

Guéret smiled mechanically. This fat man's waggishness made him feel a little awkward, but it was a great relief to know that André's mother would not be present at the lesson that day. He was standing, book in hand, before Monsieur Grosgeorge, who had ensconced himself in the Louis XIV armchair. The owner of the Villa Mon Idée carried his sixty years with the good-humor that comes with age when bad health does not prevent it. White hair still grew over his ears and at the back of his head, but his pink, scarcely lined forehead and the whole of his cranium were bald. He had coarse, thick, wide lips, and a powerful jaw. A large hooked nose gave his profile a fierce, stubborn look that was belied by the merry glint in his brown eyes. He was dressed in a gray sporting-suit, but a spotted tie worthy of more sober attire drew a thick black line beneath his double chin, as though to put a limit to his sportsmanship.

"Sit down," he said. "You can spare a moment, hang it. I don't suppose André will complain at having five minutes' recreation."

At these words André, who was sitting at the table, turned a sly childish face to his father and laughed, hiding his mouth behind his fingers. Then, after reassuring himself by a glance at his tutor, he slipped from his chair and went and looked out of the window. Everything about this frail little creature proclaimed him to be the child of elderly parents—his narrow shoulders, his feeble wrists, and that grown-up quietness and carefulness not to make a noise.

Monsieur Grosgeorge indicated his son with a jerk of his chin and said, in a low voice:

"Poor little devil! What he wants is fresh air and violent exercise, but his mother won't hear of it. Oh! His mother! Come, sit down, my boy."

Guéret put down his book and sat down in a chair opposite Monsieur Grosgeorge.

"I hope you won't think me very inquisitive," he went on, leaning his head to one side, "but how long have you been here? I am told that you lived in Paris before coming to Chanteilles. Good God! Fancy leaving Paris to come to the provinces! I suppose you moved for financial reasons?"

He asked all these questions with the air of a rich man to whom the possession of money gives the right to cross-examine a poor one.

"Yes, monsieur, financial reasons."

"And you are thinking of working up a little

practice teaching in the neighborhood. Why not, after all? Tell me, are you married?"

"Yes, married, monsieur."

"And your wife helps you, I know. That's very right and proper. What work does she do?"

"She is employed as a seamstress by a shop in Paris. She works here and goes to Paris once a week to deliver her orders."

"Do you go with her?"

"I, monsieur? No, never."

"I see you're not jealous, my dear Guéret. Oh, don't be frightened! What I said was only by way of a joke. Don't I know what marriage is?"

A little laugh shook him. He paused a moment as if to give Guéret a chance of making a remark, then, seeing that the tutor had nothing to say, he went on in his coarse, rather rapid voice: "Good, good! Now tell me; you must be very bored here, after having lived in Paris?"

"Yes, I get bored sometimes," answered Guéret, after a slight hesitation.

Monsieur Grosgeorge stretched his legs out in front of him and crossed one over the other.

"Do you feel the lack of anything?"

"I, monsieur? Why . . . no, I can't really say . . ."

"Good Lord! my boy," exclaimed the old man, between his teeth. "If I were your age . . . !"

And he waggled his feet, staring straight into the tutor's embarrassed eyes. A few seconds passed in a silence which Guéret did not dare break.

"Damn it, yes!" observed Monsieur Grosgeorge, finally, as though concluding a short meditation. "I don't want to give you advice, but it makes me think when I hear that you are bored here. As for me, thank Heavens, I'm glad I didn't waste my youth. I can assure you that *I* was never bored at your age. However, that's that."

He rose and went to the other end of the room.

"Come here, will you. What do you think of this little picture?"

When Guéret came up he took him by the arm.

"Stand there, a little to one side. Now give me your candid opinion. I may tell you that I paid fifteen hundred francs for it last week in Paris. It's a nice little thing. . . . It came this morning."

"Fifteen hundred francs!"

"Don't let yourself be dazzled by the price, my friend. Give me your opinion of it as a work of art. It's price doesn't really matter. Beautiful things are beyond value. And then, damn it! A Chacornac. . . . "

Around a table covered by a rich lace cloth three prelates clothed in scarlet satin were finishing a dainty dinner, the remains of which could be seen on the gold dinner-service before them. A bottle of champagne was cooling in a silver pail reposing sumptuously on the red carpet, while one of these gentlemen, the stoutest of the party, was holding up his crystal glass and looking at his friends. One of the others was apparently preparing to reply to the compliment that was being paid to him, for he was smiling at the toaster and was pouring out a glass for himself. This action seemed to strike the third prelate as being unwise, for he, fearing, perhaps, a lack of attention on the part of his neighbor, was touching his arm with the tips of his fingers and, with a look of alarm, seemed to be warning him not to let his glass overflow. Lastly, as a final detail which crowned this good-natured and precious effort, a white cat was rolling on the floor, playing with an oyster shell at the feet of these gentlemen. Such was the subject of the picture which Monsieur Grosgeorge proffered for the tutor's admiration. Guéret knit his brows for a moment and let his eyes travel over the work of art.

"It's very pretty," he said.

"Pretty!" repeated Monsieur Grosgeorge, impatiently. "Is that all you've got to say? Good Lord! my boy, look at the thing from an artistic point of view. Don't these warm, living, harmonious colors mean anything to you? The vermilion of the robes, contrasted with the white of the tablecloth, and the white which, in its turn, shows off the dark red of the carpet. Isn't that fine? And the cat, the dear little animal placed at the bottom of the picture like a signature? And then, good God! Just look at the detail in that lace. You could almost pick it up. Look here, and here . . . "

His short, pointed finger lovingly indicated the lace pattern which the artist had reproduced with such scrupulous accuracy. Guéret leaned closer, with sudden interest. Was it possible that there were people in the world who took a pleasure in painting lace tablecloths and cardinals having a drink, when it all meant so little to him? He felt that the violent desire which never gave him a moment's peace ought to be universal and to occupy all men's minds night and day. He was amazed at everything that did not concern Angèle. It was easier for him to believe that the whole town was in love with Angèle than that three people were indifferent to her. Deep in his thoughts he did not notice that Monsieur Grosgeorge had been looking at him for the last moment or two with puckered eyebrows and moist lips.

"Don't tell me, my boy," observed the old man in a voice whose very softness made the tutor jump, "that you are not thinking about something at this very moment. You are in a state of melancholy, that's quite clear. . . . "

He placed his hand on Guéret's arm.

"You are no more thinking of my Chacornac than Chacornac is thinking of you. Don't be alarmed; I am not annoyed about it. A moment ago, when you told me that you were bored at Chanteilles, I did a little quiet thinking. 'Damn it,' I said to myself, 'When one is bored at his age, there can be only one reason for it. . . . ' "

The tone in which he said this showed Guéret exactly what he meant.

"Only one reason," the old man went on, insistently. "Yes, my boy. Don't be shocked. The whole of life is made up of that. It is a constant preoccupation with everybody."

His voice became declamatory:

"Follow the dictates of nature, my boy, exacting nature. Do you think I don't know something about you already? My good fellow, I'm going to say something to you that will perhaps shock you, but never mind, it's for your good. You must know, then, that the other day I was taking a walk near the station when I saw a tallish woman dressed in black. . . . I won't describe her to you; the person with whom I was told me that she was your wife. Well, my boy, my dear friend, listen to me carefully, I'm sixty years old and I've a certain experience of life. I tell you to your face, you have not got the right woman."

"Monsieur!" cried Guéret, amazed.

"Stop!" ordered Grosgeorge in a voice of authority. "Let me finish. When I say that you have not got the right woman, I mean, solely, the woman whom nature destined for you. I have no doubt that Madame Guéret is good, hardworking, and anxious to please you. That is obvious, indeed. But is that all you ask of her, *all?* When you go home after a day of hard work and worry, do you find her beautiful, your Madame Guéret, and seductive? My boy, it is terribly important. Think of the years that pass. Do not store up for yourself an old age full of regrets."

"But, monsieur," said Guéret, with an effort, "why do you talk to me like this?"

"Because it irritates me to see you wasting your youth, my boy! You are as dull as a brick wall; it's pitiful to see. And you think I don't understand you, that I'm too old to understand you? Would you like me to confide in you, my friend? You've seen my wife. Take thirty years off her, and imagine the most delicate, the prettiest face . . . At the end of a month she disgusted me, and yet she was beautiful. But there it is; she was not destined for me by nature, and I found it out too late. Well, you may be sure that I've made up for it since, and I don't regret it, I promise you. After all, damn it! one must be loyal to oneself and know how to look after oneself; in a word, one must know oneself, that's the whole secret, to know oneself. Aren't I near the truth? Haven't I put my finger on the sore spot? Good God! my boy, can't you answer? There you stand . . . "

"All right; yes," breathed Guéret, hanging his head. "You are quite right."

He felt relieved and furious at the same time, but he dared not lift his eyes to Monsieur Grosgeorge. The old man waited a few seconds, then he went on in a warmer voice which shook a little with triumph.

"My poor friend! I have long suspected as much. The first time I saw you, I said to myself: 'There's a fine fellow who is eating his heart out!' You seemed to me like a man calling for help, except that you just didn't call. Do you understand, my boy?"

A sudden fit of gayety made him lift his arms to heaven. The pleasure of having extracted a secret, an admission, was too much for him for the moment, and it was some time before he could find words to express what was in his mind.

"Life is opening before you," he said lowering his voice as though he were telling a secret. "Ah! if I were only your age! Damn it! you don't mean to tell me that there isn't a single woman in the whole of Chanteilles who interests you? Or do you think that there are no love-affairs in the provinces?"

He screwed up his face and looked the tutor in the eyes.

"Even I, my boy, I who stand here talking to you. You think, perhaps, that because I am old there is no romance in my life now? Don't make me laugh! It all began in this very house, in the Villa Mon Idée, almost under my wife's nose. The person in question is only eighteen years old! Eighteen! What a complexion! What hair! And a good girl! Of course a little present now and then makes things a bit easier, but, as we were saying just now, beautiful things are beyond price, eh? I have been seeing her twice or three times a week for the past month . . . Don't go away with the idea that she's a tart, my boy. Far from it. My presents to her are just the presents one would give anyone who was hard up, and she is naturally grateful to me for them. I take her out to dinner sometimes. All she asks is that I should be discreet. Oh! on that score . . . "

"Discretion!"

"Yes, my boy. How strange you look! Don't you feel well?"

"Yes, quite, thank you."

"Here, just listen to this little note she sent me this morning."

He took from his pocket a note which he unfolded and held close to his face as though he were going to put his lips to it.

"*If you would like to see me tomorrow,*" he began, and interrupted himself to explain: "Tomorrow, that's today. *Tomorrow at half past nine . . . at half past nine near* . . . I can't read it without my glasses."

And putting the paper down on the table, he began to fumble in his jacket pocket. Guéret gazed for a moment at this old face blazing with passion. He felt as if his senses were failing him, one by one. For some seconds a buzzing sound had filled his ears and prevented him from hearing all that Monsieur Grosgeorge was saying. He had only grasped the beginning of the letter, but these few words had struck him as though with a sledge hammer, and now a sort of mysterious echo kept on repeating, tirelessly, somewhere at the back of his brain: *If you would like to see me tomorrow, tomorrow evening at half past nine* . . . Suddenly the room seemed to grow dark, as it sometimes does when a cloud passes over the sun. Monsieur Grosgeorge could not find his spectacles. Impatience drew in the corners of his mouth and his greedy lips became thin and shiny. That was all that Guéret could see in the darkness that seemed to rise around him, the shameful, cruel mouth that swelled and contracted alternately, wracked by a hunger which life would never satisfy. And then abruptly his eyes fell on the letter, and everything became clear again in a flash. In the hastily scrawled pencil lines he recognized Angèle's handwriting.

Chapter Eight

MADAME LONDE sat, as usual, near the window, and cast frequent glances out on to the little triangular, wind-swept space in front of her house. Her house was the last one in the town. Behind the row of trees the scanty grass extended down to the Sommeillante, and it was this that she saw every day. The rounded cobbles of the highroad, the twelve lime trees planted so as to form an angle, the almost motionless water of the river, and lastly the deep afternoon silence, all combined to give this scene the somewhat dreamy and thoughtful character of places which no traveler ever visits. Even nature becomes vague in these places; trees, there, are not like other trees, and the sky behind its clouds seems to be concealing some secret thought whose mystery is communicated to the stones of the houses, the water of the river, and gives them all a certain crafty and sinister air of complicity.

"There are not many people out for a walk now," said a little girl seated at Madame Londe's feet on a low footstool which she had placed near the window. She was about twelve years old, and wore an alpaca pinafore; she was leaning her rather prominent forehead against the window and with her dirty little hand held aside the muslin curtain yellowed by

time and dust. The restaurant proprietress looked
for a moment at the intent profile and the mischievous schoolgirl eye which nothing escaped.

"People out for a walk," she repeated, slowly.
"Do people out for a walk amuse you, dear?"

"Yes, they do," answered the child without looking up.

"I suppose you like seeing new faces?" asked
Madame Londe.

"I like recognizing the ones I've seen already,
too."

"You little imp! You've always got an answer
ready," said Madame Londe.

She sighed and looked out of the window herself,
as if she wanted to make sure that the trees hadn't
moved; then she took from her lap an old stocking
into which she thrust her hand.

"A hole," she observed in a low voice. "How on
earth do I manage to wear my stockings out so
quickly when I take so little exercise?"

Arming herself with a needle and a violet wooden
egg, she set to work to mend the hole she had discovered. Long minutes passed in complete silence.
The little girl looked first one way and then the
other, absorbed in her rôle of lookout man, and her
short pigtails seemed to move stiffly, as if an invisible hand pulled them to make her turn her head to
the right or left. Her head bowed over her work,
Madame Londe was absorbed in a revery that one
guessed became deeper and deeper, although the
activity of her fingers did not react to it and her

needle rose and fell in the same patient and regular movement.

The room in which this conversation took place was a long low one. A vast mahogany bed occupied the whole of one corner, between a yellow door and a gigantic walnut wardrobe. The faded paper on the walls showed, here and there, where damp had not destroyed its pattern, large patches of vague color, neither red nor violet, with lines of brown running through it. Little circular or rectangular rugs partially covered the tiles on the floor, from which rose an icy cold. A miserable coal fire slightly modified the temperature in the immediate vicinity of the fireplace, close to the place where Madame Londe was seated; besides, her feet rested on a foot-warmer and her hands were warmly incased in black mittens. Several cretonne-covered cushions wedged into the depths of her armchair gripped her body and helped her to keep upright. She was dressed in black serge, for she kept her taffeta dress for the dinner hour, and she had thrown a short gray wool cape over her chilly shoulders.

"Are you cold?" she asked, suddenly rousing herself from her revery to look at the little girl's bare legs.

"No, Madame Londe," she replied, brightly.

"You must not call me Madame Londe, dear. I have already told you that. Has anyone passed lately?"

"No, no one. Aren't you looking out of the window, too?"

"I was far away, dear," she muttered. "Three seconds' distraction are quite long enough for anyone to pass without my seeing them."

"What shall I call you, please?"

"Well . . . I told you, call me 'auntie' for instance."

"Why 'for instance'?"

There was a moment's silence. Madame Londe appeared not to have heard. Then abruptly she said: "You've got to call me auntie, and that's all about it."

The child crossed her hands over her left knee and began to rock sulkily backward and forward. She was pretty, in spite of the extreme pallor which heightened the brilliance of her black eyes. She was a little offended by the harsh way in which Madame Londe had just spoken to her, but her sullenness did not last long. Catching sight of a ball of wool that had fallen beneath the armchair, she picked it up and handed it to Madame Londe, hoping to put an end to their little quarrel by a graceful act.

"Oh! Thank you!" said Madame Londe with a smile. "You're a good little girl," she added, patting her cheek with the tips of her fingers. "Tell me, what do you tell your mother when she asks what you do here?"

"She doesn't often ask."

"Not often? Then she has asked sometimes? What do you tell her then?"

"I tell her that you send me on errands . . . "

"That's true. You went and bought me some coffee, the day before yesterday."

" . . . that I help you to mend your linen."

"Good! Your mother is an excellent woman, dear. You may tell her that I have my eye on you and that I mean to employ you in the restaurant one day, when you are bigger. Is she satisfied with the wages I give you?"

"She said, one day, that I should certainly not earn more anywhere else."

"To say nothing of the fact that you would get tired anywhere else. Are you sure you're not cold, dear? I don't want you to get ill here. I know if I went about with bare legs like you . . . But then you are young and healthy. Have you got enough on, though? Have you got anything warm over your chest?"

"I've got a vest."

"Your vest. There are vests and vests, dear. Let's see." And leaning forward, she slipped two fingers into the opening of the black pinafore. The child gave a little scream which was half giggle, and made as though to draw away, but the seriousness of Madame Londe's expression warned her to stay still. Madame Londe's face suddenly darkened, and she pursed her lips.

"It's just as I thought," she said, after a few seconds of painstaking investigation. "A little cotton vest as thin as paper. Why do you shrink like that?"

"You're tickling me," said the little girl, with a snigger.

Madame Londe quickly withdrew her hand and leaned back again; the blood mounted to her cheeks. "I'm tickling you!" she repeated, indignantly. "Impertinence! Perhaps you'll say I'm tickling you now?"

"No."

"That's lucky! Do you know why I put my hand inside your pinafore? To see if you didn't need a good warm garment, a woolen vest, something really good, which I would have given you, my girl. Now, if you are not satisfied you can go. Do you hear? I can get hundreds of little girls like you in Lorges. It's no good crying, miss!"

"I never said I wasn't satisfied," sobbed the child.

"You looked as though you were thinking it. And don't contradict. Now go away!"

She spoke the last words harshly, but with an effort and not quite steadily.

"What are you waiting for?" she asked as the little girl went on looking at her miserably, without moving.

"What have I done wrong, auntie?" asked the child.

"Obstinate little wretch!" cried Madame Londe, furiously. "Are you going to obey me?"

She was suddenly seized with violent rage. The shame of having been frightened of a child sent the blood flying to her cheeks, as though some one had slapped them, and she half rose from her chair, pushing away the foot-warmer, which slid over the tiles with a little squeaking sound. Her black eyes flashed beneath her thick eyebrows. The sole of her slipper had already touched the ground when the terrified child fled from the room. Madame Londe sat down again victoriously.

"There now!" she muttered, excited but satisfied. "Little vixen! She would murder me for twopence."

She reached out her foot, brought the foot-warmer back to its former position, and took the stocking up again; her fingers trembled a little as she looked for her needle among the wool; at length, after one or two deep breaths, she felt calmer. She glanced out of the window and then went on with her work.

Some one knocked.

"Come in."

It was Angèle. She put her basket down on the table and said, quickly:

"You didn't expect to see me at this hour, auntie."

"You are always welcome, dear," said the other, putting aside her stocking. "Have you thought about Monsieur Blondeau?"

"I will tell you tomorrow," said Angèle, pushing away the strands of hair which fell over her forehead.

"Tomorrow! But he has been worrying me for three days, dear. It's Thursday already. You may be sure he'll ask me what you have decided this evening again, and what shall I look like? Remember he has been waiting for a long time. He was to have his answer today at the latest."

"I know."

She sat down before Madame Londe and bent her brown head. On her cheeks, which were colored by the wind and also, perhaps, by ill-concealed emotion, her lowered eyelids traced long black curves and added the charm of a thoughtful melancholy expression to her young face. She had never appeared so beautiful as she did in the waning light of that autumn afternoon. Her neck retained the delicacy of childhood; in all her movements a certain awkwardness betokened a creature whom life had ripened too soon and which preserved deep down in itself, like a secret of whose very presence it was unconscious, the mist and uncertainty of earlier years. But her mouth was firm and serious, and her eyes, when she raised them, were averted, though there was understanding and no trace of hesitation in them. She clasped her hands on her knees.

"You know!" repeated Madame Londe. "It isn't enough to know; you must answer. I don't know why you are making all this fuss. Monsieur Blondeau is a good customer. The last time he went out with you, you told me he was very kind. And that reminds me, I want to talk to you about my new customer."

"Your new customer?"

"Yes. What's the matter with you?"

"Nothing at all, auntie."

"Well then, this gentleman came last Thursday, as you know, and he's coming back again this evening. Naturally I thought of you."

"Of me?"

"Yes, of course, you. Everything I say today seems to be a surprise to you. What's the matter with you?"

"Nothing. Nothing at all. Really."

"He's a nice-looking gentleman, very well behaved, perhaps a little shy. I thought I might be able to arrange something this evening for Sunday week. You can come and talk to me at the beginning of dinner just to show yourself. When you go out with him you must make him talk. There are all sorts of things I want to know. First of all, why did he come here at all? I've made inquiries everywhere, but the wretched man doesn't confide in anyone. It's only by chance that I found out that he was married."

She did not see the girl wince, and went on chattering away, saying the first thing that came into her head.

"You must admit that it's really extraordinary for a man to come and settle down in Chanteilles after having lived in Paris. But to come back to Monsieur Blondeau; there's something I want to ask you. What's all this about an old cousin of his in Lot-et-Garonne? Is that story true?"

"I don't know any more about it than you do. He certainly did talk to me one day about a Mademoiselle Bourgeron."

"Bourgeron," repeated Madame Londe, quickly, pretending to have remembered the name just as the girl uttered it. "I knew her name. Is she rich?"

"Really, I don't know anything at all about it."

"You must find out, Angèle dear. I mention it because Monsieur Blondeau has just bought a new overcoat. You haven't seen it yet. The color is dreadful, but the material is good. He certainly didn't do it out of his salary. I know quite well that he can only just live on what the Agence Walther gives him. On the other hand, he gave you ten francs in September. Where did that money come from? I thought of this relation of his in Lot-et-Garonne, but then why should she send it to him? Is it a loan or a gift? At any rate, you may be quite sure I shouldn't have promised that you would go out with Monsieur Blondeau on Sunday if I hadn't been impressed by his new overcoat."

"You promised him without asking me?"

"Yes, I did. Good Heavens! If I had to consult you every time an opportunity arose there would be no end to it. I tell you I am sure he has got hold of some money from somewhere."

"I don't care if he has. I shan't go with him on Sunday."

"What's that? Are you going out with some one else?"

"No; I'm not going out with anyone."

"With no one? Are you mad?"

"No, I'm not mad. I tell you I don't want to go out on Sunday."

"What have you got against Monsieur Blondeau? He's quite nice."

"Perhaps so, but he disgusts me."

"All right then; if Monsieur Blondeau disgusts you, take Monsieur Guéret."

"Monsieur Gué . . . No! Once more, I'm not going out with Blondeau or with anyone else."

She got up as she said these last words and walked across the room in such a determined manner that the older woman hesitated for a moment before answering.

"Here's a pretty pass!" she said, at length. "What's come over you? Is this what you came here to tell me?"

"Partly," answered Angèle, facing her again.

"Well, I congratulate you," returned Madame Londe. "If the rest of what you have to say is in keeping, we're in for a jolly time. And without wishing to be inquisitive, may I ask what you're going to live on? Will the Widow Brod pay your rent?"

"My rent?" repeated Angèle, leaning against the table. "But I've got my room . . . "

She stopped and stared at Madame Londe.

"Well, dear," she said, "go on. 'The room that Madame Londe lends me.' And if Madame Londe told me to clear out, this very evening? . . . "

"Auntie, you wouldn't . . . "

"How do you know I wouldn't?"

"You're not going to turn me into the street simply because I don't want to go out on Sunday?"

"And what's to prevent me? Have you thought of the mischief you are doing me in refusing to go out with my customers?"

"Auntie, I've got something to tell you. Perhaps I ought to have told you of my plans before. I'm looking for another job. You see, the one I've got now tires me out and brings in practically nothing. It's stifling in the laundry, and leaning on the iron all day . . . Anyway, I'm looking for something else."

"What else?"

"Something not so hard which will bring me in more. I had thought of becoming a housemaid."

"Housemaid to the Grosgeorges, for instance?"

"Why do you sneer at me, auntie?" said the girl, on the verge of tears. "I'm quite serious. You know quite well I couldn't possibly go to the Grosgeorges."

"All this doesn't explain why you don't want to go out on Sunday."

"Because I'm looking for a situation in which I shall be independent of all these people—of Monsieur Grosgeorge as well as your idiotic Blondeau."

"You're doing what?" cried Madame Londe, getting up suddenly. "Are you mad? Leaving me with all my customers on my hands?"

She had gone quite white, and strode up to Angèle, who waited for her unflinchingly.

"You forget that it's I who brought you up . . . " she began.

"Brought me up as you are bringing little Fernande up," answered the girl, a little more firmly.

"Ah! So I'm bringing up little Fernande, now?"

"Of course you are. You're teaching her to call you 'auntie,' as you did me at her age."

"And what does that prove?"

"It proves that she will finish like me. That one day you will serve her up to your customers."

"*I* serve you up to my customers? *I?* Are you mad, talking to me like that? I don't know what on earth you're talking about."

"Don't you? And when I come home in the evening, and you come into my room and ask me how much I got from Monsieur Blondeau, how much from Monsieur Goncelin, I suppose you've no idea of why they give me money?"

"I'm not responsible for your behavior. What passes between you and these gentlemen is no business of mine."

"Really? I suppose all that really interests you is to hear what they tell me, how their little family affairs are going on, and to find out about them through me so as to be able to cut a fine figure in the restaurant downstairs . . . "

"What an idea! If I do ask you questions sometimes, it's only to know what sort of people come here. Don't you understand? I can't have any sort of person here. I have to keep myself informed . . . "

"And what do you care what it costs me? I suppose you don't know what they do with me? Where they take me?"

Madame Londe's face went gray.

"I have already told you that I'm no longer responsible for you," she said. "You are quite old enough. . . . These things are nothing to do with me."

She waved her hand as though she was trying to get rid of some one who was being too insistent.

"All right! But I prefer to go away, anyhow," said the girl. "I won't stay in this house any more."

"Be quiet! Be quiet, do you hear?"

"Don't come near me or I'll scream. Yes, I'm going to pack this very night. Oh, you can't frighten me any more. You'll be in a nice hole when you haven't got anyone to spy on your customers any more, you old bitch!"

She made for the door, but Madame Londe planted herself in front of her and looked at her, arms akimbo.

"Don't delude yourself, my girl," she said in a calm, hard voice. "I've got some one who'll take your place perfectly, some one who is already in great demand."

"Who?" asked Angèle, involuntarily.

Madame Londe did not answer at once; her eyes remained on those of the girl.

"Fernande," she said at last.

"Fernande! You dare offer these men a girl of thirteen?"

"What a thing to say! 'Offer them'! These gentlemen are kind enough to want to take Fernande out with them for a walk. I let them do so, that's all. Her parents know all about it. I've got nothing to hide, and the child is quite happy."

"And how much do you get for it, eh?   How much do you make out of Fernande?"

"How much do I get?   What do you take me for, insolence?   I tell you that Fernande's mother is very grateful for what I do for her daughter, and she has absolute confidence in me.   Why, if she were here now she would have slapped your face long ago, to teach you to treat me with more respect."

The girl colored suddenly as though her face actually had been slapped, and for a moment she was on the point of answering, but she controlled herself and simply said:

"Well, I'm going.   Let me pass."

"No, I won't," cried Madame Londe with all the determination of which she was capable.   And as she spoke she gripped Angèle by the wrist.   "I'm not going to let you ruin yourself, you little fool. And, anyway, where could you go?"

Angèle struggled.

"Let me alone.   I want to go."

"Go where?   There!   I've let you go.   You want to pack your trunk?   Your trunk belongs to me. Do you think they'll let you into a hotel with a brown paper parcel?   I forbid you to touch the trunk! You're hiding something from me, dear. Don't deny it.   I know you are."

"It isn't true."

"You're hiding something from me. I ought to have suspected it before.   When I saw you come in looking so bewildered, and with that nervous laugh,

I guessed something was up at once. Something
has happened. What is it?"

In desperation and out of sheer weariness the girl
was on the point of surrendering and answering,
when she suddenly had a confused feeling of danger,
and seizing her basket she retreated toward the door.
Terror gave her back her energy.

"Leave me alone!" she cried, sharply. "If you
meddle with what doesn't concern you, I'll go at
once. Whatever you may say, you know that the
day I go you won't have a single customer left."

"What? You dare to threaten me, you little
slut?"

But the girl had already opened the door and
fled.

Madame Londe's first impulse was to run after
Angèle and beat her, but, apart from the fact that
her slowness of limb would have prevented her from
catching her up either on the staircase or in the
street, she reflected that it would be better not to
make this little family tiff public. So she contented
herself with opening the window and glaring furiously after the girl as she hurried away.

"Hussy!" she said, shutting the window again.
"Hussy!" Her armchair and footstool were in her
way, so she pushed them away roughly and walked
toward her bed. No doubt the girl was right; now
that her customers had tasted this kind of extra
titbit that Madame Londe had provided for them,
they would never go without it. They wanted

Angèle, easy-going Angèle with her pretty face. Hussy! She had had her head turned by flattery during the past three months.

She sat on the edge of the bed and sighed as she thought of the time, so very recent, when the girl had showed herself so obedient and amenable. On Sunday evenings, and sometimes on week-days too, she would come and tell her all she had learned about various people, with a faithful simplicity that did not always make distinctions between futilities and essentials. In this way Madame Londe quenched that pitiless thirst for knowing about people's affairs which devoured her incessantly. It would have been impossible for her to have lived surrounded by strangers unless she found out all about them. At first, every newcomer was to her an enemy who had to be besieged and captured, and in accomplishing this she experienced a mixed emotion of pain and delight which could only be compared with the impatience of love. She dominated her group of customers by the intimate knowledge she had of their narrow daily lives. This passion of hers exaggerated everything. Things which a person less inquisitive than herself would have found a meager fare were to her a royal banquet. To her eyes nothing was unimportant. Frantic with curiosity, everything that came to her mill was grist, and the origin of a tie interested her quite as much as the origin of a fortune, for hunger knows no discrimination.

But, as a kind of cruel jest, nature had not endowed this woman with those faculties of divination which would seem to have been her due; it had been content with putting her at the mercy of one of the most tyrannical instincts in the world without furnishing her with the means of satisfying it. The only gift that had been bestowed on Madame Londe was that of being able to divine, not a secret, but the presence of a secret. She always knew when a mystery existed, but she could never probe it alone. Thus it was that fate mocked her, for, if she had remained in complete darkness she would have enjoyed, if not happiness, at any rate the peace of ignorance; whereas her passion was never allowed to doze; a demoniac voice was always booming into the wretched woman's ear: "There's something up there. What is it? Why is this rich man miserable? Why does that man always wear clothes of the same color? So-and-so always turns up at the restaurant three minutes after all the others. Why? Why? Why?" Questions like these surged into her mind all the time, and tortured her. She sometimes thought that people deliberately concealed things from her, and then a general hatred of all mankind took possession of her, and if she was to have a moment's peace it was essential that Angèle should bring her the solutions to all the enigmas that strewed her path from the beginning of the day until the end. Yet the solutions always disappointed her, doubtless because there was no proportion between the eagerness with which she yearned to know them, and the pleasure which they gave her. "Was that all?" she would think. And she would be secretly an-

noyed with Angèle for not having brought her the
magnificent booty of secrets for which she always
hoped. Although she was over fifty and had had
long experience of curiosity, she did not yet understand that the object of her passion was not to trans-
form the unknown into the known, but to seek out
the unknown for its own sake and to live close to
it always. This was, perhaps, what nature tried
to make her understand in depriving her of the
ordinary intuition of women.

She was like a mole longing for sight, and Angèle's
help was indispensable to her, for the girl, less com-
plex than the woman she called "auntie," possessed
all the qualities necessary to put men into a confidential mood. Madame Londe had brought her
up as she was bringing little Fernande, but Angèle
was wrong in attributing mercenary motives to her,
for she was not avaricious. One passion is enough
for each person. Sometimes, it is true, she asked
Angèle for some of her ill-gotten gains, but this very
rarely happened and only when she found it difficult
to make both ends meet. In return she gave the girl
a room, not a very good one, perhaps, and nearly
all her meals; so that she really had the whip hand
when Angèle talked of going elsewhere. Where else
would she find free board and lodging?

There had already been several scenes between
Madame Londe and Angèle, for the girl grew more
and more restless as time went on and was straining
at the leash; but she had never before dared to talk
to Madame Londe with such brutal frankness or to

reproach her with her one great fault. Besides,
she had not only shocked Madame Londe by talking
to her of her inquisitiveness; she had surprised her.
"Inquisitive!" she thought with mingled astonishment and indignation. "The little wretch called me
inquisitive. Of course I have to know all about the
people who come to the restaurant." And she added,
inwardly, with that speciousness which the humblest
person makes use of when he wants to lie to himself:
"Besides, if I were really inquisitive, I should make
it my business to know what she does with my customers.

"But that is not my business," she added, aloud,
emphasizing her words as though she were in the
witness box. Of course she knew, from having frequented them in her own youth, the sort of places to
which her customers took Angèle; her imagination
was quite untroubled on that account, and her instinct warned her that it was more prudent not to
enter into details about relationships of which she
already knew the essentials. So long as she pretended to be ignorant of them, she could not, she
decided, be held responsible for them. Yet on Sunday, the day which she modestly referred to as
Angèle's day out, she was always nervous and
anxious until the girl's return. She kept thinking,
with an uneasiness that she could not explain, of
the familiarities which her niece had, no doubt, to
suffer. It was no use her asking herself, "After all,
what does it matter to me?" She could not regain

her calm until she heard Angèle come in and go up to her room.

And now Angèle, in her turn, was hiding something from her; the only person whom she thought she knew really well was eluding her like the others. This seemed so unjust to her that she was tempted not to believe it.

"She's only doing it to tease me," she told herself. "To tease me—*me!* What have I done to her? I brought her up. She has eaten my bread and slept beneath my roof for four whole years."

She shook with silent laughter for a moment and mentally promised herself the pleasure of giving Angèle a couple of good cuffs, but as she suddenly remembered the look in her eyes and her voice, despair settled down upon her.

"Why didn't I look after her better?" she groaned, aloud. "I'm sure she's up to something. Now she's escaping from me. And it's my fault, my own fault."

The violence of her sorrow contorted her features and compelled her to rise and walk about the room, as though she did not know what to do with her body. Tears trembled in her black eyes and made them shine like enamel. She had a sudden awful vision of a lonely life, with long dreary evenings. How could she have spoken so lightly of Angèle's departure? She hadn't thought of what she was saying. Death would be better. Yes, it would be better to disappear than to see her customers leaving her one by one, taking with them the secrets of which she seemed to see the signs in their faces, in their movements, even in their clothing. What was to hold them, in future? She thought of Fernande. But no! They would never confide in anyone but a grown-up person, and besides, from any point of view, Fernande was still too young. So that was the end of the restaurant. She would have to bear first the disappointment and then the general dissatisfaction of her customers. A strange fancy to crown her humiliation, to lacerate her own feelings, compelled her to imagine Monsieur Blondeau's face when she told him that Angèle was not coming any more, and Monsieur Goncelin's face, and Monsieur Pellatane's and Monsieur Trept's. And then their voices! She could hear their voices, whining, furious, imploring. Her head was spinning. She saw herself at her desk, her fingers clenched on the little tin vase, pale, erect, explaining, explaining.

Her hands covered her face, which was burning with emotion and shame. The girl would have to be kept from going. If she only could manage to discover why she wanted to leave her!

"Of course she won't go," she announced, firmly. "But what is she hiding from me?"

She sat down and got up again at once.

"I *must* know," she groaned, resuming her tireless striding up and down the room. "It isn't fair to tell me nothing. What can it be? What's the matter with her?"

Over her bed a metal Christ spread His arms upon a plush cross. She stopped before Him abruptly and stared at Him with the concentrated look of a person whose thoughts are far away. Then suddenly she saw Him with His head on one side and His eyes closed. He looked as though He were tired of this woman and of her troubles.

"What's the matter?" she repeated, as though she were addressing the Divinity. "What's the child hiding from me?"

She stood still for a few moments, and fell into an impassioned meditation on her misfortunes, which at least gave her an outward appearance of calm. The deep lines that appeared on her face showed that her thoughts had dragged her into the lowest depths of misery and left her to wallow there. Behind her the sky was growing paler, with a reddish line above the house-tops which promised a fine morrow. The rays of the setting sun, split up by the window-bars, were already illuminating the floor tiles and moving slowly across the walls. The brilliance of their light roused Madame Londe from her reflections. She sighed and, with a heavy heart, clasped her hands. Tears which she could no longer control trickled down each side of her majestic nose.

"If she goes . . . " she muttered. But her voice broke and she could not finish the sentence. She bowed her head and walked from her bed to her armchair and from her armchair to the center of the room like a traveler who has lost his way in the depths of a forest.

"Heavens! it's late!" she said, after a moment,

hearing the waiter go downstairs to the kitchen. "Dinner's in three-quarters of an hour!"

Behind her back her hands unhooked her skirt, which slid down over her massive hips. For she had to perform her evening toilet and put on the taffeta dress sacred to the dinner hour. But her heart was breaking with bitter sorrow, and now she was crying unrestrainedly, standing in the splendor of the twilight, dressed only in her faded serge bodice and her gray flannelette petticoat below which appeared the shapeless calves of an old woman.

Chapter Nine

WHEN Angèle had crossed the open space in front of the restaurant, she took a road which encircled Lorges, following the course of the river, and then went on to Chanteilles. As a rule, if she had a few minutes to spare at the end of the day, she spent them in walking through the town and passing the time of day with all and sundry, for she hated being alone, and it amused her to exchange trivialities with her neighbors. Like all people who, because of their beauty, are accustomed to friendliness and compliments, she had for a long time felt the need of being surrounded by people, of seeing faces light up at her approach and hands stretched out to greet her. Of course she knew quite well that they thought badly of her, and that many of the people who were nice to her when they met her, said harsh things about her behind her back, but she did not mind that much. She was satisfied with the outward signs of cordiality. Her own peace of mind depended upon the apparent good temper of the people she saw every day. A hasty word or a scowling face could wound her deeply and cast her into the depths of depression. Perhaps that explained why she had yielded so easily to the men who had pursued her and courted her ever since her sixteenth year. With the tacit approval of Madame Londe, and egged on, also, by the desire to be thought affectionate and a "good sort," she had let herself go, weakly, from one to another, delighted by the attentions and the flattery which they lavished on her. The reputation she had acquired did not worry her at all, because, like all weak natures, she imagined it to be inevitable. Life appeared to her, dimly, as a kind of lottery, something good or bad according to whether one were lucky or not, but in any case irrevocable. It never occurred to her that she might be wrong.

That evening her first impulse had been to leave Lorges and thus to get away from her aunt. But as she passed before Saint-Jude she yielded to a desire to go in. Half Gothic, half Roman, restored in the seventeenth century, it was one of those churches that fade sadly away into oblivion and are nearly always empty, but in which generations of the faithful have left a kind of memory of their devotion. As the girl entered the nave, the choir was already in darkness and one could scarcely make out its Corinthian columns alternating with Gothic arches. She sat down not far from the door and drew a deep breath as she looked around her.

Although she was by no means pious, she liked resting in Saint-Jude. Her faith was limited to the occasional recital of a short prayer, with a hazy feeling that it did not commit her to much and couldn't do any harm. And she did not like her aunt's customers to sneer at priests. But that was all; services bored her.

After her recent outburst she felt the necessity of remaining quiet and reflecting on all she had said and all that had been said to her. Madame Londe's infuriated voice still echoed in her head. During all her monotonous life no one had ever yet spoken to her as her aunt had done, nor had she ever seen such rage flaming in anyone's eyes. The sight of it had affected her. It was as though a firm, relentless hand had shaken her and roused her from a deep sleep. For years she had believed in the compliments of men and in Madame Londe's affectations, and had never for a moment questioned the sincerity of their kind words and their smiles; and now, suddenly, she saw something real, a woman who had lost her head from sheer fright, who drew herself up, palpitated, threw herself about and tried to stop her from leaving the house by main force. And this had so upset her that now, a quarter of an hour later, her heart still beat violently and seemed unable to calm down again.

To try to quiet herself, she began to recite "Hail Mary's," but the thoughts that kept crowding into her head were stronger than the words of the prayer, and though her lips moved they could not soothe her mind. The first time she had met Guéret was in a street in Lorges, toward the end of one afternoon. He had followed her for some time, then he had accosted her and spoken to her, but in such an abrupt way that at first she thought he was angry

with her about something. The impression he gave
her was that he was in a hurry to tell her something
and then go away. He had not spoken to her about
money; he had simply asked where he could see her
again, and she had fixed a time and place, but rather
against her inclination, because he spoke in such a
strange way, as though some one were compressing
his throat, and because he dropped his eyes when
she looked at him. Naturally she had been disappointed that he had not offered her anything, disappointed but surprised, and the surprise, after all,
had been greater than the disappointment. Was it
because he excited her curiosity that she had kept
the appointment? With his anxious face, his drawn
and haggard features, she found him anything but
handsome, and his broad but bent shoulders had
frightened her for no reason that she could give; he
looked as though he were carrying something very
heavy, or as though he were trying to hide from
justice. His hands had never once left the pockets
of his gray overcoat, which came down below his
knees, and yet Angèle had a feeling all through their
conversation that he was holding her arms, her
wrists. Perhaps this was because he had gazed at
them so intently, for his eyes had never left them.

At any rate, she had kept the appointment. But
if she had been afraid of him, why had she met him
in a secluded spot, at nightfall? No one ever ventured anywhere near the railway footbridge after
sunset. She remembered that it was he who had
suggested the road leading to the footbridge and

that she had said yes, without thinking, probably to get rid of him. He was already there when she arrived, and began to talk to her at once, and she, in a sudden panic, quickened her pace, telling him that was not the right place, and that she did not want anyone to see her with a man. She had said that to gain time, even though each step took her further away from the town and people. She thought of running away and hiding herself behind a bush. But what if he found her? She had read so many stories of women being murdered in woods. Then he had run after her. She stood still with a beating heart and spoke to him in the firm voice one uses to an infuriated animal that one wants to intimidate. And near the footbridge he had rejoined her and had spoken to her angrily, as she had expected him to do, but she had stood up to him, hiding her own terror by pretending to be angry, too, and to her great surprise he had apologized. Then they had crossed the footbridge, and in the road, at the other side of the railway, he had offered her a ring, and it was at that moment that she felt she was mad to have been afraid of such a poor-spirited creature. And, with her heart full of contempt for this man with his lowered eyes, she had accepted his gift, the ring which he tried to place on her finger. For now he was holding her by the arm, there was no mistake about it this time, and she saw an enormous gnarled hand which shook at the end of his muscular arm with its white wrist; but in spite of the power and ugliness of this hand she was not afraid of it, and she only

felt pity for his awkward movements, and in her
impatience she had taken the ring, which was of no
value, she could tell that at a glance, and put it on,
herself.

How different, she thought, from her aunt's customers. They didn't waste time in ridiculous hesitation, and the money that was to buy them Angèle's
good graces was never long in forthcoming. It is
true that in this case she was dealing with a stranger,
but could anyone be so simple, such a booby? The
man's timidity communicated itself to her and made
her feel awkward, too; she was not used to such long
silences, to that attitude of his full of respect and
humility. Naturally she had no illusions about
what the man wanted, but by a monstrous caprice of
her nature she resolved to refuse him everything because he did not despise her.

She had seen him once again. She had written
to him of her own accord, because it seemed to her
that he was purposely putting off asking her to
meet him, and that perhaps he was trying to forget
her, to cure himself of her. Now that he did not
frighten her any more, she wanted to play with him,
to hear what a man like that said to a woman, to
watch his expression. His impatience, his sadness,
his anger, all amused her. It was delicious to remain
calm in the presence of some one so profoundly
moved, because she had no doubt at all that the man
was suffering, and she was not indifferent to his
suffering; on the contrary, she encouraged it; sometimes even, in a sudden wave of pity, she felt herself

on the verge of taking his hands and smoothing his
forehead, just to see his wounds heal and joy come
into his eyes. But the strange thing was that she
always suppressed this impulse; perhaps she was
afraid of the bother that such a spontaneous act on
her part would cause her; an affectionate gesture like
that would call for others, and so on until she finally
yielded to Guéret's desires, and she did not intend
to yield. Besides, there was always the risk of
being seen. For instance, the day she had met him
for the third time, below the Boulevard de la Preste,
it would have been quite enough for some one to
have passed at the moment she stretched her hands
out to him, for it to be all over the town an hour
later, and she was afraid of some one discovering her
little intrigue, for she was ashamed of this man.

She was ashamed of him, and that was why she met
him only after sunset, or, as on the last occasion, in
some deserted spot near the river. He looked so tall
and ungainly in his ill-fitting overcoat, and his long
gloomy face would have been treated as a joke by
people who were inclined to jeer. Of course, it was
surprising that a girl like Angèle should be so particular; one had only to cast a glance over the Restaurant Londe, one evening when all the regular
customers were there, to see that the gentlemen to
whom she accorded her favors were neither hand-
somer nor better made than this man with whom she
would have nothing to do. But their graceless
bodies and stupid faces were indifferent to her. Her
aunt's customers had always been like that, it ap-

peared to her, and she could not imagine them to be anything else; they formed part of her life in the same way as the walls of the houses she saw every day, the banks of the Sommeillante, and the little plane trees on the promenade. It was not the same in the case of Guéret, who represented, in her eyes, so far as she thought about him at all, the element of chance. Besides, she was scarcely angry with him for not being handsome; she was humiliated by the fact that he was not younger and richer, that he had large hands, dirty cuffs, and a hunted look. Surely she deserved something better than that? How she longed to find herself swept into a romantic affair with a boy of her own age, with a quick wit and a jolly face! Instead of which . . . Fate scoffed at her, clearly.

And in spite of everything, she felt herself obliged to see this man again, however little satisfaction she got from it, in the same way that a gambler refuses to leave a game once started, and goes on with it, even if it bores him, merely to see how it is going to end. Hadn't she gone too far to draw back now? She could not very well tell a man that she did not want to speak to him after having herself asked him to meet her.

It was with this mixture of false logic and caprice that she invented reasons for seeing him again. Guéret had appeared at a moment when many things around her filled her with repugnance, for even habit had not been able to make her accept cheerfully the life that had been imposed upon her, her work at the laundry, her "outings" with her aunt's customers, and clandestine visits to other gentlemen in the town. In certain moments of solitude, at night when it was too hot to sleep, and in the daytime if she was too tired to go out, she caught a glimpse of her future as a long succession of weeks each exactly like the last, or only varied by illness and misfortune. And being by nature inclined to consider events from their gloomiest side (a cautionary measure to avoid disappointment), she would put herself difficult questions to which her mind could suggest no answer. Where would she go if her aunt died? Or if the customers of the restaurant, sordid source of wealth though they were, went away? What would she do if, as had already happened to Madame Pellatane, the butcher's wife, an attack of erysipelas were to disfigure her? For the butcher's wife it had been of only relative importance, but for her, good Heavens! it would mean that her livelihood would be seriously jeopardized.

But now a man, a stranger, came to her. Not a man like other men, like the coarse *habitués* of the Restaurant Londe who lusted after her, paid her, and did not give her another thought, but a lover, yes, a man who respected her, idiot that he was, and who offered her a little ring as a man does to his betrothed, and never even mentioned money to her. As she reflected upon all these things, a strange feeling crept into her heart. She did not love him, poor Guéret, because he was neither handsome nor young nor rich. And yet she wanted to see him.

Even now, in this church, she missed him. She would like to be with him, in the street, hearing him talk in his low, rather flat voice, a voice into which something savage crept from time to time. Beside him she felt herself handsome and powerful and happy —she who was so small beside this tall strong man who none the less lowered his eyes before hers.

To have treated her as he did he must have known nothing of the real circumstances, but must have taken her for a person much less promiscuous than she really was. That was because she did not flaunt herself like those peroxided women who walked about the Boulevard de la Preste between eleven o'clock and midnight; she did not make up her face or accost people; and, anyway, what could she have in common with those dreadful creatures? The most spiteful tongues in Chanteilles would hardly dare to confuse her with those unfortunate women. She seemed so quiet and shy! That is what had deceived Guéret, undoubtedly. But if he found out one day that she got paid like the Chanteilles ladies, what would he say? He would certainly change his attitude toward her. Does one stand on ceremony with a girl whom anyone can buy?

A sigh broke from her and she clasped her hands together. She was not a girl whom anyone could buy. The proof of that was that she had refused to go out with Monsieur Blondeau. It was only that she had often been weak and had yielded to a lot of men because her aunt had egged her on, and because it was the only way to make people nice to her. But what pleasure had she ever got out of these dreary affairs of hers? These "outings" with the restaurant gentlemen always bored her and often disgusted her, for Madame Londe's customers were neither young nor handsome. There must be good-looking young fellows somewhere in the world, and yet by a sort of fatality all the poor and unattractive ones seemed to have congregated at her aunt's restaurant. One day, not quite a year ago, she had watched an infantry regiment pass on its way from maneuvers back to barracks. Hundreds of young soldiers had passed before her. She had stood at the corner of a street, a little afraid at being so close to them, embarrassed by a great deal that they said to her, but neither daring nor wanting to run away. What strange feelings she had experienced on that occasion! With their red caps on one side and their dusty cloaks, some of them had seemed to her so handsome and so gay that the mere thought of them sent the blood to her cheeks. And that scene seemed to her to be the image and substance of her whole life; she stood beside a road, motionless, while these happy, vigorous men passed her by without her being able, because of some mysterious order of things, to put out a hand to detain them. She had to watch this crowd of young men go by, when a single one of them would very likely have made her happy all her life. It was as though some one had said to her: "Follow them with your eyes. The road leads them to other towns where the women who love them await them; for you may be sure that they are not starved of love, or that women want to starve them of it; but see, they are passing by, and not one of them is for you."

And since that occasion, each time that one of the customers of the restaurant asked her to go out with him, the memory of those bitter moments came back to her, as though to scoff at her dreams. Yet at Chanteilles there were young men at whom the poor girl looked longingly when she passed them in the street. But no doubt she lacked boldness, because her instinct urged her to hide herself when they looked at her, and so she gave them the impression that she was proud and did not want to speak to them. Besides, they never appeared to be particularly interested in her, for they never followed her. This sometimes made her think that she was not so good-looking as she imagined, or, at least, that good looks were not enough unless their charm was enhanced by a certain pertness and confidence of expression and manner. Not that she was lacking in pertness with Monsieur Blondeau, for instance, who was sometimes stingy with the drinks, or with Monsieur Grosgeorge when he imagined he had the right to talk to her as though she were a servant, because he was rich; but one of them was weakly and the other was a sexagenarian and they represented between them all that she could imagine as most despicable and dreary. They were the kind of men who said nice things to her about her face and her figure. Good Lord! A perfect fright who was as accommodating as she was would have received the same attention; so that she could have no faith in even these poor men's flattery. She would perhaps believe she was pretty when a healthy, handsome man of her own age spoke to her and begged her to be nice to him. But in the meantime, how ugly and insignificant she felt under the gaze of the people she would have liked to love. She remembered one summer afternoon, a terrible afternoon which she had spent at the window of her room, looking through the shutters, because some workmen were repairing the roadway in the little triangular space in front of the house, and because she had been lost in admiration of one of them, who with his bare neck and arms had seemed to her to be a sort of prodigy. And, as though his companions recognized his superiority over them, the noblest task seemed, as it were, to have been allotted to him, for he knelt in the road, and his work consisted in fitting together the stone cubes which the others handed to him; from time to time he moved along by a slight shifting of his legs, but he remained squatting on his heels, his body erect, like a prince to whom vassals were bringing gifts.

And the years passed without these memories growing less painful, and without healing the open wound which they left in her mind. She was not wanted; her pretty bright eyes and her full cheeks allured merely dreary old men or feeble men, or timid men who dared not pay their addresses elsewhere. Oh, what a cry she could send up to Heaven if she had faith! Who was she to pick and choose?

And now a man came to her, less repulsive to her
than the others because he loved her, because he
spoke to her with that shy deference which she also
had felt in the depths of her heart for other men,
for those whom she had looked at from the roadside
or through the slits in the shutters. How well she
understood, now, the trembling of that man's hand
when he touched her arm! Could she rebuff a man
whose suffering linked him to her with so many
bonds? And this idea put her into such a violent
state of emotion that she rose from her seat. Was
not happiness, after all, love—love no matter whence
it came? And even if that love were not the love of
her dreams in her restless solitude, was she for that
reason to despise the mysterious gift that was offered to her? Would it not bring her bad luck to
spurn love, who never thought of anything but
love? She leaned her hand on the prie-Dieu and
looked around her, suddenly seized with terror at
the thought of what life might hold in store for her.
Was there no way of averting future misery? Wasn't
prayer meant for that? Without much conviction
she made the sign of the cross on her breast.

All at once she seemed to understand that life did
not give you a second chance, and that you should
grasp what little it gave you with eager hands. And
her gloomy imagination pictured life to her as a
capricious and terrible creature, a tyrant with whom
it was not wise to argue. In that ancient church full
of deep shadows, the sound of a chair being pushed
back, the step of a passer-by in the street, the most

ordinary sounds, took on an abnormal character.
The silence deepened and enfolded the high vault
of the choir and of the side chapels where so many
unhappy women had come to sit and sigh a little
and try to ease their sorrows by telling Heaven of
them.

She turned her back on the altar and took a few
steps down the nave. The smell of incense still
hung in the air and she breathed it in deeply with
melancholy pleasure; this smell so full of childish
memories suddenly made her miss all the things that
had been denied her. Long ago when she was little,
she had always thought of heaven as an endless
meadow beneath a spring sky; clumps of blossoming
trees broke the monotony of this vast, gently un-
dulating space; and here and there children danced
in rings, and sang. It was thus that she imagined
the eternal happiness of a soul united to God, and
now once more this childish idea came back to her,
but she did not smile at it, even though it was a far
cry from her longings as a little girl to the desires
that now haunted her youth. She asked herself
whether true happiness did not perhaps lie in these
illusions of early years, in which the soul let itself
drift gently along with the sweetness of its dreams
and in which reason has not yet the power to close the
delicious paths along which imagination wanders.

As she reached the end of the church she suddenly
thought of Guéret, and of his voice by turns harsh
and humble. If ever he discovered that she had sold
herself to others, to many others, what would his

voice be like then? Was it possible that he had not yet heard about it in Chanteilles, where everyone gossiped so? And if, filled with disgust, he gave her up and refused to see her any more? The thought of such humiliation brought the blood to her cheeks and she pushed open the church door, wondering whether it was really worth the trouble of spending a quarter of an hour in a church to come out like this with one's heart full of anger and despair.

Chapter Ten

THIS time he did not have to find a place for himself: as he was hanging up his hat a waiter came to tell him that his place had been laid at the *table d'hôte*, and he went and sat there between Monsieur Morestel and Monsieur Blondeau, thus interrupting an animated conversation, carried on in a low voice, about politics. The table was full. Out of shyness he affected a certain abruptness of manner and coughed once or twice as he unfolded his napkin. And yet, if these gentlemen had been able to see him, five minutes earlier, in the shadows across the way, irresolute, as nervous as though he were committing a crime, changing his mind twenty times before daring to enter, they would have smiled at these acts of self-assurance and the defiant look he cast round at his neighbors. "I know I'm late," he seemed to be saying. "Are you annoyed? I am indeed distressed." Actually his two minutes' lateness gave him a prestige of which he was quite unaware. His was the dangerous glory of having braved Madame Londe, to whom punctuality was no laughing matter. But Madame Londe did not appear to be angry. Quite the contrary, in fact; she smiled at him and bowed in his direction with an air of royal condescension.

"Damn it!" exclaimed Blondeau in a whisper. "He seems to be in the old lady's good books."

"I was just going to say the same," said Morestel, full of admiration; "no one has ever been late before without hearing about it."

"Well," said a customer whom Guéret could not see because of a large potted plant that hid him from view, "if the gentleman is new to these parts, it is hardly surprising that he doesn't know our habits."

"Lunch at midday, dinner at seven," said Morestel, leaning toward Guéret as though he were imparting a confidence.

"Thank you, monsieur."

"At your service."

There was a short pause during which the soup that remained at the bottom of the plates disappeared loudly, then the diners resumed the interchange of remarks, either aloud or in whispers, in the peculiar tone always observed at the Restaurant Londe.

"I see," said Morestel, wiping his mouth and turning toward Guéret, "that you are not what I may call a regular daily customer."

"No," replied Guéret. "You see, I can only come once a week."

It was an effort for him to talk to this man whose appearance revolted him, but on the other hand he had to find out certain things and the opportunity was a good one. He examined his neighbor furtively. He was a narrow-shouldered young man, dressed in a blue serge suit which had grown shiny with long use. His face, the bloodless face of an underfed fair man, was crisscrossed with premature wrinkles which seemed to take a delight in lining his hapless flesh. His mouth, which was much too small, was surmounted by tufts of yellow hair; it had practically no lips, with the result that every time it opened to speak, it went through a series of appalling grimaces. His thick pince-nez glasses partly disguised the insolent yet nervous look in his pale-blue eyes, but all the moral hideousness of the man was embodied in his nose, which nature had thinned out into a bird-like beak, an inquisitive nose without self-confidence, always ready to flinch before a blow, the only part of that wretched face which had any blood in it.

"And in my turn," Guéret went on, "may I ask if you come here every day?"

"Every day for the last two and a half years. I am, indeed, one of Madame Londe's oldest and best customers."

"One of the oldest?" put in a diner who did not appear to have been listening. "There are two of us here who beat you by six and eight months, Monsieur Morestel."

"So far as length of time is concerned, I yield to no one," then said Monsieur Blondeau's right-hand neighbor. "Ask Madame Londe if she didn't herself serve me my first dinner. And when I tell you that Madame Londe herself served, I am taking you back more than three years."

These words were uttered in a dull, dreary voice, with a strong provincial accent, by a man whose massive carcass and powerful shoulders were practically completely concealed behind the napkin which he had knotted behind his neck. His black curly hair hung down over his forehead and relapsed into whiskers along his blotchy cheeks. While speaking he glared at the people dining opposite to him.

"Certainly, Monsieur Borges," replied the gentleman behind the plant, a trifle sharply. "It was actually of you that I was thinking when I explained to Monsieur Morestel that he was not, strictly speaking, among Madame Londe's oldest customers. However, let us be accurate. You must deduct four months of absence from the three years you speak of."

And he spread his hands out in a rhetorical gesture, looking confidently around him, as though to invite his neighbors to support him.

Guéret had a glimpse of a long, bad-tempered profile to which the joy of triumph gave a glimmer of intelligence.

"Four months?" repeated Monsieur Trept, a stout, pasty-faced youth seated at the end of the table. He had a high voice and all the others turned toward him with looks of curiosity or indignation, because he had spoken too loud. However, his question was welcomed, and caused considerable relief; Monsieur Borges's immediate neighbors would never have risked annoying a man so violent as the

poulterer, but this youngster was only a recent arrival; as for Monsieur Palisson, the man who had
apostrophized Monsieur Borges from behind the
plant, he had acquired a reputation for "cheek"
and he was allowed, even by Monsieur Borges, to
say anything that came into his head. He was said
once to have acted in a comedy produced by some
theatrical society. He was the extremist element in
this parliament of idiots.

"I said four months, Monsieur Trept," he repeated. "But you are both new customers of
Madame Londe's, so you cannot be aware, unless
you have been told, of the fact that Monsieur Borges
was away for four whole months last year, which
reduces his months of attendance to thirty-two, or
two years and eight months."

"You bore me with your calculations," cried
Monsieur Borges, his voice rising in anger. "Is it
my fault that I had an attack of pneumonia which
kept me in bed for six weeks, to say nothing of six
weeks' convalescence, all to the detriment of my business, Mister Clever?"

"Your attack of pneumonia? Why not simply
say your attack, your apoplectic fit?" flung out
Monsieur Palisson in an icy voice. "That would be
nearer the truth."

"An apoplectic fit!" roared Monsieur Borges, half
rising from his chair, his face scarlet. "I have
never had an apoplectic fit, monsieur, and whoever
says it is a liar!"

At this point the voice of Madame Londe rose from the end of the room:

"Less noise, a little less noise, gentlemen! You are forgetting where you are."

Every eye turned toward the proprietress. So high was her desk that only her motionless head and her broad shoulders could be seen, but, with an invisible movement of her hands, the little bunch of marigolds passed quickly from right to left.

"It's a bad sign when she touches her flowers," whispered Morestel to Guéret.

There was silence for a further moment or two. The waiter was going noiselessly around the table, handing the meat. Monsieur Borges had sat down again. Drops of sweat trickled slowly down the furrows on his forehead and met on his little short nose, where they shone like glass. Suppressed rage darkened his eyes and gave them a wild, desperate look which would have aroused compassion in hearts more sensitive than those of his neighbors. When the dish was handed to him, he thrust his fork into a cutlet with such ferocity that his neighbors smiled, and the uneasiness which Madame Londe's words had caused dissolved.

"I was there when he had this famous attack of his," muttered Morestel. "Funny thing, he has always maintained that it was his lungs, saying that he got them congested in a draught, but Monsieur Palisson is a chemist and you know you can't bluff them. From time to time he speaks to Monsieur Borges about his attack, out of revenge, because he didn't buy his medicines from him. It wouldn't need much to give him a second attack, he's so fat."

"Poor man!" said Guéret, disgusted by all this spite. Morestel's eyes opened wide with surprise.

"Do you think so? You don't know old man Borges. If he wasn't afraid of the police he would have throttled Palisson long ago."

Monsieur Blondeau had caught these last words, even though they were whispered, and, screwing his mouth up on Guéret's side so as not to be heard by Monsieur Borges, who sat on his right, he said:

"If you want to annoy him, ask him how many chickens he sold at the big fair at Pont-Emiliard last year. You've no idea how funny it is."

Then he quickly put his glass to his lips, as though to put Monsieur Borges, whose suspicions were suddenly aroused, off the scent, and drank four or five gulps of water trying to look innocent.

"Hurry up, can't you?" suddenly cried Madame Londe to the waiter. "Can't you see they're waiting for the salad? Put those cutlets down and run and get it. Quicker, my lad, quicker!"

"Oh dear!" said Morestel. "I told you there'd be trouble."

It was the fact of feeling herself out of it that made the proprietress irritable. She guessed quite well that something was happening at the *table d'hôte*, but she could not catch a single word. She would have liked to fling herself bodily into the abyss of hatred which she dominated from the height of her desk, and to explore its very bottom and all its hollows; to find out, oh, to find out. "What are they saying?" she thought. "Why does Monsieur Borges look so upset? And what is Monsieur Guéret saying to his neighbors?" She folded her hands and closed her eyes sadly. "The girl will find out on Sunday," she told herself, by way of consolation. "Yes, but will she tell me?" And she began to feel unhappy again.

"For my part," went on Morestel, cutting up his meat, "I think she'll get into trouble over the girl."

Guéret heard this remark, but he paused a moment before putting the question of which he had been thinking since the beginning of dinner. His throat suddenly tightened. A little while ago, while walking round Saint-Jude, he had seen Angèle; she was running and he had followed her. She had entered the restaurant. He had seen her cross the room and disappear behind the screen at the end. Why had she not told him that she knew Madame Londe?

"Whom do you mean by the girl?" he asked for a moment.

"Angèle, of course," said Morestel, with his mouth full.

A fresh silence followed this reply.

"Aren't you going to finish your cutlet?" asked Morestel, suddenly.

Guéret shook his head.

"Then will you let me have it? Thanks, thanks very much," he went on more amiably, as though the gift of this piece of meat deserved something in return. "It is not surprising that you don't know the girl. That's what we always call Madame Londe's niece."

"Ah!"

"Yes, but it surprises me that you don't know about her. We have known her for so long. She and I are on quite intimate terms."

"Your neighbor seems to be pulling your leg," interrupted Blondeau. "To hear him talk, one would think he was a . . . seducer."

"A Don Juan," announced Monsieur Palisson. Morestel looked down his nose. Blondeau smiled. Borges, who had not followed the conversation at all, but saw Morestel's discomfort, choked with laughter behind his napkin.

"The truth of the whole matter," explained Blondeau, putting his finger and thumb together as though he were holding a flower between them, "is that, in point of fact, Angèle is not very austere."

He had a round, jovial face, so fat that its skin was stretched until it shone. His mouth, which he never shut completely, was well shaped and full, and from the way in which he rolled his eyes it was obvious that he was proud of their large brown pupils and thick lashes. The grease with which his hair was plastered exuded a sickening smell of violets and perspiration. The whole of his little plump person inflated his black serge suit until it was nothing but curves.

"All you need," he went on, conceitedly, "is to know how to talk to her."

"Oh, be quiet!" interrupted Palisson, contemptuously. "Anyone always knows how to talk to a girl like that if he has five francs in his hand."

"Except on the days when she snubs chemists," returned Blondeau, furious at being taken up like this.

"If you are addressing me," retorted Palisson, "I have the honor to tell you that you are lying, my little man. She herself suggested that we should go out last Sunday, and it was I, you understand, I, who refused."

At this point Borges broke in.

"It isn't true," he said, with an explosion of bestial joy. "It was she who refused him, and, by Jove! she was quite right; you've only got to look at him yourself to see that!"

The whole table was in a state of suppressed uproar. A flood of bile turned Palisson's face yellow, and half rising from his place he pointed his finger over the plant.

"And I refused," he went on, "because after you've touched a woman I don't want her any more, Monsieur Borges! And if you want a piece of advice, free advice, Monsieur Borges, I advise you to be careful of women. With a complexion like yours and a neck like yours . . . "

"Gentlemen, I cannot allow you to talk so loud," cried Madame Londe after straining her ears vainly to hear. She was exasperated at not being able to grasp even the subject of their quarrel, and was at one moment on the point of demanding to know the reason of the noise of which nothing but a kind of rolling echo reached her. Her voice produced a general silence, but was powerless to subdue Palisson, who did not even turn his head, but went on, his finger still pointing at Borges:

"With a neck like yours, Monsieur Borges, I should be afraid to."

And he sat down again. A horrified silence was the only commentary on his words, as though death had suddenly appeared at the table. Borges looked gapingly around him without being able to articulate a syllable, trying to find some reassurance in the eyes of his neighbors, who turned away and seemed merely to be annoyed by the sight of such anguish.

"At last!" exclaimed Madame Londe, with the expression of some one who has won a hard victory. She would have given one of her fingers to know what Palisson had said, but she curbed the wretched impulse that urged her to interrogate the diners and vented her spleen upon the waiter:

"Bring in the stewed fruit, quickly, my lad. You've done nothing but dawdle the last few days. Be careful! You know I won't have it."

There was silence for a further few seconds, during which nothing was heard but the sound of forks scraping against cutlet bones and tearing the last shreds of meat from them; then some one sighed, and his neighbor ventured a remark which was immediately taken up, and conversation started again.

"At any rate, that girl can pride herself on having made plenty of enemies at this table," murmured Morestel to Guéret. "Women are so deceitful."

He was still smarting under the affront he had been compelled to endure a few minutes before, and was consoling himself by giving vent to generalities, but Guéret did not answer at once. He had clasped his hands as though to master the violent emotion which was making them tremble. Finally he opened his lips and, leaning toward Morestel without looking at him, asked:

"Tell me, has she been with everyone?"

"With everyone here? Yes, of course," he whispered. "Beginning with Palisson, whom she won't have any more to do with, down to Blondeau, who is going out with her on Sunday. But don't let's talk about it too loudly. If you get them on the question of priority they'll tear one another's eyes out. Madame Londe is scowling at us enough already."

"And what does one have to do to go out with her, as you put it, Monsieur Morestel?"

"Why, you just speak to Madame Londe and ask to be put on the list for a particular Sunday. Naturally you have to pay something, but you won't regret it, I can assure you. When you first see her you may think she is a little young. Her manner may deceive you at first, but at heart she's more shameless than a Chanteilles tart. Angel eyes, you know, and all the time . . . You look as if you're not pleased with what I'm telling you. But I'm doing it for your own benefit."

"Thank you, Monsieur Morestel. You say she is going out with Monsieur Blondeau. Which is Monsieur Blondeau?"

"Not so loud. Your right-hand neighbor."

"And if I don't want to wait until Monsieur Blondeau has had his turn, eh? Can Madame Londe arrange that, too?"

"Well, I don't know. Such a case has never arisen. I should ask the proprietress. Don't hold my arm like that; you're hurting me."

"I'm so sorry, Monsieur Morestel. I don't know what I could have been thinking of. Would you like my portion of fruit? You may have it. And, look, you may finish my wine, as you have no more of your own. I don't seem to have any appetite this evening, but I particularly want to drink your health, Monsieur Morestel."

Chapter Eleven

To WAIT. That was what he had to resign himself to, in spite of the throbbing impatience
that he felt within him. For weeks his mind had not
known any rest, but went floundering on, never leaving the barren paths along which his desire led him.
A perpetual hunger devoured him, and though he
suffered from it, everything but this hunger disgusted him. What was life and its little anxieties
compared with the terrible reality of this torture?

He had not gone to bed to sleep, but, since night
had come, it was better to take advantage of its
coolness and its silence. At least he could abandon
himself to his misery, for he felt a desire to aggravate
his wound, to lacerate himself, to poison himself with
his nails, since he could not cure himself. What
is the use of trying to distract oneself from a pain
that dominates both one's body and one's soul? It
is easier not to resist it, and to let it wreak its havoc
with its full force.

He had been lying on his back for more than an
hour, his eyelids burning, his head so heavy and tired
that he thought several times that he was going to
lapse into slumber, but somewhere at the back of his
brain a thought kept watch, like a flame which no
breath could possibly extinguish. In the darkness he

distinguished before him a long white surface which seemed to shimmer slightly, the wall, and then a black shape, the door. One day he would cross the threshold of that door and would never return to that room where he had already suffered so much. Would he be alive or dead? And if he were alive, where would he go? What could ever happen to him better or worse than he had known until then? Was it not appalling to be thus confined to a knowledge of the present, not to know whether the future was going to aggravate or to relieve one's miseries? How strange was this parsimony of time that spread one's misfortunes over hours and days, only giving one a little at a time so as not to kill one too quickly.

His bedclothes scorched him, even though he felt the cold air on his face and on his shoulders. He rose and sought on the round table in the middle of the room the water-jug that his wife left there every evening, but in his impatience he could not find it at once and he opened the shutters a little to see better. It was a fine night; in the cold hard light which came through the opening between the shutters the room looked strange to him. The night was so profoundly still that the three chairs around the table, the remains of food, the ceiling, and everything else seemed plunged in ineffable slumber. It was that hour of the night at which the most poignant sorrows lose their bitterness, at which trouble seems to sleep, and at which the sick fall into a kind of merciful unconsciousness and regain their strength and power of suffering. There was no breath of wind. In the two towns of Lorges and Chanteilles there was perhaps not a single soul who was not at peace at that moment, whereas he was awake, his body damp with fever, like a damned soul to whom sleep is denied. And he pictured hundreds of sleepers, old men huddled up in their beds, young men lying on their backs with their hands along their sides like corpses, and girls with their plump white flesh and voluptuous breathing—a whole lifeless world gravitating toward the dawn.

He pictured her, too, lying a little athwart her bed, her head back, exposing her throat to crime or to love, and her arms raised like wings and half hidden by the black waves of her heavy hair. She slept like a dead thing. The blood had grown sluggish in her veins and no longer colored her cheeks. If anyone were to kill her one night it would be thus that she would be found, surely, but she would be naked, and her arms and hair would be trailing upon the floor; if a man were to crush her to him until the breath left her body forever, she would have that same pallor, that same half-open mouth that would never cry out again.

Now he hated her! Only the day before yesterday, when he thought of her hands and her ears like a little girl's, a sudden tenderness had seized him; there had been something friendly and consoling about these memories visiting him in his loneliness; it was as though she had whispered to him, "Don't suffer too much." But now that his eyes were opened and he knew she had belonged to everyone

and refused herself to him alone, his heart seemed
to him to be too small to hold all the hatred he felt
for this one woman. He hated her all the more because she still attracted him to an extent that nothing would ever diminish. When one person falls in
love with another, he abandons all his liberty forever; lust may fade, passion may die altogether, but
at the bottom of his heart there remains something
inalienable which he can give but never take back.
The man who is in love has sold his soul, and hatred
can never succeed in supplanting his love; one belongs to those one has loved until death. He understood that. His instinct warned him of the altered
view he would take of Angèle in ten years' time, in
twenty years, and of the subjection under which he
would always be, and of the slavery of memory. And
until the end of his life he would be subjugated by
his mind, his heart, and perhaps by his senses, to
a woman in whose eyes he had made himself
ridiculous, a woman who must laugh at him and his
deference toward her.

Now that he had rebelled against love, his desire
seemed to have increased. Sometimes in a fit of
rage he would think of the sufferings that had been
inflicted upon him, and the need of triumphing and
hurting in his turn overwhelmed him. How good
violence was! How delightful it would be to see the
woman who had humiliated him groveling in the
dust. It seemed to him as though new strength were
spreading through his arms and along his fingers;
and his hands, like two creatures endowed with

separate life, opened and shut, clasped and unclasped
each other unceasingly, joyously and eager for action.

There was one strange result of his perpetual
thinking of her. For whole hours he forgot what she
looked like. He remembered, indeed, the shape of
her nose, and her bright open lips, like some red
fruit, but he could not succeed in visualizing her
face as a living face, a face which he could recognize; and then suddenly she would appear to his
eyes with a clearness which astounded him; there
she stood with her hair blowing over her forehead,
with that mysterious expression in the depths of her
dark eyes in which he seemed to see both a challenge
and a prayer. She would sigh and move her head.
Each movement she had made seemed to make her
richer by some marvelous grace, as though her
beauty, working for its own perfection, grew more
and more perfect every moment until it intoxicated
him. And he would shut his eyes the better to be
able to retain within him this sweet yet terrible
vision; she would hover before him for a moment,
hard and quizzical, and then abruptly efface herself.
She had gone again, and it was in vain that he called
her name, or buried his head in his hands to recon-
struct her image. She had gone completely.

In his agony he walked round and round the table
and finally let himself fall on his knees. Perhaps
if she could have seen him like that she would have
had pity. Why did he suffer for so long? Did that
make him any better? Better? His whole being

was nothing but violence and craving. And overcome by the weight of his sorrow he fell upon the
floor, and lay at full length between the bed and
the table. Why did he not die? How much misery
did it take to kill a man, for his heart to break?
A few hours earlier he had spoken to Madame Londe
as he had been advised to do. She had taken the
two five-franc pieces which he offered her, and had
promised to "arrange" everything with Angèle.
Then he had been seized with joy, a hideous joy
which had driven him from street to street right up
to the edge of the river, and he remembered that in
the throes of his delirium he had flung himself down
on the bank with his face buried in the grass, listening to his labored breathing in the silence of the
night.

He had remained there for half an hour, perhaps
more. But now his joy had changed to despair. He
had come home sadder and more downhearted than
ever. Why should his fate be suddenly linked with
that of a woman he had met in the street? What mad
laws regulated people's lives? If he loathed this
woman, why didn't he avoid her? And if it was
nothing but lust that attached him to her, why did
he not rejoice in the facility with which life "arranged" things?

He got up and drank some water. His wife's
door stood open. A chair pushed against it prevented it from banging, and a gentle draught came
through it like the passing of an invisible person.
A sudden curiosity seized him. He went to the

door and looked at his sleeping wife. Exhaustion had overcome the wretched woman and gave her body complete immobility; she lay on her side, one arm across her body and the other hanging out of the bed, and she looked like some one who had fallen into the bottom of an abyss. Her face, from which all youth had fled, was faintly outlined by the light. On her forehead and in her sunken cheeks age had installed itself forever; triumphant lines laid stress upon the imperfections of her features, the bitterness of her lips, and the weariness of her eyelids. He looked at her and thought: "I have never loved you." And as if she felt his hard, unjust gaze upon her, she made a vague sign with her hand and drew a deeper breath.

He stood still. A strange pleasure held him there, the pleasure of contemplating this woman and measuring the distance that separated him from her more and more each year. Nothing about her pleased him —neither her face, nor her body, nor her love. She was meek before him, but he preferred Angèle's disdain and cruelty to his wife's docility; she loved him without ever suspecting his treachery, and yet this ignorance and simplicity of hers merely excited his contempt. And he asked himself, always with the same surprise, how he had been able to marry her. There, too, life had cheated him. Doubtless this woman had been pretty once; he still remembered her face, now ruined by care, her pure white body broken by labor. Something should have warned him that she would soon lose her charm, and that six years would be enough to make her ugly and tiresome. Her hair was quite gray on one side. Even by the uncertain light of the moon he could see it shine like steel. And he compared it, mentally, with the hair that spread all over Angèle's pillow, like long motionless tongues of black flame. Then such a horror of his own existence gripped him, such a disgust with himself and the world, that he crept back into his room and hid his face in his hands. At that moment it seemed to him that in some way he reached the very dregs of his misery, and that, though he could still suffer, it was impossible for him to suffer more. It was as though the knife which was being used to torture him suddenly grew blunt in his muscles and his bones.

After a moment's hesitation he dressed and went out. Two o'clock had just struck. What was he doing? Could he have guessed, the day before, that at dawn on the following day he would be running through the streets like this? Why was there suddenly such perfect peace in his heart? The movement of his limbs, the cool air upon his cheeks, made him almost happy. The taste for life came back to him with the resolution he had taken. He was suffering because of this woman. He was going to see her. She didn't want to see him die, did she? Well, he would explain to her that if she did not love him he would throw himself into the river, into the Sommeillante that flowed quite close by the restaurant, for he would see her there, in her room. He would ring, and the door would be opened. It was obviously the only thing that could possibly happen, but it was necessary for him to have lived in agony for days to succeed in understanding it. It was not easy to talk to Angèle on the highroad, to offer her money, to make an appointment to see her, that wasn't what life, that secret goddess, had foreseen and prepared for him. He knew now what was going to happen; he would force his way into Angèle's room that very night, in five minutes' time, and he would speak to her, hold her by the arms, force her to listen.

He ran swiftly and noiselessly. Street by street he descended toward the little triangular space before the restaurant and the river. He had the impression that the streets were running with him, that they were carrying him, and passed him to one another like players passing a ball. The one he was going down was steeper than the others. Five hours earlier he had walked up it, his back bowed beneath a terrible weight of misery. Now it seemed to him as though each of his steps flung him forward, almost against his will, and that he was being thrown into the little triangle which he reached at last.

At first he recognized nothing—neither the plane trees, nor the stone bench upon which he sat, nor the house that awaited him. Everything had lost its color in the strange light of the moon; the leaves of the trees were as pale as the crumbling walls; the slates on the roofs seemed just as white as the cubes of granite with which the road was paved. In the corners occupied by shadow, it was so deep and so black that it seemed to have annihilated whatever was behind it. It was as though not a single soul had ever tarried in that place, and this silence and the immobility of things had never been interrupted.

He looked at the house. It was a very ordinary three-story house. On the ground floor were the long restaurant windows hidden behind iron shutters. Then came six windows equally divided between the first and second floors; all the shutters were closed. Angèle was behind one of those windows. Guéret had been told that her window was on the first floor at the north corner of the house. Stretched there on her bed, she was breathing, oblivious of the fact that her very breath was a cause of suffering to a human being. In her sleep she no doubt turned over, freeing her arm from beneath her side, her head heavy with dreams, but the niggard night kept to itself these movements that would have enraptured the unfortunate man. What was the use of her body being beautiful, of her neck being round and white, of her shoulders shining? She might just as well have been ugly, or not have existed at all, during those few hours when the light did not fall upon her face.

He crossed the triangle at a run. These thoughts drove him frantic. A sudden fury possessed him against the shadows and the walls, against everything that kept him from his love. For one moment he was on the point of ringing, but he immediately changed his mind. The first floor was not high. The iron shutter that protected the restaurant window

had a ledge an inch or two wide. He put his foot
on this, one hand placed flat against the metal surface, and the other trying to get a hold on a corner
of the door frame, but he lost his balance and had
to jump back to avoid falling.

He was panting now with excitement. He let
his eyes wander over the front of the house, raging
at the bare wall which offered no hold to his fingers.
The idea of ringing came to him again, but he dismissed it as he had done the first time. After a
moment's reflection he picked up a pebble and flung
it against the shutter. As soon as he had done so,
the folly of it struck him. He did not want to put
Angèle on her guard against him; he wanted to
surprise her. That was why he hadn't rung just
now; his instinct had warned him not to. And in
the fear of having compromised his chance of success, he went and hid himself beneath the trees, determined not to move if the window opened.

However, the noise made by the pebble against
the shutter had probably not been loud enough to
rouse Angèle from her sleep, for several minutes
passed without the window opening. This gave him
time to consider his next move. From where he stood
the first floor seemed so near the ground that a child
could have climbed up to it; the whole question was
to find the simplest means of accomplishing the
ascent. It was not a question of strength, but one
of patience. He had plenty of strength, and this
would come in handy later when it became necessary
to open the shutters from the outside.

He returned to the iron shutter and raised his arms to calculate the distance that separated him from his goal. With his hands and fingers stretched out as far as possible he could almost touch the top of the ground floor window. This inch or two was sufficient to defeat his object, for if he jumped to reach the top ledge of the window, he lost at the same time the strength necessary to keep him there, the impetus of his spring causing him to lose his hold. Nevertheless, he tried again and fell back for the second time.

Then something clutched his heart, a sudden dumb rage that flung him to the ground. It was better to die than not to reach that window; it was better to smash his skull on the pavement and let his miserable life run out with his blood. But he suddenly pulled himself together with a start. To be there, a few yards from Angèle, and not to be able to climb the wall, to open the shutters, to touch her, to ravish her. He felt a wave of rage and violence come over him and ran once more to the plane trees, to hide there like a wounded animal and take council with himself.

After a moment he emerged into the light again, charging at the house as though it were an enemy. He reached it in three bounds and nearly succeeded this time. The strength that comes to us, we know not whence, when our own is not sufficient, seemed to lift him from the ground and attach him to the iron shutters in such a way that his entire body was above the ledge which he had been unable to grasp before.

If his arms had been raised his hands could easily have gripped the actual shutters he wanted to open, but he lacked the necessary presence of mind. For two or three seconds he remained there, his arms and legs outstretched, his hands flat on the wall, held in place by will-power alone, like one of those great night birds which a whitewashed wall fascinates and attracts in spite of themselves, and who rivet themselves to it as though to intoxicate themselves with the detestable brilliance of its whiteness. Then he suddenly relaxed and fell back to the ground.

Then, blinded by rage, he began leaping straight up, clinging as best he could to the inhospitable surface which only offered handholds too high or too low, clawing at the stone and iron with his nails. Several times he managed to stand upon the lower ledge of the big window, but his success ended there; his arms stretched vainly right and left to try to find some roughness, some corner, anything to keep him from falling, but everything seemed to have been designed by an astute architect to frustrate an enterprise of this nature.

He sat down on the pavement to recover his breath. It ought to be easy enough to reach the first story of a house. Was it possible that with all the strength of his wrists he could not do it? The idea came to him of looking for something that would serve as a step. One of those big stone cubes, for instance, that he had seen piled up beside a road in process of repair. But he did not want to leave his post; it seemed to him that his fate was to be

decided there, and that he would destroy all chance
of success if he left the house. He would enter the
room on the first floor before dawn, or never, for
never again would he be able to make the frenzied
effort of will that had flung him against the iron
shutter; with daylight qualms and hesitation would
return. He must make the best of that kind of hallucination under which he had been living for the last
few hours, and take advantage of the extraordinary
fact that he was there and that he was trying to
break into a house like a burglar. What did he care
what people thought of him? He had the impression that his whole existence was crowded into the
minutes that were speeding by so swiftly. What
would his joy be when he flung himself into the
room where Angèle was sleeping! Would she dare
resist him then, lie to him, try to put him off with
words, as she had done on the highroad?

When he had rested a little he rose and, gripping
the framework of the door, as though he were trying
to pull it toward him, he placed his left foot in the
angle made by the splaying a few inches from the
ground. At first he thought he could not keep his
foothold, and the sensation of being pushed away
by the wall and of struggling with it almost made
him let go; the blood was gathering under his nails
and burning his flesh, but his elbows rose slowly.
All the strength of his great body was concentrated
in his wrists, which shook beneath the effort. He
could not fail now; he was gambling with life itself;
to fall back was to die. He raised his left foot a

little and put his right foot in a similar position at the other side of the door. His head was buzzing; all the veins in his neck were beating and swelling. When his elbows were level with his face, he rested his feet against the door frame and hoisted his body as high as he could. His forehead, his nose, and then his mouth passed the top of the door. He threw his head back and rested his chin on the narrow stone ledge; this fresh hold gave him the use of his left hand during the space of a second, time to seize the top corner of the door frame. This compelled him to throw his body on one side so as not to lose his balance, and to place himself diagonally, both feet propped against the door and touching one another. His head returned to the height it had reached before he had got into this new position. He began to despair of ever succeeding and was on the point of abandoning the attempt altogether; everything seemed to be against him. However, he realized that he had everything to gain by being bold, and he suddenly shifted his right hand and placed it near his left. His legs immediately left the door-frame and for a moment he swung, hanging by his fingers, nearer the ground than he had been since the beginning of this attempt.

His head throbbed with dizziness and exhaustion. Little by little his strength was leaving his hands, which trembled beneath his great weight, and in ten or fifteen seconds they would abandon their prey, that narrow stone ledge to which they still clung. He thought to himself, "If I let myself fall I shall not see her." By a sort of jerk he raised his knees, striking the panels of the door with them. His heart beat louder and louder, sounding to him like the footsteps of some invisible being walking on his chest. His whole body was taut. He bent his elbows and took a purchase with his feet on each side of the door-frame. His muscles were so tired that he felt as if he were being drawn and quartered. His body, raised by the movement of his elbows, hoisted itself up again. Suddenly he gave a shout and, pressing on the tips of his toes with all his strength, he flung his hands up into the air, pressed them to the wall above the door, and reached up. The palms of his hands were bleeding from contact with the wall; he felt the wood creak under the pressure of his toe-caps and realized that he was going to slip. Nevertheless, he made a last effort and bent his feet in such a way that he was now supported merely by the ends of his big toes; he felt as though a knife point was being thrust into his flesh, and the pain was so sharp that it drew a groan from him; almost at the same time his feet abandoned their position and beat against the door; but he did not fall, for his fingers were clinging to the window bars.

He swung for a moment or two, his whole body bruised, and blood running down his wrists. Yet in spite of everything, his inactivity was a kind of rest and gave him time to pull himself together. Now that he had reached the window and that his hands were firmly gripping the window bars, he could employ his legs as he liked without fear of losing his balance. After a moment, scrambling up the door with his feet and knees, he managed to stand up on the ledge over the door, with his hands on the hand-rail of the window. But this was not Angèle's window. He was gasping for breath, and letting go with his left hand he began to creep along the upper ledge of the big window that occupied the ground floor. Over two yards separated the first-floor windows. He stretched his arms out as far as he could, still clinging with his right hand to the hand-rail of the window he was leaving behind him, and feeling along the wall with his left. The ledge upon which his feet rested measured a little less across than his shoes, but was wide enough to bear him. He advanced thus, imperceptibly, his body glued to the stone-work, without daring to breathe or even to think. At last he felt beneath his fingers the hand-rail of the other window and gripped it. Then he let go with his right hand and brought it up to join the left.

Now, with his shoulder against the join of the shutters, he began to overcome the last resistance and to bend the little iron catch. But the wood gave way first. After one or two wrenches, each more violent than the last, one of the shutters split with a crack that echoed in the silence like a rifle-shot.

He let himself fall into the house and rolled on to the floor. The blood was singing in his head; he lay there panting for a moment and then got up, amazed by his success and hardly daring to raise his eyes to the room and the furniture he had so often seen in his imagination. The first streaks of dawn had come into the room with him, lighting up the dirty walls and threadbare carpet. And then he saw that the room was empty and the bed had not been slept in.

The decisive moment had passed. For one moment destiny had hesitated, not knowing what to do with him next, abandoning him to his blind volition, but since then the path had once more been cleared before this man; a ready hand thrust him along it and the night's hallucination came to an end.

Lying on the bed, he felt drenched in the fragrance of her absent body; he found the place where her head must have rested and laid his own cheek, his lips, his eyes, in the same place, running his bleeding hands over the sheets and the pillow, full of a perfume which intoxicated him.

Steps began to run up and down the corridor. A door opened and shut again. A voice asked, "What is it? What's the matter?" and then, emboldened by the silence, it began to shout: "Help! Help!!"

He heard without understanding, as one hears a voice that wakes one from deep sleep. Then the voice drew nearer until it was outside the door. It was Madame Londe shouting; fear gripped her by the throat, but for all that she shouted louder and louder, and once she called Angèle.

After a moment he pulled himself together and, leaning on his elbow, he tore the pillow-case from the pillow and stuffed it into his coat pocket. Then he rose and took a few steps round the room. His eyes wandered from one object to another, from the iron bed that had creaked beneath his weight to the little mirror that reflected his haggard face. He saw the damp-stained walls, the two straw-bottomed chairs near the door, the table which had lost its drawer. He meant to carry away with him the memory of that room into which life had led him to deceive him, in the same way as he was taking the pillow-case over which Angèle's hair had spread.

As he stepped over the hand-rail there was a loud knocking at the door; then the door opened, but he had already slipped from the window and fallen in a heap at the foot of the wall. From the road he could hear Madame Londe's exclamations as she broke into the empty room and discovered the blood-stained bed. She had only to lean out of the window to see him. He stood erect, in spite of a pain in his side caused by the fall, and crept along the side of the house until he reached the road at its corner. There he waited to recover his breath. In his anguish, and to stifle the harsh sound of his breathing, he pressed the stolen pillow-case to his face. The smell of it made him dizzy, and he closed his eyes. A whole world of memories sprang up before him. So many things had come into his life since the moment he had met Angèle, so many little things the sum total of which was such that it seemed to him that there would be enough for long years of suffering.

He was suddenly recalled to his danger and opened

his eyes. Madame Londe was shouting from the window. From where he stood he could see the yellow light shed by the lamp she held in her hand. He put the pillow-case back into his pocket, and buttoned up his jacket as though he were about to take to his heels. The voice which alternately rose and fell with terror was shouting dreadful things into the night: "Angèle has gone! She has been murdered! There's blood all over everything! I heard a man here! It was he who did it!"

He looked undecidedly to right and to left. To the right lay the town which would soon be roused by the woman's screams. To the left lay the Sommeillante and the open country, but to go to the left was to risk being seen and recognized by Madame Londe. So he began to run uphill to the right. A light had already appeared in one window and people were shouting to one another from their houses, but no one had come out yet; it would be some time before they plucked up sufficient courage to do so. He hugged the wall, his knees sagging, his chest crushed by a relentless pressure. His heart beat like some frantic animal hurling itself against the bars of its prison in its efforts to escape. He had never experienced such terror. This murder they accused him of, this death he had inflicted on Angèle, would it not seem probable? Was it not even true? What else would he have done if he had found the young woman in her bed? He might perhaps have cut her throat to be revenged on her, to keep her quiet, and his hands would have been as they were now, hot and heavy and sticky.

He crossed the road and plunged into a side street which Madame Londe's cries did not reach, but he dared not stop. After dragging along for about twenty yards he came to a street which he knew well because he had followed Angèle along it; he knew it led to the river. In broad daylight Madame Londe would have seen him, but the night was still dark enough for him to risk it, and gathering his strength together he began to run again. On one side of the road stood a row of little low houses; along the other ran the coal-yard. He followed the line of the wall. At the end of the street he hesitated. He began to hear shouts again, distinctly. He looked to the left, saw nothing there, and turned sharp to the right.

The road was wide and was paved with resounding stones that made his footsteps echo. He reached the slope that ran down from it to the river and ran along the grass, beneath the plane trees that accompanied the Sommeillante in its lazy journey through the town. As soon as he reached the last of these little short trees he would be safe. For at that point began a dense wood in which he could hide.

The sky was growing gradually lighter, and a dull pale glow began to outline in the darkness the last houses of the town, which ran along the right-hand side of the highroad; then a fine rain began to fall. It was about four o'clock. Without stopping he held his burning hands out to the little fresh drops

which glittered in the gray air. His exhausted body
was beyond any feeling of fatigue. After a certain
degree of weariness is passed, one's limbs do not
suffer any more, but obey of their own accord the
will that no longer has the strength to command
them. If he had had to walk for another hour, for
more than another hour, he could have done it.

At the edge of the wood he stumbled over a fallen
branch and, letting himself fall on the ground covered with dead leaves, he fell asleep almost immediately.

He awoke toward ten o'clock and left his hiding-
place. He was on the road again, but now he made
his way toward the houses from which he had fled
the night before. The breeze dried his clothing; he
dared not use his hands, for fear of reopening his
wounds, and he walked along with his hair tangled
and his body burning with a fever that sent the
blood to his cheeks. One thought alone filled his
mind—he must find Angèle. He had set out to do
so, and he must succeed. It was impossible that this
awful night, in which he had endured so much concentrated suffering, could be nothing but a mean-
ingless nightmare. It must have a price; there
must be somewhere in the course of time an hour, a
minute, that would redeem it.

People passed close by him. He did not see them
or return their greetings. He would go to the
restaurant and ask where Angèle was. Little did
he care about what they said of his appearance or of

his hands black with blood, or about the suspicions which he would arouse. He could not be arrested because his hair was untidy and his hands scratched. But what if something really had happened to Angèle, what if she had been assassinated in the night? What if she were dead?

What if she were dead? The thought made him stop as though an invisible hand had suddenly struck him full on the chest. He repeated the question aloud, without any fear or emotion, but with surprise at uttering strange words whose meaning was difficult to grasp; and he began to walk faster. She could not die before he had held her in his arms; she was his; life had given her to him, that mysterious will that rules our destinies, that force that dominates the world, had given him this woman. She was his because he loved her and because he had suffered for her.

When he reached the Avenue de la Sommeillante, he quickened his pace so as to avoid the attention of a group of five or six women who were talking beneath the plane trees. He could already see the open space before the restaurant and his heart beat faster. A woman in front of him was walking in the same direction. He passed her, but she ran after him and put her hand on his arm.

"What's the matter with you?" she asked.

It was Angèle.

Chapter Twelve

SHE repeated her question:
"What's the matter with you? Where are you going?"

With the back of her hand she brushed away a strand of hair that lay across her forehead. Her eyes were wide open and bright. He looked at her for a second, then he seized her arm convulsively.

"Where did you sleep last night?" he asked her.

"They lent me a room at the laundry," she answered. "So it was you who broke into our house last night? In that case you had better not show yourself yet. Go back home quickly. Let me go."

"No."

"Come, don't let's stop here. There are people about."

"I won't let you go. Come with me."

"At least let go my arm. After all, it was I who came and spoke to you. . . . You passed quite close to me without seeing me."

"Why did you come and speak to me?"

"I won't tell you if you don't let me go. Look, there are a lot of people coming this way and looking at us. We can't stay like this."

"I will go anywhere you like, but I won't let you go."

She turned her back on the restaurant and began to walk toward the little wood. Her imprisoned arm hung by her side.

"Aren't you afraid of my calling for help?" she asked.

"No, I'm not afraid."

"Listen," she said, after a moment. "You must go home and tidy yourself up. Your clothes are all torn. People will suspect you if they see you like that."

"Will you come with me?"

"No; I don't want to walk through the town with you."

"Why not?"

"Let me go," she begged. "Please let me go. I'll tell you all that later."

"Where did you sleep last night?"

"I've told you. At the laundry."

"It isn't true. Whom were you with?"

"Don't talk so loud. There's some one coming."

There was silence for a moment; then he began again, in a lower voice, without looking at her.

"Just tell me whom you were with."

"With no one."

"I know you've sold yourself to everyone in the town. Whom were you with? With Monsieur Blondeau?"

She suddenly burst into tears and tried to free herself. But he held her firmly.

"You were with some one," he went on. "Who was it? Was it Monsieur Grosgeorge?"

She made no reply. They walked along for a moment in silence, then he asked her again, shaking her arm:

"Tell me, was it he?"

"Neither he nor anyone else. I was alone. I did not sleep at Madame Londe's. I was sure that she would come and talk to me about Monsieur Blondeau."

"You've promised to go out with him on Sunday."

"I haven't promised anything. On the contrary, I have said that I wasn't going out at all."

"You lie. He told me himself that it was all arranged."

"It isn't true. Let me go. I am unhappy enough already. Let me go, I tell you! You're hurting me!"

He dragged her along with all his strength and compelled her to leave the road and climb down the embankment.

"Since you are afraid of people seeing us," he said, "we will walk on the river bank."

The voice in which these words were uttered and the look that accompanied them terrified the girl; she suddenly had the impression that the slope down which she was going against her will was cutting her off from life. The idea of calling for help crossed her mind again, but Guéret seemed to read this intention in her eyes, for he looked at her and said:

"I am stronger than you now. If you shout I'll

throw myself into the water with you and we will drown."

"Alas!" said she, mastering her emotion. "I never dreamt of calling out."

"Why do you say, 'Alas!'?"

"Because you are in such a state. . . . You look as though you were ill."

For the first time since she had known him she saw him laugh. But he became serious again at once.

"I bet that worries you!"

"Yes, it does."

"No, it doesn't," he said, shaking her arm again. "It doesn't worry you in the least, but you are afraid of me. However much you may persuade yourself that some one will pass in a moment, you know quite well that if I want us to drown I've got about four times as much time as I need. And then you say you're worried about me. You may keep your worry for other people."

She felt the heat of his breath on her face and turned her head slightly away.

"Go on! Tell me that I disgust you," he said, suddenly.

"No, no!" she said, quivering. "On the contrary, it was on your account that I left Madame Londe. I wanted to explain to you."

"Tell me that I disgust you," he repeated, fiercely. "I order you to."

"But I tell you it isn't true."

He thrust her violently away from him, without letting her go, and forced her to her knees.

"Say it, if you value your life!"

"All right, yes!" she moaned, horrified.

"Say, 'You disgust me.' "

"Yes," she sobbed. "All right, you . . . disgust me. Let me go!"

With her free arm she tried to reach one of the little bushes that bordered the Sommeillante and whose tops could be seen from the road on the embankment.

"What are you trying to do?" he asked.

"I'm trying to get up. You see I am."

He was standing before her, his whole face aflame, hiding the sky from her with his great height and his gigantic shoulders. He let her struggle for a moment without letting go her arm, which twisted and turned in his grasp. She succeeded in raising one of her knees and placing her foot flat on the ground. Then her eyes sought those of the man as though imploring him to let her take advantage of this victory; but he suddenly pushed her back and she fell on the river bank; in her surprise and terror she uttered a scream.

"Stop it!" he ordered, bending over her.

But she was no longer mistress of herself; her heart was beating too fast; a terrible shriek broke from her throat, in spite of herself, the scream of a trapped animal that sees no other expedient than in its cries of pain and despair. The sight of her fear drove Guéret mad. First he struck her with his open hand, then, dropping her wrist, he took her head between his hands and struck it several times on the ground. She was panting now, but she still screamed. He put his hand over her mouth and she bit it. Then a kind of frenzy took possession of him, a frenzy of rage and misery. He gazed around him with the look of a man who has fallen into the sea. He waved his arms about, striking the branches of the trees around him, and then suddenly he seized one of them and clinging frantically to it, tried to break it off. It bent once or twice and finally broke with a horrible tearing sound, leaving a great white wound in the tree from which it was torn.

Angèle had risen and was running along the Sommeillante; when she was twenty yards away from Guéret she tried to climb back up the embankment, but it was six feet high there and too steep for her to climb; she was not strong enough. So she started running again along the bank.

He caught her up in a few strides and seized her by the head. The wretched woman's heavy black hair came down and rippled over the man's arm. For a second he paused as he felt the coolness and weight of her tresses against the back of his hand; then his fingers closed again. She cried out and tried to turn round to face him, but he flung the branch he held to one side and, putting both his arms around her struggling body, he let himself fall to the ground with her. The girl was panting, overcome with exhaustion and terror. In the rage

which made him lose all control of his actions he
suddenly had a spasm of pity as he saw the whiteness of the skin throbbing with her labored breathing, and he murmured the girl's name; but she
looked at him through the long strands of hair which
half hid her face and began to scream again, beside
herself at the thought that perhaps the man was
going to kill her. She saw the fury return to his
eyes in a kind of wave which changed their color;
then she closed her eyes. He held her by the neck,
stifling her screams in her throat.

"Stop it!" he repeated, in a voice of supplication
and fury. And as she tried to free herself and
scream again he struck her several times on the
chest and on the face. It suddenly seemed to him as
though the river, the trees, the air, everything, was
whirling around him and that a continuous roaring
filled the sky. His fists rose and fell mechanically.
His only thought was to stop the abominable screams
whose shrillness pierced his brain like a knife. Then
terror, the same terror as that of his victim, suddenly gripped him. He could no longer escape from
himself or his crime, or stop his hands from acting,
or stop the girl's screams. Her eyes no longer
looked at him; they were turned back in an effort
to escape the sight of the face leaning over her, and
as she lay there she looked like a blind mad woman,
and a little like the vision of a murdered woman that
he had had the night before.

Then he suddenly seized the branch that he had
thrown on one side and which still lay within his

reach, and in the violence of his anger he raised it and beat the girl across the face with it, on her cheeks and forehead, until she stopped screaming and the sight of those beloved features was hidden from their conqueror by blood.

Chapter Thirteen

ALL day long the wind had been blowing, chasing the dead leaves from one side of the highway to the other, or scattering them over the sluggish surface of the Sommeillante. On the river bank the thick grass gleamed in the sunlight, flattened as though exhausted bodies had stretched themselves upon it to absorb the freshness rising from the earth and the water. The sky was quite clear, and each branch cast upon the ground its clear-cut, shifting outline which the wind seemed to be trying to blow away. There is no time of year more delicious than those first autumn days when the air is stirred up by swirling currents and breaks among the trees like the waves of an invisible sea, while the sun, looking down upon this violence and tumult, casts from the smallest flower a shadow which will move around it all day long. Out of this mixture of calm and fury comes an impression of strength and gentleness which no human language can describe. A kind of restfulness without languor, an excitement to which there is no reaction; one's blood flows more gayly and more freely, and one's heart goes out toward life. In these bountiful moments nature brings happiness to those who do not know what it is, with the scent of the woods and the chirping of the birds, with the rustle of the leaves and all things quivering with youth.

All day long he had walked beside the river and across the fields. People had seen him and followed him with their eyes, and he had taken fright and quickened his pace, only to meet fresh faces turning slowly toward him, and eyes which took the same surprised and careful note of the disorder of his clothing. Toward evening he returned to the place from which he had fled some hours earlier, and the calm which he now felt in his heart was a direct contradiction to all that he seemed to remember. His anxiety and fatigue had gone and he was enjoying the fresh air and the twilight hour. The memory of the girl's screams and sudden quietness had obsessed him for so long that all at once he found he could no longer believe in them. It was all too utterly unlike the rest of his life to be true, and he could not recognize himself in the deeds that kept on being reënacted before his eyes. Had anyone told him of the horrible struggle by the river bank he would probably have laughed, and he followed the bank of the Sommeillante to verify the fact that there was nothing there, searching for the exact spot to prove to himself that it did not exist.

But there it was; he had seen those broken branches in his nightmare. Could he, in his frenzy, have noticed so many little things, so many flowers and trees and reflections? Something within him had remained awake while all the rest of his being was lost in a sort of horrible dream in which acts took place which he could not believe possible, acts of crime and lust. He could deceive himself no longer. The whole truth flashed before him; he had killed the woman, and people had come and taken her away; people had stood around her and had gazed on the dead woman and the horror of that mutilated face; then some one had thrown a coat, a piece of sacking, anything, over the unfortunate woman's head because it frightened them. And what if she were not dead? He could no longer remember whether she was breathing or not; all he could remember was that suddenly, after several minutes, he had seen the wounds he had made in her face and that he had been seized with terror and had run away.

He had run along the river, and then, climbing the embankment, he had turned round, in spite of himself, to look at her again. She was still there, motionless, lying across the path, with her hair spread about her. Then he had begun to run again, only to turn round a little further on; but from this new position he could no longer see her. It was at that moment that he experienced the greatest relief of his life; nothing could have happened, since he could see nothing on the bank, and he set off again, plunging into the wood as quickly as his legs could carry him, for fear that he would be tempted to return to the little path to go and look.

But now that he was once more near the river, at the spot where these things had taken place, now that the path was empty, it all seemed to him as real

as if the girl's body were at his feet. He took a few
steps to right and left, not knowing why he remained
there instead of running away. He derived a sort of
pleasure from staying there and he did not feel
strong enough to abandon it at once. He knew that
if he went away he would come back again. He felt
no remorse for his violence. A little while before
he had been haunted by the fear of what he had done,
and yet he did not believe it; but now that his intelligence furnished him with proof of his crime, he
was calm. He looked at the grass and bent down
as though trying to trace the outline of the body
that had lain there. His heart was racing, not
from fear, but from a new emotion which he did not
try to repress, an extraordinary curiosity concerning
everything that gave this place its peculiar character
—the smell of the river, the coolness that rose from
the earth and the perpetual waving of branches
above his head. "It was there," he kept saying to
himself in a low voice. He closed his eyes once or
twice and breathed deeply; he plucked a tuft of grass
which he put in his pocket, and then he suddenly
flung himself on the ground, lying where he had lain
a few hours earlier. And, as in the morning, he
heard the rippling of the water against the bank and
the rustling of the leaves. If he opened his eyes,
he saw the Sommeillante almost above him, but he
could not see its other bank, and before him he had
nothing but grass stalks among which the light and
shade played as in a forest, and then the river, high
and flat as a wall. He lay there motionless, flat on

his face, and gradually all his strength left him; he felt as though he was losing all consciousness of existence, and as though some invisible element was taking possession of him, a mysterious emanation which was everywhere around him, and came from all that vegetation whose odor pervaded him. He had become light-headed, and a kind of dizziness threw his thoughts into confusion. His arms, his legs, his whole body were ceasing to have a separate existence, and were mingling with everything that breathed or rustled around him. Although he could not sleep, he fell into a kind of stupor in which for some time his soul forgot its existence.

He was roused by the sound of voices—the voices of people passing on the road and talking excitedly. Once or twice they stopped and seemed to be arguing as to whether they should go forward or turn back. Although they kept raising their voices, he was unable to hear what they said. The only phrase he could catch was "farther on," and that terrified him. These men were looking for him, and to discover him they had but to look over the embankment which hid him from view. The idea of stealing away crossed his mind, but he dismissed it at once. The slightest sound would betray him. It was better to wait and try to control the terror that sent the blood rushing to his heart. If they went away, so much the better; if they came down the embankment he would throw himself into the river.

They moved off. The wind bore him the sound of their voices growing more and more excited as

the discussion proceeded.   After a few seconds he
crawled away in the opposite direction, until he had
increased the distance that separated him from them
by fifteen or twenty yards.   He rested there for a
moment and then, rising, he scrambled up the embankment and lay down in the ditch that ran beside
the road.   By raising himself on his elbows he could
see them.   There were three of them, and although
they walked slowly, they were already some distance
away. One of them, who was small and thin, looked
like Monsieur Pinsot, and it was he who, taking his
companions by the arm, compelled them to stop and
pointed with his walking-stick.

He waited until they had gone a little farther,
then, fearing that they might return, he got up
quickly and crossed the road. Fortunately for him, a
side turning led out of the road at this point, and
down this he dived; then, preventing himself with an
effort from running, he walked along the sidewalk in
the direction of the town.

Night was falling fast, and in a quarter of an
hour it would be dark, and that part of Lorges was
not lit up at night; prudence told him to stay there
and to wait, yet how could he wait when his limbs refused to be still?   He wandered without volition,
from one side of the street to the other, as if, in order
to be safe, he had to be continuously on the move,
and it were dangerous to remain in the same place.

He was incapable of any clear or reasoned chain
of thought, and in this state of mind he kept walking
about in a way that could not have failed to arouse

the suspicions of anyone passing by, had the street
not been deserted, for all his actions betrayed an
ill-concealed terror, and it was obvious that he had
almost lost control of himself. Looking around him,
stopping suddenly, doing everything that could
attract suspicion to him, he reached another street,
wider, but just as deserted as the one which he was
now leaving behind him. There were no trees in it,
and grass grew between the stone cobbles of the highway. He remembered having seen this road at dawn
on that same day, and that its sinister aspect had
prevented him from taking it. Now, however, it
appealed to him. On either side of the road was a
row of shabby houses with closed windows and, seized
with a panic which bereft him of all freedom of action and completely overpowered him, he broke into
a run. It seemed to him that the impact of his footsteps accompanied him and grew louder in the silence
like the noise of an ever-increasing crowd. When
he reached the end of the street, would he go to the
right or to the left? He did not know. His legs
would bear him where they would, where they could.
He no longer relied on anything but that last resource of the desperate, the sudden whim of chance.
The important thing was to run, in spite of the terrible drumming of his heart against the walls of his
chest, in spite of the giddiness which numbed his
brain and blurred everything before his eyes. A
roaring came from his contracted throat. Far away,
behind him, he heard a window open, and, reaching
the end of the street at that moment, he quickened

his pace and turned to the right, doubtless because
he would have had to run uphill to the left, and felt
too weak to do so. Then a short distance ahead he
saw some one who seemed to be waiting for him.

It was a man dressed in a black overcoat. He was
leaning on a walking-stick, and the large black cap
which fell over his eyes helped to give him the air
of an old pensioner who had obtained permission
from his almshouse to go for a walk in the town, for
he was bent with age and there was something
vaguely military in the cut of his clothes.

They looked at one another for a moment,
separated by the width of the road. The fugitive
had stopped dead. He had pictured being pursued,
but he had never foreseen that people might come to
meet him or that anyone would stand in his path.
He was too surprised to do anything. What would
this man do if he went on running? He was obviously too feeble to chase him, but he could shout and
rouse the town. Who was he? Did he know anything? Why didn't he move?

His ribs ached with fatigue; he gripped his sides
with his hands and made an effort to recover his
breath. Each movement of his was noted by the old
man, who never opened his lips or gave a hint of any
intentions that he might have. Several seconds
passed in complete silence. The street was long and
narrow; to the left it rose, winding through the
town; to the right it went down steeply toward the
river. The wind had fallen, as though it had only
been blowing since the morning in order to drive

away the day from this part of the earth; it grew
darker every moment. Not a sound broke the silence,
and so deep was the stillness of everything that all
life seemed to be suspended. Guéret felt himself
being slowly cast under a kind of spell depriving
him of his liberty. Probably not more than two or
three seconds passed, but even this short time
weighed upon him, somehow, and crushed him. The
few hours which he had lived since dawn gave him
the strange impression of a life in the midst of his
life, an appalling life, full of agony and blood,
neither long nor short, incapable of measurement
according to human standards; but complete in itself, interpolated into his real life like a dream in
the twenty-four hours of the day, and no more re-
sembling that life than the visions of night resemble
the actions we perform during the day. It would
soon be over, and he would awake to return to his
every-day worries, the boredom of morning, the
boredom of evening. But supposing he awoke with
those bleeding hands, supposing all this horror were
true? Was it possible for a nightmare itself to become to reality and to confuse itself with everyday
matters?

Then he suddenly shouted:

"Why are you looking at me?"

"I didn't ask you for anything."

It was a thin, worn-out voice that replied, a slow
voice that found difficulty in forming its words
properly.

"If you think you can frighten me . . . " began Guéret, with terror in his heart.

After a moment he added:

" . . . with your stick. You old sneak!"

The old man shook his head, red with anger.

"Me! a sneak?" he quavered. "I don't know you. I'm only taking a walk. Why are you afraid of people? Have you done something wrong?"

"Afraid?" repeated Guéret.

He shook with rage. He made the violent gesture of a man tearing off his coat, and stepping off the sidewalk he advanced a yard.

"So I'm to be afraid of you, am I?" he asked.

He saw the old man shake his head again, with his mouth open, and he leapt roughly at him and tore his stick away from him. They both rolled on the road. The black cap came off, revealing a head with close-cropped white hair. The old man was shouting feebly, so his aggressor seized the cap and tried to stuff it into his mouth. He was helped by a superhuman strength which he felt merrily and impetuously running along his limbs like electricity. After a few efforts to free himself, the old man's legs stiffened and his imprisoned arms ceased to defend themselves. Terror paralyzed his body, which had been felled like a dead tree; only his face still preserved some signs of life, of life reduced almost to nothing by an appalling fear of death, and which had concentrated itself, not in the eyes whose gaze was already vacant and staring, but in the desperate movement of his jaws, which opened and shut on the hand that was suffocating him. The raised stick fell first on the victim's chest, and then with frantic violence on his forehead and temples, until blood came.

When he saw the black threads running along that yellow skin and joining each other, he suddenly stood up. Not a single cry had warned him that life was leaving the old man, and the only herald of death had been the sharp rapping of the stick. He stood there and gazed at the little man he had beaten to death. After a moment he moved a few paces away and looked around him. It was a miracle that no one had either seen or heard him. He was still grasping the stick he had used; he let it drop, then he picked it up and threw it down a drain close by; he heard it rattling several times against the stone walls; then it was carried away by a stream of dirty water toward the Sommeillante, which would engulf it and carry it far away where it would not be seen again.

He went on down the street without looking back. It was almost dark now. A window lit up, and then another just as he was passing beneath it. Then he began to run again; the slope was so steep that he stumbled and almost fell. His stride grew longer in spite of himself, and he knew he was running too fast and making too much noise. What was he going to do when he reached the avenue that followed the river? He could already see the lime trees bordering it, black against the colorless sky. He was following a white wall, so white that it seemed to

light up the narrow street. He noticed this as he
ran along and hastened to reach the end in order to
escape from this vague light that might betray him.
In a moment he would reach the gates of the coal-
yard. When he reached them he would stop to recover his breath and to consider what to do next,
for the river was only a few yards away and Guéret
did not feel brave enough to follow it again, and to
race along that river bank the memory of which
terrified him. In the confusion of his mind one
thought stood out clearly, namely that the banks
of the Sommeillante, the highway, the wood, the
whole region in which he had suffered that morning,
were out of bounds to him at present, as well as the
street he had just left. It was impossible to retrace
his footsteps, however greatly he wanted to do so.
He must go forward, and carry the plague of his
crimes elsewhere, into the streets he had not passed
through since the beginning of his nightmare.

His legs were trembling so much that he doubted
whether they would be able to bear him as far as the
huge blot of shadow which the entrance to the coal-
yard made in the long white sheet of wall. He tried
to slow down his speed and to walk, but to change
his pace required an effort which he was not in a
condition to furnish. An exhausted man does not
stop running to walk; he pursues his course until
he drops. It seemed to him as if his chest was bursting and was incapable of holding the frenzied heart
beating against its walls and the scorching breath
that filled it and devoured it.

Suddenly he asked himself, "What am I afraid of?" For the street was empty and the only sound that broke the silence was the clatter of his feet on the pavement; and for the space of a second fear seemed to waver within him. At that moment a man's figure appeared at the end of the pavement where the wall reached the avenue; he, too, had a walking-stick in his hand. Hearing some one running toward him, he stopped and called out, "Hi, there!" but his challenge went unanswered, and, besides, the sound of footsteps had ceased. He let a moment pass, then he walked up the street, warily, keeping to the middle of the road. After passing the gates of the coal-yard, his courage failed him, and he stopped and peered into the darkness around him; then becoming first suspicious and then frightened, he turned and walked rapidly back to the avenue. Guéret had dived into the coal-yard. If the gate had not been open he would have lost his head and would have given himself up to the terrified pedestrian, himself raising the cry of "Murder!" to have done with it all; but now that he lay stretched on the ground behind the gate, his body relaxed and the sweat which bathed his limbs dried in the cool evening air. With his head back and his eyes closed he seemed to be gazing at a sky full of revolving stars.

When he reopened his eyes, a quarter of an hour had passed and night had come. Voices gradually roused him from his slumbers; they came, judging from their sound, from a building that occupied the farthest corner of the yard, and he heard them discussing the question of lighting the lamp over the gates. He was too weary to stand up, but he managed to drag himself round a big wood-pile, behind which he lay down again.

In his stupefied condition he was incapable of any further sensation; as in a dream he heard footsteps going diagonally across the yard, and heard them stop at the gates; then he heard iron-shod boots climbing up one of the stone posts that stood at the entrance. Then some one whistled. After a moment the boots leaped from the post to the ground and the footsteps went back across the yard. A door opened and shut again.

He waited. The light of the lamp was cut off by the wood-pile and did not reach him, but he could picture it above his head. A fresh heavy smell of earth and wood rose around him and he breathed it in eagerly, as though to recover his strength by doing so. Both his hands had begun to bleed again; he realized this each time he closed his fingers over his palms, but he no longer dreamt of getting up or running away. The impression of having somehow reached the uttermost limit of his misfortunes gave him a new feeling of calm. Even if he were discovered behind the wood-pile and arrested, he could never suffer more than he had suffered that day. He had reached the end. In the silence he hardly noticed the regular sound of his own breathing, measuring perhaps the last minutes of liberty left to him.

A clock struck in the distance; at first he did not think of listening to it, and when he started counting there were only five strokes more, but it must have been seven o'clock, for it was quite dark. In front of him bits of coal caught the reflection of the lamp and shone like glass. He stared at them, heavy-eyed, then, relaxing his head, which he had raised for an instant, he fell asleep, his cheek resting on the ground.

He slept on until midnight. Something running persistently to and fro quite close to his face, almost touching him, woke him. In the incoherent dreams that were passing through his brain it appeared as a giant hand trying to seize his hair, and to avoid its contact he was jerking his shoulders convulsively this way and that. In reality it was only one of those great bloated glossy rats that seem to be born spontaneously in coal, sleeping during the day and roaming about their coal-yard at night, as if it were a marvelous garden full of sweet-perfumed flowers and winding paths.

He got up and staggered to the wall, which he followed to the gate; it was shut and the lamp had been put out, but the moon shed a hard strong light whose brilliance forced him to rub his eyes. The coal-yard was rectangular. A space of about fifteen yards separated the corner which contained the gates from the one in which stood the coal-order office, a little one-storied building, to the right of which a door opened on to the street. Along one of its walls ran a gently sloping lean-to shed, which projected far enough to shelter an empty van and a large pile of firewood heaped against the house.

In the middle of the yard rose three piles of coal, of equal size, quite independent of one another, in spite of the continuous slipping of the coal, which tended to blunt their apexes and to bring their bases closer together by widening them. They stood powerfully reflecting the light which bathed them; a whitewashed wall would not have seemed whiter than the sides which lay toward the moon, but whereas whitewash gives a dull surface, the scintillating facets of the coal shone like sparkling, ruffled water. This motionless rippling gave the dumps of coal and coke a peculiar character; they seemed to palpitate like creatures accorded a few hours of mysterious and terrifying life by some magic star. In the side of one of them a long horizontal rent made a furrow into which no light penetrated, and this black line gave one the impression of a grin on a metal face. Behind the dumps their shadows almost met, looking like triangular chasms from which they seemed to have risen to the surface of the earth as from some hell. The haphazard way in which they were grouped, like three people deep in conversation, imbued them with a sort of sinister grandeur. If one looked at them for a long time in the midnight silence, standing there beneath the black sky from the vault of which the moon seemed to be permanently hung, they became as awe-inspiring as gods looking on at some tragedy in which the very fate of creation was at stake.

Not a breath of wind stirred the air. As though
in some enchanted spot, all life seemed to be suspended within these walls. Objects, transfigured by
the crude glare, seemed to have ceased to belong to
this world, and to have become connected with a
universe unknown to man; so moving was all the
magnificence and desolation of this place, that one
seemed to be standing among the ruins of a city, but
not a city of this world.

Guéret stared in front of him for some time, uncertain as to the exact point at which his dream
ended and wakefulness began. When, five hours
earlier, he had slipped out of the way to avoid the
man who was approaching him, he had been too
weary to take much notice of the character of the
place into which he had fled; his brain was too exhausted to hold any more impressions. His head
still full of dreams, he took a few steps and reached
the first dump. So far no recollection troubled him;
he was like a child astonished by the sight of this
glittering pyramid at whose foot he stood, and as a
child might have done he bent down and plunged
his hand into it as though it were a stream, drawing
out a black stone whose fractured surface seemed
covered with sparks.

A piece of coal. He held it in his hand for a
moment and then let it drop. Then he walked
slowly round the first pyramid, and passing in front
of the second he made for the middle of the yard with
the gait of a sleep-walker, his feet stumbling on
the cobbles. His eyes were fixed on vacancy, yet he

gradually recognized the coal-yard, but the haziness
of his mind remained just as complete. Incoherent
images began to form in his mind, without his being
able to coördinate them or give them a semblance of
reality.

He was no longer in a dream as he crossed the
yard. The hand which, a little while before, had
tried to seize his hair, was a dream, but the footsteps that were taking him to the house at the end
of the coal-yard were real. He distinguished the
sound they made; he saw his shadow preceding him,
small and black, then longer and longer from second to second, as though it were in a hurry and were
dragging him along by his feet.

On reaching the house he halted. Three steps
led up to a door from which some one had removed
the latch. The window shutters were closed. He
mounted the three steps and, leaning his back
against the door, he considered the coal-yard as a
whole. The three pyramids in an oblique line, the
wood-pile in whose shadow he had slept, the closed
gate, the high white walls, the black lean-to shed,
the van with its shafts on the ground as though
sleeping, the whole of this fantastic landscape worried him. He descended the steps again and walked
toward the van. By getting closer to things he
could divest them of that visionary aspect which
they took on in the peculiar lighting of the moment.
Moreover, he now remembered this coal-yard. He
had followed that wall and entered this place by the
gate; he knew all about it from having heard it

talked about; indeed his own coal came from it. Anyway, he must not get unreasonably alarmed, he must try to find some means of getting out. Perhaps the gates were not locked. In any case he could climb them. He had easily climbed to the first floor of the Restaurant Londe.

This recollection drew him up as abruptly as if he had been struck in the face. His conscious life was returning after having hovered in a kind of mist, and his memory suddenly came back to him. It had been no use his trying to cheat it; it was stronger than he was. Only sleep or death could get the better of it. That was what he feared most. He could no longer deceive himself; he must continue his life in the direction he had given it the day before.

Twenty-four hours earlier he was at liberty to do as other people did, to stay at home or go out or lie down or take a walk in the country, to speak to people he met in the street or pass them by; now he could not take a single step except with the object of protecting himself from men, and as soon as he ceased moving he must hide at once. If he remained in this yard he ran the risk of being discovered; if he left it he ran the risk of being recognized in the street, on the highroad, in the middle of the fields. Even now he was no longer free. It was as though his prison life was beginning already. The first person he met might be his gaoler; a woman, even a child encountered at the corner of a street held his liberty in their hands, unless, of course, he killed them as he had killed the old man. But he could not do that again; he knew that. The power of homicide, that sudden gift that had been bestowed upon him the day before, had been taken away again. He was once more weak and timid, as he used to be, but his mind was burdened with memories which he could not succeed in dismissing from it and the horror of which made him groan aloud. He felt hot, and the sweat was trickling down his spine and making his shirt stick to his skin. In his despair his hands moved aimlessly, fingering his waistcoat and fumbling for the skin of his chest as though to rend it. A craven fear kept him in this corner of the yard, the fear of being seen if he left the shadow which the shed cast upon him. When the light shone on him he felt as though it shouted out to denounce him and he lost his head; whereas there, in the darkness, he could consider the situation calmly.

The first thing to do as soon as he got out of the yard—and he was going to get out—was to get back home as quickly as possible. His latch-key was in his pocket. He would get in without waking his wife and would take all the money he could lay hands upon. He would then go on foot to the next town, where he would board the first train that passed. He had four, five hours before dawn; that was enough, if he were only sufficiently determined enough.

He walked a few steps along the pile of firewood in the shadow, as though this shadow constituted a place of safety along the edge of the abyss of light.

His cowardice outweighed even the instinct that urged him to escape. Any pretext served him to prolong these dangerous moments of hesitation. He must have ample time for reflection and to gather his wits together.

As he reached the van his foot struck a wooden bucket full of water standing between the two shafts. A sponge was floating in the water which had been used to wash the van. As he looked at the water it occurred to him that he might wash his hands so as to get rid of the suspicious stains that might be noticed, and as he leaned over the bucket he was seized with a sudden longing to see what he looked like. It was a day and a night since he had seen himself; it was the first time he had felt this desire and it was all the more imperative in consequence. What did he look like after all he had done? He wanted to know. A vague form appeared in the surface of the water, a sort of shadow in which he could only distinguish the shape of his head and shoulders. He was kneeling so close to the bucket that his breath made the water ripple, but he could not distinguish his features or his expression.

Then, forgetting the fear of light that had prevented him from leaving the shed, he seized the bucket by its handle and carried it into the moonlight. He was panting, as though the weight of the water had exhausted his strength. He knelt down and leaned over the bucket again, but this time his shadow was in the way and prevented him from seeing himself. He went round to the other side of

the bucket, threw the sponge on one side, and waited
for the surface of the water to settle down.

By not leaning over too much and kneeling almost erect, he succeeded in seeing himself. The
water was not clear, but the moon made a mirror of
it; little by little the ripples on its surface died down
and the reflection he saw became sharper and sharper
until it was quite steady. That motionless man was
he.

He remained without moving for some minutes.
His tangled hair, the beard shading his cheeks, the
disorder of his clothing, all these things he had expected and they did not surprise him. And yet he
stayed there as though fascinated, his arms hanging
by his sides and his knees upon the ground. In the
image of himself which he saw, he noticed the slight
trembling which shook his body. He would never
be able to tear his eyes from that magic reflection.
It was not the moon, in whose sinister light he was
bathed, that he feared now, but the look which met
his own and held it as though by a spell. He had
seen those eyes too often to notice them, but now
they clung searchingly to him, speaking and living,
in fact, as much as that mouth whose lips quivered,
as though they were about to part and break into
a scream. The face at the bottom of the bucket
seemed about to rise, lifting itself slowly out of the
water. For a moment he had recognized it as his
own, but then terror had worked an extraordinary
change in it and it was no longer the same. It was
going to leave the water, float in the air before him,

and scream. His legs stiffened abruptly. He suddenly rose and turned the bucket over.

Around him, in his ears, the very silence created a tumult and seemed to sound an alarm, as though the noise of the bucket rolling on the cobbles had aroused the night. With his hands to his head he ran behind one of the coal dumps, then rushed to the gates which he tried to open, turning the handles violently first one way and then the other, maddened by the creaking sound they made. But the gates were locked. He stood on the stone post as the man had done to light the lamp, but when he got there he realized that by no conceivable effort could he reach the top of the wall. He had not the patience, the strength, or the time. Dawn was not far away now.

He leaped down and ran back to the house. What little energy he had left was being rapidly exhausted; if he did not get out at once he was lost. Perhaps he had been shut into this yard on purpose; perhaps they had guessed that he would come there, and he had a feeling that he was being spied on from behind the coal-dumps and that people were laughing at his terror. He mounted the steps of the house, descended them again, and tried to open the little door, which was as firmly locked as the gates were.

Everything was going black before his eyes; his knees were shaking. His fear was so great that tears began to roll down his cheeks. He caught sight of the van and climbed into it, without realizing what he was doing. It tilted slowly, lifting its shafts. He tried to leap back, but it was too late and, seeing that he was about to fall, he sprang almost to the top of the pile of firewood. This supported him for an instant and then he felt it beginning to give way beneath his feet, but the top of the wall was now within his reach. He had only to lift his arms and to scramble up, with the aid of his knees, tearing his body on the stonework. He was climbing the wall of his prison.

Below him the bundles of firewood clattered to the ground with a sound like hail. He paused a moment on top of the wall, his chest aching from his effort. Then he grasped the stonework with his arms and let himself down on the other side of the wall, his legs dangling over the street. How many feet was he from the pavement? He did not know and could not calculate. His fingers relaxed little by little. He must let himself slide down the wall. But how? Suddenly, with a scream, he let himself go.

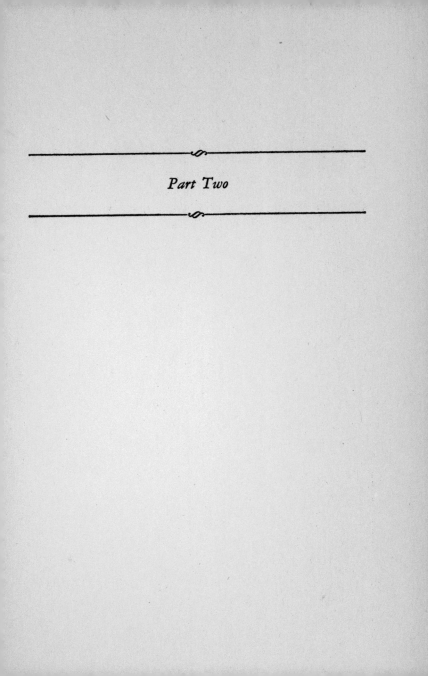

Part Two

Chapter One

"SHOCKING weather, Madame Londe. You may
say it's the time of year for it. But some years
winter comes sooner than others. It's bitterly cold.
Don't you think so?"

"You've always been a chilly person ever since
I've known you, Madame Couze. As for me, I'm
quite happy if my hands and feet are warm. With
my foot-warmer and my mittens I'm first rate."

Madame Couze gave a little mirthless laugh.

"Mittens!" she said. "Can't you see me cook-
ing with mittens on! Luckily, it's warmer in my
kitchen than here."

Madame Londe preserved a dignified silence.

"No offense meant," went on Madame Couze.
"Many apologies if I've annoyed you."

"Not at all, Madame Couze. The temperature I
maintain here is the one I think best. If I suffer,
it's my own affair."

She said this in a calm, firm voice, glaring at her
interlocutrix as though to defy her to argue the
point; but Madame Couze had no intention of doing
anything of the sort; it was easy to browbeat this
little woman who shivered and rubbed her hands
together without daring to lift her eyes. The
rough work of her profession had exhausted and

shattered her body, and she sat bent in two in her dark flannelette stomacher, perched on the edge of her chair like a child that is afraid of taking up too much room. With her bright eyes and her flushed forehead and cheeks, she seemed still to have the light of her kitchen range upon her, and she looked as though the fire, that wild animal which cooks are always irritating in its pit with their pokers, had leaped out at her face one day, for she had neither eyelashes nor eyebrows and her hard shining skin seemed to be permanently reflecting a conflagration.

"I shall have to be going soon," she said, after a moment's pause. "It's getting dark already."

"You needn't go just yet," said Madame Londe, in a decided voice. She did not like being alone.

"I'm afraid I have my dinner to get ready, Madame Londe, and I don't like being out alone these days."

"Bah! You're afraid, like the rest of them. What are you afraid of?"

"An unprotected woman has always something to be afraid of, on the highroad."

"A young woman, perhaps. But you're quite old enough to be safe."

"I might have my throat cut for my money, or my brains beaten out with a cudgel like poor Monsieur . . . "

"Come, Madame Couze, don't get such ideas into your head. The whole countryside has been in a state of panic for six weeks just because an unfortunate old man was murdered at a street corner.

As if murders weren't committed everywhere. What would you say if you lived in Paris, where at least ten people have their throats cut every night?"

"Oh! Please! Madame Londe. You frighten me. You talk about it so calmly . . . "

"I don't see why I should worry myself over such a trifle."

"Monsieur Grosgeorge was telling his wife the other day that the desire to commit crime was as catching as the 'flu' and that was why crimes always went in series."

"And what did she say?"

"She said nothing. She never does say anything."

"Well, that shows she didn't believe it."

"I'm not sure. She looked so queer. It's like the newspaper. For some time now . . . "

"The newspaper?"

"Yes, she fairly flings herself on it."

"Well, so do I, so do you. She wants to see if there's any more news."

"You haven't seen her as I have, Madame Londe. Do your hands shake when you open your paper? They don't, do they? Well, hers do, and it's only since this business about Mademoiselle Angèle."

"Well, what does that prove?"

"Why, that she's afraid!"

"If she were afraid, she wouldn't go out at night."

"As a matter of fact, she went to the station to fetch a parcel the day before yesterday, after dinner."

"I know. The parcel came from Paris."

"How do you know that?"

"You're very inquisitive."

"Not at all, but it's exactly what she said to her husband when she came in. A parcel from Paris containing boots."

"There you are, you see."

"But I can't think you could have guessed that. Once I could have understood it. Monsieur would have told Mademoiselle Angèle and Mademoiselle Angèle would have told you. But now that he doesn't see her any more . . . "

"Leave Mademoiselle Angèle out of it."

"Oh, forgive me, Madame Londe! I know I ought not to have spoken to you about that. It must be dreadful for you. Such a pretty girl, with a scar like that on her face. What a dreadful monster that man Guéret must be. He seems to bring misfortune upon everyone he knows, and on his wife more than on anyone. Do you know what has happened to her?"

Madame Londe greeted these last words with a scowl. She hated having to answer no to a question of this sort.

"I know as much as you do," she said at length. "The only thing certain is that she's gone."

"I heard she'd gone back to her people, in Brittany. The other day the housemaid heard Monsieur Grosgeorge tell madame that Guéret ought never to have married a woman like Madame Guéret, and that that was the cause of everything."

"Ah! And what did she say to that?"

"Nothing. I told you, she never does say anything. If she didn't speak to give orders, you might think she was dumb. Heavens! Here I am gossiping away while night falls. Now I really *must* go."

"Just as you like."

"Well, good night, Madame Londe. I shall walk quickly and keep to the middle of the road. If you hear screams you will know I am being murdered."

"Don't you worry about that, Madame Couze!"

"You always say that. You are lucky to be staying at home. Well, I must go. Good night, Madame Londe. Don't get up."

"Good night."

"Get up, indeed!" she muttered, when she was alone. "As if I were going to put myself out for her, now. Run, you old coward," she added, looking through the window.

She had uttered these last words with a mixture of animosity and contempt and so loud that she even surprised herself. She gazed around her with embarrassment and coughed, as people often do when they talk to themselves, possibly in order to try to make anyone who might hear them believe that they were only clearing their throats, and what sounded like words was really only the noise of coughing.

Still, if the fact of muttering and talking to oneself is one of the little misfortunes of old age, Madame Londe could be forgiven, for during the past few months time had been very unkind to her. Her sight was failing, and she could not see prop-

erly without the help of recently-acquired glasses,
which she did not dare to use in public; for what was
the good of the fine black hair she still kept if she
had to disfigure herself with this ridiculous instrument? After all, she was only fifty-seven. She
could still see well enough to recognize her customers, and if she wanted to read or to sew she
could shut herself into her bedroom. But what
alarmed her much more was that recently her hearing had not been so keen; at first she thought that
the fault lay with the people who addressed her not
pronouncing their words distinctly, but now she
had to bow to the evidence: her senses were betraying
her, one by one. No one but Angèle could make
herself understood to her now. The young woman
knew exactly how to pitch her voice so as to pierce
the mists of her incipient deafness.

Thinking of these things made Madame Londe
shake her head; then she gazed out of the window
for an instant, and got up. A short black wool
cape protected her shoulders from the cold and gave
her the appearance of a priest in a rochet. She
went slowly round her room, rubbing her hands together, and as she approached her armchair again
the thought of Madame Couze returned to her mind.
"All these women are frightened," she muttered,
angrily.

The panic that gripped the town after sunset
caused her some uneasiness. If the men allowed
themselves to be influenced by the cowardice of the
women, it was all up with her restaurant; for they

had to come down long badly lit streets to get there, and in winter it was not a very cheerful walk.

She stood before the fireplace and lit her paraffin lamp. "They've got into the habit of coming here," she told herself, replacing the shade over the glass chimney. "They don't like change. Besides, I'm the only person in the district that charges such low prices. And they're frightened of me, too. Perhaps not quite so much as they used to be when Angèle went out with them . . . "

Her thoughts suddenly trailed off into generalities, as though to escape from the pain of too precise a memory:

"Why do I have all these troubles?" she asked aloud. "Why should fate suddenly afflict me like this? Three months ago I thought I was unhappy, but I was happy, yes, happy. I ate well and slept well, without realizing it. My daily life seemed to be settled forever. . . . "

She took the lamp and, crossing the room, opened the wardrobe.

"And now I'm even afraid of the morrow," she continued, plunging her hands among the dresses and wraps. "Every time I hear a knock at the door I am frightened of something, Heaven knows what. There's no one here. Of course there's no one in this wardrobe. In the first place, how could he stand up? He would have to be about four feet high. These old women's fancies! But it doesn't alter the fact that three months ago I never dreamt of examining my room."

Shutting the wardrobe door, she went over to the bed and placed the lamp on the tiled floor.

"I can easily believe that Madame Grosgeorge's hands shake when she opens her paper. What about mine! I can't bear blood. The thought of anyone touching me with the point of a knife! Ugh!"

She knelt down as though in prayer in front of the Christ who held His arms above her and her fears, but she did not see Him.

"Going down on my knees and looking under the bed at my age!" she groaned. "I shouldn't know what to do if I found anyone there. Which proves that I don't believe there could possibly be anyone, and yet I wouldn't leave this room before I was sure that there's no one hiding here."

She put her hands flat on the tiles and leaned forward until her hair touched the floor; the blood rushed to her head and made it sing.

"I can't see a thing," she sighed; "I ought to have put on my glasses. This lamp doesn't light it all up. Anyway, I don't believe anyone could slip in under there, however thin he was. . . . And yet one never knows; people are so clever when it comes to annoying honest people."

Her voice lost itself beneath the bed. Crouching down there and sighing, she was like a fat animal snuffling dejectedly beneath the door of its cage. Behind her the winter twilight came feebly through the window. At the moment she was neither moving nor speaking; her scowling glance traveled from right to left. Her enormous bottom in its sheath of shiny serge protruded insultingly into the last rays of daylight.

That evening, after shutting up the restaurant and putting the latch in her pocket, she went up to Angèle's room. The girl had been in bed for some time and her lamp was out; so she was surprised at Madame Londe's visit and feared for a moment that something unusual had happened.

"What's the matter?" she asked, shrinking beneath the bedclothes.

Madame Londe sighed and placed her lamp upon the mantelpiece.

"What could be the matter?" she asked with a forced air of joviality. "I just came to say good night. I hope you weren't asleep."

She drew a chair up to the foot of the bed and sat down.

"This evening," she went on, "I was depressed, downstairs." "Why are you doing that?" she suddenly asked, seeing that the girl was holding the sheet over her face.

"The light's in my eyes."

"That's right. Always interrupt me when I begin to speak."

She rose, grumbling, and put the lamp on a table in a far corner of the room, so that Angèle's bed was in shadow.

"I was telling you that I was depressed. Yes. I am catching the customers' depression. They don't talk as they used to. That's a fact."

"They never did talk very much, except to quarrel."

"I would rather see them quarrel. I don't care what you say. Their silence is a bad sign. They've never been like that ever since I've known them."

"What does it matter? Just let them be quiet."

"Thank you! And if they go away?"

"Who said they wanted to go away?"

"No one. But if they don't talk it means they are dissatisfied, and if they are dissatisfied they may go. I have a sort of presentiment about it."

"Personally, I've got a presentiment that they'll stay because it's cheaper here than anywhere else."

"And what about comfort, my girl?" said Madame Londe with sudden warmth. "Do you think it is comfortable for them to come and dine at Lorges, when many of them live at Chanteilles, and Chanteilles is gay and full of lights and people? Whereas Lorges has a sinister reputation and its streets are badly lit. Even the poorest of them would pay twenty-five centimes more for his dinner in some place from which he could get home without having his throat cut."

"Why are you telling me all this, auntie? You promised me . . . "

"Let me finish!" interrupted Madame Londe, unable to contain her irritation any longer. "I must talk and you've got to listen. I've got this thing on my mind, don't you understand? A little time ago I had a visit from Madame Couze, another of these women who almost die of fright every time they set foot outside their houses. It's all getting on my nerves. When people begin to be frightened in a little town like Lorges, it's bad for everyone. I don't want people to think they take their lives in their hands every time they come and dine in my restaurant. Winter has come. After six o'clock it's pitch dark. Come, you're surely not going to cry again. You make my life quite impossible here with your sniveling. It wasn't so very gay even before. Angèle! Do you hear me, Angèle?"

"Yes."

"In your interest as well as in mine, I am going to ask you a question, a serious question. You know the name of the man who attacked you. Who was it? Tell me."

Angèle shrank still farther into the bed, with her arms over her head. Her tears prevented her from answering at once; then she suddenly cried:

"You promised me not to talk about that again. Can't you leave me alone?"

Madame Londe did not move, accustomed, perhaps, to the girl's violence.

"I can't stand it any longer," she said at last, in a lower voice. "Many people say that you know the man's name quite well, and that it's your duty to assist justice. Don't you understand, that by not speaking, you are putting the whole town against us? If anyone is ever attacked in the street this winter, people are sure to say that it wouldn't have happened if you had denounced the man who attacked you. Then there would be nothing left for us to do but to clear out."

"But I can't tell you the man's name if I don't know it."

"Do you expect me to believe that you had never even seen him before? Come, what was he like?"

"I was standing on the river bank. He came behind me and hit me on the head. That's all I know."

"But you were seen with him in the road, you wretched girl. Madame Koppé saw you. And a little farther on the chair-woman at Saint-Jude saw you, too."

"Then you had better ask them whom I was with, since they saw me so well."

This reply was followed by a long silence, broken only by Angèle's stifled sobs and Madame Londe's noisy wheezing. Madame Londe was trying to sit bolt upright in her chair, no doubt to appear more formidable to the young woman and to overawe her. Half her face was lit up by the lamp which she had placed behind her, and her long hard profile appeared silhouetted in a kind of halo. She reflected for a moment, her eyes glittering as she thought what unkind thing she could say that would hurt most.

"We'll see what you'll answer at the assizes," she said, finally.

Angèle said nothing for a moment, then:

"You'll make me laugh in another moment," she observed, calmly. "What have I to fear from the assizes?"

"They'll say that you're sheltering some one, that you've taken money to hold your tongue."

"They'll have to prove it first."

"Lawyers can prove anything they want to, and you'll go to prison."

"Do you think I'm a baby to be frightened so easily? When did they start putting the victims of crimes into prison?"

There was a very short pause; then Madame Londe resumed with the patience and ferocity of an insect:

"Of course your aggressor will be punished, but you will be made to pay for your silence which will have prevented the law from laying hands upon him sooner; and, who knows? Perhaps you will have been the cause of other, even more appalling crimes, because that man at large is a public danger, and he is at large thanks to your silence, my girl. If he took it into his head to cut my throat tonight, do you know that you would be held partly responsible?"

"I, auntie? But how? How?"

"By refusing to give his name."

"But I keep on telling you I don't know it. I don't know anything about him. I couldn't tell you what he looks like, even."

"And yet you were seen talking to him on the road. There are witnesses to that."

"The witnesses are lying."

"You can explain that to the public prosecutor, darling."

"Oh, do leave me alone, auntie! Why do you go on tormenting me?"

"Just tell me whether it was Monsieur Guéret or not. A good deal of suspicion rests on him. If it isn't he you will be doing a kind action in telling me so. You don't want to get an innocent man into trouble, do you? And his wife. Think of his wife. She hasn't heard anything of him at all. Perhaps he is only keeping away because people are accusing him of having done this crime. Tell me, is it he? You've only got to say yes or no."

Angèle stiffened in her bed.

"I'm not going to answer any more questions," she said, violently. "Leave me alone, I tell you!"

"You won't answer, won't you?" repeated Madame Londe, rising and coming close to the bed. "And what if I've had enough of you, eh? What if I showed you the door? You weren't so proud the day they brought you from down there."

Her voice rose higher and higher until it became a scream, and she leaned over the young woman's white shape outlined beneath the bedclothes.

"They'll arrest the ruffian, all right, in time, do you hear? And you, you'll get what's coming to you, too. You are his accomplice. You got money from him to hold your tongue. Everyone says it. It's obvious."

"It isn't true," said Angèle, half rising in bed. "I tell you it isn't true. You used to believe me." She was speaking like a person being suffocated. "Isn't the sight of me enough to make you believe that if

I knew the man's name I would be revenged upon him? I hate him far more than you do. I should like to see him on the scaffold."

She fell back on to her pillow, sobbing. Madame Londe straightened herself and said nothing; she stood in the dim light and seemed to be thinking.

After a moment she left the bed and went to pick up the lamp standing on the table. Her face was strongly lit up, as though by limelight. Old age was triumphing at last in the deep furrows that lined her cheeks and in the quiet eyes whose stare could almost be felt. Her long large nose and thick eyebrows made her look like a man, and the paint she had put on with a trembling hand struggled vainly to impart a little freshness to her skin, from which life seemed already to be departing. She gazed for a long time at the bed, which she saw but dimly; then she sighed. Her heart was heavy. As she opened the door she shrugged her shoulders more in disappointment than in indifference.

"Well, good night," she said, almost regretfully.

And without waiting for a reply, she left the room.

Chapter Two

IN SPITE of the ugliness of its furniture and color scheme, it was difficult not to feel happy in the little sitting-room which Madame Grosgeorge had established on the second floor of Villa Mon Idée, and that impression was no doubt due to the log fire that gave out a delicious heat on this bitterly cold afternoon. The red velvet curtains, the scarlet carpet with its dark flowered pattern, the furniture itself, a sofa and armchairs of Turkish design, were all impregnated with pleasant warmth and betrayed a fastidious love of comfort. A person of taste would certainly have said that the room contained too many things for its size; he would have deplored the distressing mixture of colors and the quantities of pictures with which the walls were covered, but for anyone coming in from outside, buffeted by the December gale, it was a real delight to be in the room.

And yet Madame Grosgeorge, who had just come in, did not seem to notice the warmth. She threw her muff on the table and, without removing the long beaver coat that enveloped her completely, she sat down by the fire and then rose again almost at once to walk across the room. The cold had made her eyes water; she stripped off her gloves and wiped her eyes with the backs of her numbed hands.

For some minutes she strode restlessly backward and forward across the room. At length, as she passed before a mirror hanging on the wall, she suddenly caught sight of a look in her eyes which must have surprised her, for she stopped and then crossed over to the sofa and sat down.

She removed the fur toque that covered her head and with her long lean fingers she smoothed the black hair just beginning to turn gray round the forehead and behind the ears. It was as though she were ashamed of her recent behavior and were trying to recover her calm by doing something sensible. She rose, rang the bell, and removed her coat.

"No one called while I was out?" she asked the maid who answered the bell.

"No one, madame."

"Very well. Take my coat and hat. If anyone calls, don't say I am in until you have asked me. Is your master out?"

"He went out almost immediately after madame. He took the carriage."

"Very well. That's all."

"What am I to do?" she muttered when she was alone. She thought for a moment and then walked over to the window. The wind was howling through the tree-tops and raised a white dust on the road which appeared beyond the gate, swirling it endlessly round and round a few yards from the ground. The cold had killed all the plants. The two flower-beds which lay one on each side of the big lawn were nothing but dismal mounds of black earth. Only the grass plots and the hedges of alternate laurel and prickwood which hid the walls of the garden struck a note of color in this barren landscape.

After another moment she let the lace curtain fall and went and sat down by the fire.

There were moments in which her life appeared to her not as a succession of years, but as a living creature, a sort of double to whom she could have given a face, movement, and a voice; and that mysterious person always came to her in hours of great loneliness, or after any violent emotion; she could feel her by her side, speaking in a voice drowned by the silence, and moving about invisibly. At those moments she had the impression of being with a traveler who had returned from some distant land and was telling her what she had seen, and it was only by an effort that she was able to emerge from the torpor into which this strange revery of hers cast her.

Except in her childhood, she had never been happy. She had never lacked money or health, and nature had been generous to her, but perhaps the very profusion of the gifts which she had received was the cause of the melancholy which lurked at the back of her eyes. Was she sad because there was nothing left for her to desire? Little by little she had become detached from everything, even to the point of accepting as a husband the selfish and ridiculous man with whom she lived, and of being

insensible to the ugliness of the objects which surrounded her and met her gaze at all hours of the
day. But occasionally something which she could
not define took place within her, a sort of halt in
the course of time, as though she were being offered
an opportunity of recovering herself, of seeing herself as she really was, of seeing her life.

She had a little foreign blood in her veins; something more than the carelessness of the French;
something more than their prudence and common
sense had been required to produce a woman at the
same time so secretive and so violent. Cold and
severe as she seemed to the casual eye of the world,
she was really a mass of restlessness, and concealed
a rebellious heart beneath the appearance of a well-
regulated life. Without attaching any real importance to anything, she loathed everything which
made her life less rich and less beautiful, everything
which said to her: "It is too late. You must face
the fact that you have reached the end of your life,
for henceforth nothing will change any more." And
yet this loathing was quite vague and was not
directed against any particular person or object.
She considered her youth and all the events that had
marked it as so many games she had unconsciously
lost; and she was left now with the bitter feeling
of the man who tries to find out by what skillful
trickery his treacherous opponent has cheated him.

At forty-five she felt older than a woman of sixty,
because she had acquired the thousand little habits
that are part of an uneventful life, and all her re-

maining energy seemed imperceptibly to have abandoned her. If a feeling of revolt ever came to trouble her, her reason invariably told her that she was too old to dream of freeing herself now. Upon what could she base her happiness? Her beauty had disappeared long ago, and her fortune was no longer in her own hands. Besides, she was not strong enough. Ten years earlier she would have run away; but could she have foreseen, ten years earlier, that she would sink into such boredom, into that aversion toward everything including even herself, that now poisoned every hour of her daily life? "How do other people live?" she often asked herself. "How do they go on week after week all through the year?"

She could not bear this sort of journey across time which she was compelled to make. Where was it leading her? Toward what happiness? What could ever compensate her for her weariness? No faith had ever had any hold on this woman to whom all religions appeared to be equally false, since not one of them could explain to her why she was made to live, and why, when once this life had been given to her, the day must come when it would be taken from her again. The idea of death produced in her that feeling of dismay that is one of the signs of a youthful heart; it was not love of life that she lacked, but the gift of accepting without a murmur a life that differed from all other human lives and was hers alone.

She realized, indeed, that nothing could be altered now. Everything pointed to the probability that she would end her life in that town; she could almost predict how many more walks she would take. All her movements, almost all her thoughts, were controlled by some fatality. She was being buried alive. Death would come for her in one of the rooms of that house. Death whom she did not want, and who would tear her away from a life for which she had never asked.

This feeling of being the victim of some capricious force never left her; she was the plaything of the Will that rules the world and her liberty was nothing but a mockery. What was the use of secretly bemoaning the ugliness and monotony of her life? It would need a stronger soul than hers to escape from its prison. Although she appeared to be domineering, and frightened her husband by her severity, she was really feeble, even feebler than the people she overawed so much.

Boredom and despair made her bitter. Being accustomed to curb all the impulses of her nature, she was all the more easily able to retain the poison that had been acting upon her for years. The violence which she was constantly controlling had gradually hardened her heart until it had become indifferent to the sufferings of others. Without having ever done anything seriously wrong, her conscience was perhaps more hardened than that of the most horrible criminal. When she beat her son, she enjoyed the tears that she saw trembling in his eyes and hoped that some fresh blunder would give her an opportunity for fresh punishment. She loathed this child which reminded her of her husband; it was the living emblem of her servitude, because she felt herself incapable of abandoning it, of running away from it, and it formed part of that order of things that had been imposed upon her without her consent. Each time the child fell ill she nursed it carefully, but she was obsessed by a terrible joy; she did not know what she hoped for on these occasions.

She would soon have been living for fifteen years in this villa baptized Villa Mon Idée by its absurd owner. Ridicule was one of the dominant features of this woman's life. Her husband's very name lent itself to ribaldry. His hobbies made people smile, and the furniture with which he had filled the house betrayed only too well the mediocrity of his mind. She did not struggle against all that; to replace an armchair by another would not make her happy. Fate had chosen to afflict her; she resigned herself to being a furious but passive victim of all its injustices. At least she was proud enough to show a brave face to the world.

They say that in the Alps great masses of snow pile up and remain suspended upon the sides of mountains by a miracle of balance to which the slightest tremor of the atmosphere may put an end. A human voice shouting in the neighborhood is enough to make this wall crumble and form in its fall an avalanche which may wipe out a whole village. It was a shout of this sort that she wanted to utter, a call which would break down the equilibrium of this invisible snow. The first time she saw her son's tutor she had a curious impression which came back to her whenever the memory of that interview returned to her. She did not like the man; his nervous manner and clumsy obsequiousness were distasteful to her, but for all her lack of intuition she had guessed immediately that they had many grudges and illusions in common. No doubt her age and something rebellious in her nature had carried her beyond him along the road of compulsory self-denial, but it was enough for her to study Guéret's restless expression, his awkwardness, and the anxious, bored look in his eyes, to be quite certain that he was combating the same sort of difficulties that used to worry her. He, too, did not know how to control his life, and he showed it, whereas she had always had sufficient vanity and courage to hide her lack of skill. Like her, years ago, he probably did not see his mistakes until they were made, and did not know how to profit by them.

Other people, more tractable people, were endowed with the gift of profiting by circumstances. Many people learned happiness as one learns a profession, and resigned themselves cheerfully to accepting mediocrity in order to avoid something worse. From such wisdom as this resulted fruitful marriages, a calm old age, and family dinners to which three perfectly contented generations sat down together. But in Guéret she saw a man upon whom this happiness had not smiled any more than it had upon her. Perhaps he would never know peace. Fate would buffet him without teaching him anything, not even how to rise above himself, and to ape the appearance of a man sure of his actions. He did not even know anything about the profession he had chosen; he might just as well have been a bank clerk, or a postman, or a gardener; he had no place in the scheme of things.

She saw all this clearly, and it made her unhappy, not for him, but for herself, because he was in her eyes the symbol of her own misery. Without despising him—how could she despise a person who resembled her in so many respects?—she was annoyed with him for coming to her, but she was careful that his visits should not cease. It was painful for her to see him; but it would have been much more painful for her to have deprived herself of his presence. She longed to ask him one day about his life, and to find out what steps he, on his side, was taking to ruin his future.

Of course, he was weak, and she only liked strength; but she recognized his superiority in one respect—he was less patient than she was. Some day, thoughtlessly, in a fit of rage, which in his place she would control, he would do something more stupid than any he had ever done before, and he would upset the order of things. He would perhaps succeed in doing what she had never dared to do, because sometimes fortune favors fools.

So that when she heard that two crimes had been committed at Lorges in the same evening, and almost at the same place, it was not necessary for her husband to explain to her upon whom suspicion fell. She lived through several hours of perfect satisfaction and had to shut herself in her room so as not to betray the feelings that possessed her. And yet something inside her disapproved of her pleasure, the memory of an austere upbringing in which good works and the reading of pious books had played their part. "How wicked I am!" she thought with an involuntary smile; but this knowledge she possessed of herself did not in any way check the zeal with which she read and re-read in her newspaper the detailed account of the appalling discovery. The words and lines danced before her over-eager eyes, and without the help of her lorgnette she would not have been able to understand it all, so much did emotion impede her sight. It seemed to her that she had a share in this double crime. At first she dismissed such an absurd idea. Had she ever said a single word to Guéret that might have inspired him to commit such a crime? And all the time she read the paper she took the trouble to repeat inwardly the strange thoughts that her reading gave rise to inside her, but she was not bold enough to analyze calmly all that was going on in her mind. Her hand shook. More and more clearly, and against her will, she saw a mysterious connection becoming established between her and this crime committed by another.

"Ah, no indeed!" she cried, suddenly getting up.

She threw the paper on the floor. She was in the presence of an actual brutal fact. Everything hon-

est and conventional in her protested against the
possibility of complicity with the murderer. And
for some minutes she played the virtuous woman to
herself. How delightful to feel that one was innocent in face of such a ferocious crime! Then she
grew calm; she had known herself too many years
to enjoy this artificial delight for long. This crime
did not appall her. It astonished her and interested
her. After all, what did she care if the community
suffered by the commission of such violent acts? She
herself had nothing but contempt and hatred for
this panic-stricken community. Another person had
shown a little more hatred, a little more audacity.
What right had she to blame him? Hypocrisies of
this kind did not suit her time of life. It was much
better to face things. In the end she always came
to this conclusion, which in her mind acquired the
value of a principle and lulled to sleep her last
regrets for her lack of virtue.

Besides, it was by no means disagreeable to feel
oneself rather villainous when fate has linked one's
life to that of a man like Monsieur Grosgeorge, in
whom throve all the false modesty of a middle-class
mind. She had no qualms about her heart's not
being pure when she listened to her husband's conversation. It was enough for her, for instance, to
see the indignation with which this vicious and deceitful old man referred to the murder of Monsieur
Sarcenas, whom he would himself cheerfully have
let die of hunger, and to the outrage of a woman
whose dreary consent he had so often compelled at

the price of a few coins. That was where lack of self-knowledge led one, to this ridiculous parade of respectability.

Sitting opposite Monsieur Grosgeorge, she would listen to him without interrupting his violent harangues. In an access of mercy he decided not to insist on the scaffold for Guéret and to spare his life, provided, of course, that it should be spent beneath the avenging sky of Devil's Island. Every man has a right to his life. This axiom, which he announced as though it were the fruit of much thought, seemed to him to express the extreme limit of concession. He made up for this by the severity of the punishment upon which he would insist if he were in the place of the public prosecutor, always supposing that justice laid hands on the criminal. Many reasons which he was careful not to give explained his resentment against this man. In the first place, he had been frightened. The news of the murder committed by his son's tutor had given him a terrible shock, as though death had suddenly brushed his elbow, and for two days he had lived in a pitiable state of fear, not daring to leave the house and constantly testing his revolvers. Again, and this was probably his most important grievance, he considered that Guéret had abused his confidence in gaining admittance to his house. The ideas in his old head, fuddled by newspaper-reading, were not very clear. A criminal appeared to him to be a species of contagious invalid who ought to be forbidden to carry his disease to other people. If one is considering the commission of a murder, one should remain at home and not go rolling wild eyes in the drawing-rooms of law-abiding people; for Monsieur Grosgeorge remembered that Guéret had been wild-eyed the last morning he had seen him; he would mention that when he gave his evidence. And then, another thing, and that not the least important, either. What did Guéret think of him? The last conversation they had had together had turned upon painting and love. No doubt the wretched man had laughed inwardly at him and his expositions. Perhaps he was laughing, at this very minute, at the pictures which Monsieur Grosgeorge had condescended to show him. Intolerable thought! Had he known, had he dreamed for a moment that he was harboring a blackguard of his stamp, with what joy he would have shown him the door! And now to be an object of contempt to some one whom one might have struck across the face, and who snaps his cowardly fingers at you from the depths of his hiding-place. In Monsieur Grosgeorge's eyes the real crime lay there. The outraging of Angèle and the murder of an old man merely furnished themes for an indignation whose only origin was a seriously wounded vanity.

However, the newspapers spoke less and less of the crime. The guilty man had vanished. Several people had been arrested, questioned, and released. The investigations which had been energetically pursued at the beginning of the affair seemed to lead nowhere. But the terror had been too great for

Lorges to calm down again so soon. Doors were
bolted early, and Madame Londe was not the only
one to look beneath her bed at night. Appalling
rumors were spread about. Women no longer dared
walk along the road that followed the Sommeillante,
and after nightfall the whole neighborhood of the
coal-yard seemed cursed, as though the murderer
was bound to return there to commit fresh crimes.
Certain street corners were left to him after sunset,
and no one but Madame Grosgeorge had sufficient
courage to go out at night.

She knew that she had nothing to fear, and refused to listen to the rumors that attributed Guéret's
crimes to a band of malefactors ; for some time it had
become more difficult for her to stay indoors. Sometimes she would have the carriage out and go for
long aimless drives in the surrounding country. More
often still she took walks which brought her into the
outskirts of Lorges. The weather was cold and dry,
and she walked briskly, returning to the villa in a
state of healthy weariness that calmed her nerves
and made it possible for her to sleep. Often, again,
she was satisfied with simply following the Sommeillante as far as the first houses of the neighboring
town, and when the weather was not too inclement
she would sit on the bank and rest, watching the
river flow by.

After her first surprise, there remained to her, of
the great event that had upset the life of Lorges, a
memory upon which she dwelt with pleasure. She recalled the emotion of the first few minutes, the face

and voice of her husband as he told her of the discovery of the crimes, then the joy she had been
forced to conceal, the short period of shame that had
followed it, and the conclusions she had drawn from
all the violent and conflicting feelings which had occupied her mind for several days. She loved reviving
in herself all the phases of the little drama that had
taken place within her, but she had to have solitude
for this kind of mental exercise, and it was chiefly
so as not to interrupt her meditations that she left
her house and wandered off into the country.

Perhaps, too, certain landscapes possessed an attraction for her whose power she did not quite realize.
Was it by design or by chance that the place where
she always chose to sit on the river bank was quite
close to the trees where Angèle had been found?
What curiosity was it that drew her there, what hope
was she harboring? She was too secretive, and her
strict education had put too wide a barrier between
herself and her heart for her to be able to bring im-
partial judgment to bear upon her actions. Her
conduct was governed by irresistible impulses, and
she did not want to foresee the possible consequences
of what she was about to do. All that mattered was
the satisfaction of finding in any particular place
the memories she sought there. She liked, for instance,
to wander about that part of the town where the
body of Monsieur Sarcenas had been found. Yet
she knew the reaction that would set in on the following day as the result of these solitary walks, when
long hours of sleep had restored her to her dull morn-

ing life and the delicious excitement of the previous day fell from her.

It was in the afternoons that the desire seized her to be on the move and to feel the street cobbles or the hard surface of the main road beneath her feet, and from then until evening her mind gradually became suffused with an excitement which her face never betrayed. She walked with a light, almost noiseless, step, and only stopped from sheer exhaustion, which, toward the end of the day, sometimes made her throw herself fully clothed upon her bed, like those birds which one sees flying aimlessly round and round in the sky until a murderous bullet puts an end to their bewildered flight.

Months passed, and Christmas was only a fortnight distant when one afternoon she returned home much earlier than usual. Her heart was beating fast. She had been running, not because she was in a hurry to return to the little sitting-room to which she usually retired, but because she could hardly control herself, and it seemed to her that her body must have its share in the terrible agitation of her mind. A short while before, while walking beside the railway toward the Boulevard de la Sommeillante, she had seen Guéret. He was walking quickly in the direction of Lorges, and was probably making for the footbridge. Madame Grosgeorge had stopped. The man for whom she had been vaguely searching on all her walks was within a few yards of her; in a minute, when he was on the footbridge, he would see her, but for the moment she was a little behind him on the other side of the railway. So many ideas crossed her mind that she did nothing and stood still. Should she hide? Why? On the contrary, she wanted to speak to him. Should she call him? He would probably take fright and run away. Perhaps it was not he, after all. But it was. The rags he was wearing did not alter him in the least. If anything, they made him look more like himself, as he always looked when he was neatly dressed. He was a tramp with his coat collar raised because he felt the cold. Surprise, and a sort of vague joy, kept the woman from moving. Suddenly he turned round.

Perhaps he had felt her eyes following him. His first act was to pull his hands sharply from his pockets; then he stood still. She saw that he had recognized her and was trying to divine her intentions. To reassure him she put a finger to her mouth and then raised her other arm and beckoned him to come to her; but he stared at her and, after a few seconds of hesitation, started to return the way he had come, turning his head away from her.

Then, as he passed before her and began to run, she called out in a smothered voice:

"Stop! I don't mean you any harm."

He had not heard her, and in a moment he would be gone. But she did not lose her head. To tell him to come back would be useless. She ran a few steps in the direction in which he was going and called hurriedly to him, across the railway:

"I shall be here tomorrow at seven! Don't be

afraid!" And now that she was seated before the log fire this short scene seemed, to her mind, utterly unreal. Ten minutes earlier she had been running along the road shouting something to a man who was running away from her and did not want to listen to her. Could it be possible? She was tempted to doubt it. It was not yet half past three. In the warmth of her little room she had perhaps grown drowsy and dreamt it all. But her shoes and all the hem of her skirt were white with dust and her legs still shook with the effort she had made, for she had run as fast as she could. She remembered the muffled sound her footsteps made upon the ground, and her panting breath, her calling and her beckoning to him; she saw the man, his dirty clothing, the wild, hunted look in his eyes when he stared at her. He had hesitated for an instant before running away. He had thought: "What does she want? Will she betray me? Has she recognized me?" And he had turned and fled, running faster and faster. Had he heard what she had called after him as he passed her? What was he doing at Lorges, in broad daylight? Would he be there tomorrow evening?

These questions which she kept asking herself drove her frantic with impatience. She should have shouted, "This evening!" and not "Tomorrow evening!" She would never be able to wait until tomorrow evening. Though she made an effort to control herself and to remain seated, this inactivity was a torture which she felt she had not the courage to endure. How was she going to be calm enough to get through a whole day of waiting? She was not made for waiting; the slowness of time killed her. She would certainly not sleep that night. A long series of interminable hours was about to begin, and they had to be borne. First the remainder of that afternoon, then dinner with her husband—no, she would not come down to dinner—then darkness, the silence of her bedroom, the lamp she would re-light every quarter of an hour, the clock she would hear strike until dawn. She could not bear the idea of it. She got up and pressed her clenched hands to her breast, as though to prevent her heart from bursting.

"I can't do it, I can't do it!" she whispered to herself over and over again.

After a few seconds' reflection, she walked quickly toward the door and left the room.

Chapter Three

O N THE same day, and almost at the same time, Fernande knocked at the door of a room over the Restaurant Londe.

"Is that you, Fernande?" asked Angèle, recognizing the little girl's step. "You may come in."

"Good evening. Aren't you cold in here? You ought to come and warm yourself at the stove in the big room. There's no one there. Madame Londe has gone out shopping."

"I'm all right, Fernande. Don't worry about me."

She was sitting in a corner of the room close to the window, with her chair against the wall. As soon as Fernande came in she put down some sewing she was doing and covered her face with a corner of the gray shawl she wore over her head.

"Look!" she added, placing the back of her hand against the wall. "There's no need for me to go downstairs for your stove; it comes up here." Indeed, the stove pipe passed inside the wall and gave out a little heat. It had even cracked the plaster which appeared through a long tear in the paper.

"All the same," insisted Fernande, sitting on the edge of the bed some way from Angèle, "it's nicer downstairs . . . and Madame Londe is out."

"She'll be in at any moment, and I don't want to see her."

"Aren't you ever going to speak to each other again?"

"As little as possible, Fernande dear. Why do you ask me all these questions? You cannot understand the harm Madame Londe has done me."

"How do you know I can't? Because I'm only thirteen and a half you think I don't know anything. But you're wrong. There are many older girls than me who don't know as much as I do."

She said this with a sort of pride, leaning a little towards Angèle, who turned away her head, disconcerted by the dark eyes that seemed to be trying to distinguish her features through the meshes of her shawl.

"If you don't believe me," Fernande went on, after a few seconds' silence, "you've only to ask Madame Londe. But I forgot, you're not speaking to her," she added, hypocritically.

"I advise you not to see too much of Madame Londe. You are always hanging around her, dear. Some day you'll be sorry you listened to her."

"Why should I be? Why, you don't even know what we say to each other. She's very kind to me. She lets me do just what I want. If you only knew the confidence she has in me. She always tells me that I am quite old enough to look after myself, and that I alone am responsible for what I do. I like that so much better."

"And what does your mother say about it?"

"My mother is very pleased. She takes half the money I earn working for Madame Londe and she puts the other half in the savings bank. I've already got more than fifty francs there."

"You're lucky," said Angèle in a voice that suddenly grew softer. "It will be useful to you later on."

"I know. Mother was saying the same thing the other day. Besides, Madame Londe teaches me to sew and to wash up, which is all very useful, you know."

"Very. And what else does Madame Londe make you do?"

"Oh, I sweep out her room and make her bed. Didn't you know that? I always do her room in the morning. And I bring up her coal. No one but me has any right to touch her foot-warmer. I get it ready every day, morning and evening."

"There's a big girl! And I bet she sends you to do her errands?"

"Of course. She suffers so much with her legs. It's only in weather like this that she's able to go out; when it's cold and dry, that's what she likes."

"I'm glad of that. She must be happy today. But tell, Fernande, what sort of errands does she send you on?"

"Well, sometimes she sends me to the draper's, sometimes to the grocer's. Never to the other tradesmen, because she's afraid of them cheating me. And then . . . Oh! but that's a secret, and she made me promise not to tell!"

"You can tell me everything, dear. You know if anyone confides in me it never goes any further."

"All right, I'll tell you because it's you, Angèle. But I'm sure if she knew I'd spoken to you about it she wouldn't have anything more to do with me."

"You needn't be alarmed about that."

"Well, the other day she sent me to see a man."

"What's that?"

"Yes, she sent me to take a letter to Monsieur Domène, the chemist at Chanteilles. She said to me: 'Are you a big enough girl for me to send you to a man?' And of course I said yes. So she gave me the letter and I took it to Monsieur Domène."

"Yes. Go on."

"What's the matter? Aren't you happy?"

"Of course, Fernande dear. Your story is so interesting. I want to hear the rest of it. What did Monsieur Domène say to you?"

"He was very nice. He gave me some jujubes and a little bag of bulls'-eyes. Then he made me go into the back of his shop. Then he began to talk to me. He asked me if my legs weren't cold in socks in midwinter. You know Madame Londe won't let me wear stockings. She says I must become hardened."

"Yes. And then?"

"Then he asked me if I had a woolen vest on, a really warm woolen vest. I said yes, but he didn't believe me and insisted on putting his hand inside my pinafore. And of course I laughed because he

tickled me, and I let my bulls'-eyes drop, and at
that moment he heard some one come into the shop.
Then he gave me a two-franc piece because my
legs must be cold. And then, when I wanted to pick
up my bulls'-eyes, he told me to leave them there
and gave me another bag. After that he let me out,
not through the shop, but by a little door opening
on to a passage. You go to the end of it and find
yourself in the street."

"And did you tell Madame Londe all this?"

"Oh, I didn't tell her that he kissed me. . . . "

"He kissed you?"

"Yes, didn't I tell you? I told Madame Londe all
the rest. I even showed her the two-franc piece,
and she told me I could keep it and that I needn't
tell my mother about it. And the letter, you
know . . . "

"What letter?"

"You know, Monsieur Domène's letter."

"Well?"

"Well, he didn't even look at it. He just put
it in his pocket without reading it. It seemed hardly
worth while writing to him."

These last words were followed by a long silence,
during which Angèle remained quite still, her head
bent, plunged, to all appearances, in deep meditation from which Fernande's anxious expression did
not succeed in rousing her.

"Well then," she said, with a sudden change in her
voice, "you must tell the whole story to your mother,
do you see?"

"Why? Madame Londe told me that it wasn't worth while telling my mother."

"And I tell you that it is very important that you should."

"I shouldn't have told you," said Fernande, angrily. "But you'll never know what Madame Couze said about you and your lover."

"What?" cried Angèle, suddenly getting up, "Madame Couze said something . . . "

"Yes, I heard her. I was sewing in the next room, and she was talking to Madame Londe, but I shan't tell you what she said."

"Fernande, you have no right not to tell me. You don't know, I might die if you don't. You must tell me everything. I implore you to, Fernande. Do you hear?"

"Well, swear first that you won't tell anyone about Monsieur Domène."

"Yes, yes, I swear."

She sat on the bed next to the little girl and took one of her hands in her own, which were trembling.

"I was sewing in the next room," began the child, who asked no better than to tell all her secrets. "Madame Londe had made me leave the room because Madame Couze was there, and she doesn't like me to be there when anyone comes to see her."

"Yes, I know."

"Madame Couze began by saying that you were never about now and that the customers of the restaurant must miss you a lot. Then Madame Londe replied, 'There are as good fish in the sea as ever

came out of it.' And she seemed annoyed because
Madame Couze began to laugh, and she raised her
voice a little, adding: 'Besides, I have some one in
view to take her place.' "

"She said that?"

"Yes. And Madame Couze laughed again and
asked Madame Londe if it was me she had in view.
Me! You can imagine how surprised I was. This
time Madame Londe got angry and told her to shut
up. Madame Couze said nothing for quite a while;
then she asked Madame Londe if she thought that
they would ever find the man who killed Monsieur
Sarcenas and attacked you too."

"Yes, and then?"

"That didn't seem to please Madame Londe much,
either. She told Madame Couze that she was a
coward and that it was because of her and her gossiping that everyone was afraid of Lorges. Then
Madame Couze bridled a little and retorted that she
wasn't the only person in the town who thought that
the murderer was . . . Guess."

"I don't know. Tell me quickly."

"That Monsieur Guéret who came here twice and
disappeared the day after the crime."

"Good Heavens! What an idea! And Madame
Londe, what did she answer? Tell me!"

"She said it wasn't true, and that it was practically proved that a gang of roughs had done it.
And Madame Couze said no. They were both shouting by this time. There was no need for me to
listen at the keyhole to hear them."

"And what more did they say? Be quick."

"Wait a bit. I can't go any quicker. Madame
Couze said: 'Everyone knows that the guilty man
is Mademoiselle Angèle's lover, since the police are
looking for him and he daren't show himself.' When
she heard that, Madame Londe shouted, 'Get out
of the house!' in a voice which would have terrified
me; but Madame Couze didn't stop talking, and
she always seemed so timid, too. She jabbered on,
and Madame Londe shouted so loud that it was
difficult for me to understand what they were saying
to one another. And then suddenly Madame Couze
began to shout louder than Madame Londe. 'You
see quite well that you are standing up for him!' she
declared. And she said something else, too—something else that sent shivers all down my back."

"Go on, can't you? Be quick!"

"She said: 'There's no doubt about it at all.
He's hidden here!' "

Angèle dropped the little girl's hand and drew
away from her without a word, but she was trembling so violently that the child became alarmed.

"Why, what's the matter with you, Angèle, since
it isn't true?"

She tried to put her arms round the young
woman, who instinctively pulled her shawl back over
her face. Some moments passed before Angèle
could trust herself to speak; then she freed herself
gently from Fernande's embrace and asked:

"Did they say anything else?"

"No, she went away at once. Aren't you well? Would you like to lie down?"

"I want you to leave me now, Fernande," replied Angèle, in a low voice.

"If I'd known, I wouldn't have told you all that. I did hesitate about it. I thought it would hurt you, perhaps."

"It wasn't your fault, dear. But don't repeat what you have told me to anyone."

"No, of course not."

There was a short silence; then the young woman said in a firmer voice:

"Fernande, I am unhappy, very unhappy. If I need you one day, will you help me?"

"But of course. You know I will."

"For the last three months my life has been very hard, Fernande. I never see anyone. At first they thought that my wounds would heal in a fortnight. They've closed up all right, but the scars will always remain. I dare not show myself as I am. And yet I must go back to my work. How happy I used to be at the laundry, and I never knew it. Do you remember how pretty I was?"

"Why do you say that? You're pretty still!"

Angèle shook her head.

"You haven't seen me since . . . "

She stopped and seemed to be thinking.

"Tell me, Fernande dear," she went on after a moment, "do you really love me? Don't I ever frighten you a little bit?"

"Frighten me, Angèle?"

"Yes. You never see me except with this shawl over my head. It must seem very queer to you. Sometimes I think you look at me as though you were trying to see my face through its meshes."

"Oh no!" said Fernande, in surprise.

"Yes, you do," continued the young woman, softly. "I never talk to you about that, you see. It makes me too unhappy to think I have become ugly. Every morning I look at myself in the glass and sometimes I tell myself that I am better. And then there are days on which it seems to me, on the contrary, that it's worse. Always seeing oneself like that and thinking about it all day, in the end one doesn't know what one looks like."

"Then you shouldn't think about it so much," said Fernande, who was becoming alarmed by Angèle's tone.

"That's easy enough to say. What I want, you see, is some one to tell me the truth, some one who has not seen my face for three months and to whom I could show myself."

"Madame Londe would tell you at once."

"Madame Londe!" cried Angèle, furiously. "She would be only too pleased to see the harm she has done me."

The child paled.

"On the contrary," she said, "she told me that she hoped to see you quite well soon and at work again."

"But she is the cause of it all, Fernande. If I had never known that woman I should still be as pretty as I used to be."

She took Fernande by the hand and, getting up suddenly, stood before the little girl.

"I am going to ask you to do something for me," she said, earnestly. "I hope you won't refuse. You told me that you really loved me. I am going to take off my shawl. You must come close to the window and look at me. Will you?"

Fernande burst into tears.

"What's the matter?" pleaded Angèle, falling on her knees before her. "Are you afraid? Are you afraid of me? You used to kiss me so much, don't you remember? You used to put your hands round my neck and say you didn't want to let me go. And now that I am all alone and everyone hates me, are you going against me, too? I implore you, Fernande dear, to be nice. I assure you it isn't anything frightening. Do you think I would look at myself every morning if it frightened me? There is only a scar. But I am ashamed because I remember that three months ago I was better-looking than I am now."

These words reassured the little girl, who dried her tears.

"When are you going to show yourself in the street?" she asked.

"Why, tomorrow, if you tell me I haven't changed too much! You see what a help you can be to me. It depends on you. You see you're such a big girl."

She rose and drew the child gently toward the window.

"There," she said, placing herself in the angle

of the window, in such a way as to put several yards between Fernande and herself, "the important thing is the first impression. Try to forget what I used to look like and tell me frankly if I can go out to-morrow. Don't look so scared, dear. Anyone would think you were going to see the devil! Come. I don't want you to be unhappy. Just imagine you are at the theater."

She paused for a moment, then went on in the solemn voice of a theater manager announcing the evening's programme:

"The show is about to begin, ladies and gentlemen. The curtain is going up. There!"

A heavy silence followed this last word upon which Angèle's voice seemed to break. Then the child gasped as if some one had suddenly seized her by the throat, for she expected to see a familiar face disfigured by repulsive wounds, but instead she saw before her a stranger whose eyes, wide with anxiety, alone preserved something of the beauty that had left her tortured flesh forever. And yet the proportion of her features had not changed, and the marvelous architecture of her forehead, of her eye sockets, and of her nose subsisted; but two deep scars, wide furrows edged with white, barred the face, that would never again be anything but a pitiful sight. One of them started from the right temple, passed through the cheek, and crossed the lips as though to impose silence upon them; the other had devastated one side of her jaw and chin and disappeared above her ear. It was as though, dissatisfied with its work, a merciless hand had wanted to destroy it, tracing with sweeping chalk strokes the furious gashes that marked its condemnation.

"Well," said Angèle at length, with a painful sigh. "Don't stand there saying nothing, Fernande."

"Yes," breathed the child, without moving.

"You see," went on the young woman, "I've grown used to the idea that I shall never be as I was before, but I think that some day it will get better, in spite of everything. Don't you think so?" she asked, after a short pause.

"I'm sure it will, Angèle."

The ordeal to which the young woman had been compelled to submit her vanity had, to a certain extent, eased her mind, and she began to talk again, anxious, perhaps, not to hear what the little girl was going to say, and not realizing how tragically inane her reflections were:

"At first I thought I should die of shame when I saw myself like this. It's all a question of getting used to it. I have still got both my eyes, that's the main thing. Oh! if only the white marks would go! It seems to me that the skin has gone a deeper pink all round them. I have noticed that in broad daylight, when the sun is shining, it's less noticeable; it's only when I have my back to the window that it is really bad, but then I can bend my head, you see."

And she bent her head until she only showed the top of it where her heavy black hair was parted.

The child kept silence; pale, with her hands behind her back, she seemed to be afraid of moving.

"Admit," said Angèle, "that it isn't so awful as you thought it was going to be. What is really horrible to see is blood, isn't it? But a scar . . . Anyway, if you met me in the street, would you be frightened, eh?"

"No."

"I'm glad of that! So I can go out? If you only knew how strange I feel standing here before you without having to cover my face with my shawl. I was beginning to frighten even myself. And I had only to uncover my head to feel happy again. It's a long time since I felt like that, you know, and it's what you have said that has made me happy."

She had said all this very quickly, and suddenly burst out laughing; a sudden joy lit up her eyes and brought a flush to her face, thus accentuating the whiteness of her scars. What sudden ray of hope had come to her and made her forget for a moment so many days of suffering? She seized the little girl by the hand and went and sat on the bed with her.

"You promised to speak to me quite frankly, Fernande," she resumed, more seriously. "Listen to me. I've got many plans for the future. You quite see that I can't go on living like this; I might as well be in prison. I've had enough of doing Madame Londe's washing and darning her linen for nothing. Tomorrow I go out; that's quite certain. Now I've got another question to ask you, a serious question. You must think carefully before answering it."

"Yes."

"You are still very young, but you told me that you knew as much as anyone, didn't you? Well, look at me. If a man saw me as I am now, do you think he would think me ugly?"

"Ugly? Of course not!"

"Are you quite sure you're not saying that just to please me? Do you think that a man could fall in love with me?"

"Yes, Angèle."

"Well, he would come to me and say, 'Angèle, I love you!' And then?"

"Then?"

"Yes, what would he do then? He would take my hand, wouldn't he, and he would kiss me. That's what you mean, isn't it?"

"Yes."

The young woman began to laugh.

"Tell me," she asked, "do you think that Monsieur Domène would have kissed me in your place, the other day?"

The child nodded.

"Well, then," said Angèle, suddenly standing up before her, "you come and kiss me."

She stood between Fernande and the window, looking for an expression that would finally reassure her in the little face from which all the color had fled; but all she saw was a shrinking mouth and two eyes filling with tears. The sight of the child's fear made

her feel as though she were choking. No mirror,
however clear and cruel it might be, could have shown
her the grim truth so distinctly as Fernande's look
of terror. She felt her strength leaving her and her
knees giving way. After hovering for months between hope and despair, she had suddenly been con-
fronted with the appalling truth. She was repulsive. This child refused to kiss her. She turned
her back on her abruptly and walked to the window
without a word. People were passing by the house,
an old lady whose face was only scarred by time, a
smooth-faced little boy. What did they care if she
stood there with her heart breaking from misery?

"Perhaps she didn't understand," she thought.
"I will ask her again."

And she went back to the little girl, who had not
dared to move, and looked at her in silence. Angèle
opened her mouth, but her anguish struck her dumb;
she seemed surprised not to be able to form the words
she wanted to utter. What an awful stillness there
was in the room. She wanted to scream, to scream
until her breath left her, until life itself left her,
since death was the only means of escape from that
hell. Suddenly her legs gave way, and she fell on
her knees and hugged the little body that stiffened,
trembling with disgust at the contact of her arms.
She buried her head in the little girl's lap and, with
her hair spread over the schoolgirl pinafore she
sobbed like a madwoman, and now and then she
screamed as though in an outburst of horrible
gayety.

Chapter Four

IN THE long, dreary dining-room, the tips of her
fingers crossed and her feet on her foot-warmer,
Madame Londe awaited her customers. She sat
quite still; a knitted cape covered her broad shoulders, which had become slightly bent lately, and her
motionless eyes, turned, as it were, inward, seemed
fixed on some interior vision, the gloominess of which
was reflected in her features. The little metal vase
in front of her was empty, but she kept it there, out
of a superstitious dread of perverting her destiny by
modifying even the least of the habits of her daily
life. What, after all, did she care if flowers were
out of season? She had many other troubles. Something very serious was happening, something so
serious that in the presence of such an unprecedented
situation Madame Londe's courage entirely deserted
her and she did not even think of moving or of calling a waiter. Or was it time for her to order the
soup to be brought up, to compel these gentlemen
to appear? She dared not do it. She had lost confidence in this method of better days; last week she
had seen eleven platefuls of *petite marmite* steaming
and then cooling while waiting for the customers
who were all late.

It was twenty-five minutes past seven; she knew

it; she had counted the minutes second by second by the ticking of the black wall-clock. Anxiety and anger drove the bile into her blood and gave her face a yellow tinge under the mauve powder that covered her cheeks. She was alone in the dining-room, but if she had to die at her desk she was determined to wait until the door opened and some one appeared.

The stove was burning not far from the *table d'hôte*. She heard its roaring, which she used always to think cheerful and comforting. But now it was radiating its heat to no purpose in the air which was already warm. Physical sickness came to increase her mental distress, and she asked herself in alarm how she was going to manage to stay there without moving for an hour and a half, perhaps even more. Why was she tormented with a desire to be sick? She had not been able to eat anything at four o'clock, and now all the worry she was suffering from had completely upset her.

She asked herself why she was made to suffer like this. For long years she had calmly enjoyed an easy and uneventful life, in which everything seemed planned forever—her rising, her going to bed, her meals, and even her pleasures and sorrows. Then suddenly everything was thrown into confusion. Her most firmly established habits were threatened, the very foundation of her existence uprooted. Every hour brought some new emotion, every day threatened to dawn on disaster. Some one had come and brought bad luck. Guéret. Since the first time he dined in the restaurant everything had gone wrong.

She ought to have mistrusted his taciturn expression; and his silence had been a bad sign. Because of him Angèle had been reduced to hiding herself like a leper; because of him Madame Londe no longer knew anything that was going on at Lorges and she was gradually losing the influence she had acquired over her customers. Who was to blame for the compromising of her old age, for her agonies of unsatisfied curiosity, her humiliation, her impotent fury at seeing all that she thought she held so firmly gradually slip from her? Whose fault was all that accumulation of misfortunes, any one of which was sufficient to crush her? Whose, indeed, but that of the monster whom she had encouraged to come to her restaurant? Ah! if she could only have known, if Heaven in its charity had warned her! But she did not believe in religion in hours of trial like this. She thought of Heaven only in happy moments, as, for instance, on the days when Angèle brought her a little money and a few little tales about various people, and Madame Londe felt the need of adding to the satisfaction of slipping five francs into a drawer and of hearing some gossip, another one, namely, that of feeling virtuous. But now she considered that she had been betrayed, betrayed by the world, by that God who was said to be just and who amused Himself by clogging the well-oiled wheels of her commonplace existence. So, to avoid any further misery and to mitigate the effect of the catastrophes that were bound to occur, she would not rely upon anyone, she would sit alone at her desk like a shat-

tered idol amid the ruins of its temple. It was half
past seven. She would have liked it to have been
eight o'clock, even nine, so that the disaster should
be complete and that the iniquity of Providence
should be proven once for all.

Passing in her mind from extreme apprehension
concerning the morrow to the joy of imagining all
the worst that could happen, she saw herself abandoned by all her clients, ruined, reduced to penury,
finally handed over to the mercy of those who accused
her of concealing a criminal beneath her roof; for
this absurd rumor started by fear was gaining more
and more credence. The envy and bitterness which
had been brooding around her for so long was soon
going to break out, as a devastating epidemic may
declare itself after an incubation of several years.
There had been enough envy of the position she occupied, of this restaurant which everyone wanted to
see come to an end, of the tiny sum she had put aside
for her old age. And what reliance could she now
place in life, she who had believed in the solidity, the
permanence of things, in the loyalty of the future,
in her own power? It was twenty-five minutes to
eight.

She had reached the point at which it was almost
indifferent to her whether anyone came or not, and
whether the soup was eaten by her customers or
burnt in its saucepan. After a certain limit is
reached, we become insensitive to the blows of fate.
She was considering this fact when the door opened.
She gave an involuntary start of surprise, which she

immediately suppressed. Three of her customers
came in, then another, then three more. It was as
though they had been waiting outside, behind the
trees, on purpose, to alarm her and to be revenged
on her for the insults she had made them bear in the
past. Nevertheless, her heart began to beat faster,
and she returned the greeting they gave her, before
taking their places, with her most majestic air, in
which she introduced a touch of indifference which
cost her a great effort.

Had she been willing to put her glasses on for a
moment, the wretched woman would have beheld in
her customers' faces a self-confidence which she had
never seen there before. They stared at her boldly
and unflinchingly. Was it that they no longer
feared her, or did they guess that her sight was failing and that their impertinent looks would pass unnoticed? In a few minutes they were all eating, and
in spite of the awful humiliation of having to accept
the fact of their being late without a protest, she
began to recover her spirits, by the mere fact of
their presence. Certainly they were not all there;
even Madame Londe's veiled eyes noticed the big gap
at the end of the table, and yet happiness began to
creep timidly back to her. All was not lost. After
the agonies she had been through it was delicious to
see the room resume its normal aspect. The waiters
were moving round the table now, snatching the
soup plates in the hasty way of which they would
never cure themselves. But a problem presented itself which would have to be solved at once. Should

the plates of the absentees be left in their places, or should they be removed to the kitchen? Which attitude should she adopt? To give the order that the plates should be left would be to admit to entertaining a hope that would be farcical if it were not fulfilled, and to have them removed to the kitchen would be to admit defeat.

She felt her cheeks burn with the thought of the contempt which the words she must utter would perhaps excite, for although she could not see the diners distinctly, or hear with any clearness the remarks they exchanged, something told her they were in a difficult mood. For several weeks now she had lost touch with the pains and pleasures that filled their lives; they were disappearing into mystery as into an ever thickening gloom which her enfeebled sight would never penetrate. And according as they receded from her and became strangers, so her empire over them diminished. Who was she, indeed, without Angèle's eyes and ears, and what purpose did that instinct of hers serve except to torture her? To scent the presence of a secret of which she could not find out the slightest detail was more agonizing than the complete ignorance of a person who suspects nothing. She, on the contrary, suspected everything, but, Heavens above! the darkest night was better than this feeble ray of light! And in the way old women have when their brains are addled with age and misfortunes, she constantly turned over her troubles in her mind and attributed all her little vexations to the same cause. If she found herself faced with the difficult problem of three platefuls of soup, it was because her customers had got into an abominable habit of arriving late. And why did they arrive late? Because they no longer respected her. And whence did this lack of respect originate? From the fact that they felt themselves safe from her curiosity and were gradually regaining their independence. Angèle was no longer there to wheedle these men and find out their little secrets. How bitter it was for Madame Londe to realize that she had brought about this state of affairs by her own fault! Yes, she was definitely responsible for everything, since she had insisted on that wretch coming back to her restaurant when she ought to have driven him away as though he had been the plague. Perhaps he had planned the crime that was ruining her at that very table, at her feet; and she had known nothing about it and had let him be fed, fool that she was. Oh, let the soup go! Throw it to the dogs; pour it into the street; anything rather than give it to men!

She was just about to give orders for the three soup-plates to be removed, when the door opened again and Monsieur Goncelin (Goncelin who always used to be first) and Monsieur Pinsot walked in. They swaggered in with their hats on their heads. A violent emotion seized Madame Londe. Something was going to happen; these men were going to do her an injury. She was sure of it, and she pressed her hands to her heart as though to quiet its beating. And yet, no. They turned to her and greeted her gravely. She replied like an automaton, her face haggard with fear, her hands damp in their black mittens. Were they laughing at her? Why did they shake their heads like that and look toward the door? And why did the others laugh? She strained her ears, but only caught an exasperating rumble of words. Suddenly she started; Monsieur Goncelin, who had taken his place between Monsieur Blondeau and Monsieur Verdet, but who had not sat down yet—Monsieur Goncelin was looking at her and speaking to her.

What was he saying? She recognized the somewhat low, provincial accent of the voice that came to her as though through a mist, but she could grasp nothing definite; not one word came to her clearly. Perhaps he was mumbling on purpose. She felt beads of perspiration gather all over her forehead and trickle slowly down the skin and, passing the back of her hand above her eyebrows, she tried to protect the powder and paint on her cheeks against this stream that threatened to sweep them away. Monsieur Goncelin had stopped talking and the diners were looking at her, no doubt waiting for a reply to some question that had been put to her. Everything was blurred before her eyes; it seemed to her as though the room were suddenly flooded with an intolerable light, except for the gasolier, which had become quite black. Her clothes began to stick to her body. She was tempted to risk it and to reply, "Very well!", when Monsieur Goncelin, making a megaphone of his two hands, shouted at her in a loud, jerky voice:

"Don't wait for Monsieur Léon! He's not coming any more!"

She replied, "Very well!" because that was the only answer she had in her head, and it came out like a cry of anguish. A distressing giddiness compelled her to lower her eyes, but she had time to see Monsieur Goncelin unfold his napkin amid laughter. She had fallen; it was all over; and what the perspiration had not done tears did now, tears of despair that traced their way patiently through her makeup, from her eyes to the corners of her mouth. No one paid any further attention to her. She could abandon herself to her sorrow, intoxicate herself with misery. Through the slow tears that trembled on her eyelashes she dimly saw the little metal vase and the black book, which reminded her of so many things. What was the use of fostering vain illusions? Monsieur Léon was not coming any more. Tomorrow it would be some one else, and at the end of the week she would have to close the restaurant, kick her stock-pot over, and perhaps go away for good. For she saw quite well that they hated her and meant to make her life unbearable. She ought to have suspected that something was afoot on the day when Monsieur Léon paid her all the money he owed her, nearly sixty francs. Curse it! He had borrowed the money from friends or from his employer, and she thought she held him so tightly! As well try to grasp water in one's hand.

Now that she was resigned to facing the truth, she was better able to understand what these people

had against her. They were annoyed with her for
keeping Angèle from them. For weeks they had
asked: "How is Mademoiselle Angèle? Is she quite
well again yet?" And she had always made the same
answer: "She is not yet well enough to go out. You
must wait." She dared not risk disgusting them
with Angèle by giving her back to them too soon.
As a matter of fact, she had not examined the poor
girl's features for some time, because she hid herself from her as from everyone else, but she remembered only too well the appalling appearance of her
face on the day they had brought her back to the
house. On the other hand, she dared not explain to
her customers that Angèle's beauty had perhaps
gone forever, and that in any case the only chance
of a perfect cure depended on time. So she tried
to temporize by talking of a nervous breakdown re-
sulting from the attack; but the nervous breakdown
had been going on for three months, and her customers didn't believe in it any longer.

Besides, Madame Londe was not the only person
to have seen her niece in the lamentable state in
which she had been left by the ferocity of her aggressor. There were several witnesses, and no one
with any knowledge of human nature could imagine
that they hadn't chattered about it. So that on all
sides it was said that the reason Angèle did not show
herself was that she had kept the marks of her
wounds and that she was so ugly that she was afraid
of frightening people she met in the street. It was
useless for Madame Londe to deny this; at first she

had managed to divert public opinion, for in those days she still possessed a certain amount of authority, but now it was not difficult to see through her motives. The poor old woman was nervous about her restaurant and talked a lot of nonsense in the hope of averting disaster, but it became clear that her fortune, her reputation, all that she seemed to possess that was real and solid in this world, had rested on the most uncertain and changeable thing on earth, namely the attraction that a woman had for a few men. Everyone knew the whole sordid story. Everyone knew that before Madame Londe had begun to prostitute Angèle the Restaurant Londe was going hopelessly downhill. Since then, certainly, the old bawd must have amassed a tidy sum, but providential justice seemed only to have lifted her into a state of prosperity in order to prepare for her a fall that was all the more painful and ignominious.

The poor woman knew that people spoke intolerantly of her; but she did not suspect the extent to which they did so. It was not true that she was miserly. All things considered, she had lost more money than she had made with her system of credit meals, and the untidy way in which she kept her books betrayed the fact that dreams played a far more important *rôle* in her mind than realities. Her accounts seemed accurate, but her accuracy confined itself to noting the number of meals for which each of her customers owed her, and the end of the month always found her ten or fifteen francs out.

Did people cheat her? Did she forget to put down all she spent? This leakage, which should have alarmed her, actually did so very little. "When one owns the best restaurant in the neighborhood, one can always manage somehow," she would say to herself; and in the secret corner of her conscience in which were hidden a good many things that she did not admit, a voice would add, "Especially if one has a handsome girl like Angèle to offer to one's customers."

And suddenly this support had been swept away from her. Her house was tottering because a madman had hit Angèle in the face. To what depths did the iniquity of fate descend, and how spiteful it was to humanity! Ah! if she had only been able to mumble her prayers like the fanatics who went to Saint-Jude, she would have something to say to God, who allowed such horrors to exist. To think that a pretty girl in the very flower of her youth had been disfigured forever, and that the virtuous woman who had adopted her was in danger of becoming destitute, as a reward, no doubt for that act of charity. That was what was called Providence!

Of course Madame Londe had considered every possible means of saving the situation. What was required? To keep her customers satisfied until Angèle was quite cured and had recovered her lost beauty; and, since they had to have some one, was it so difficult to find some nice-looking young woman to take her place? For what they wanted was to compete for the favors of a pretty girl. Angèle had accustomed them to that sort of amorous rivalry, and they satisfied their vanity in this fierce little war which they had carried on for so long. They loved their treacheries and their schemings and cultivated their jealousy. And, indeed, what pleasure of love is more intense and stronger than the joy of getting the better of a rival?

A nice-looking young woman. Madame Londe had looked for one, setting to work with all the necessary caution, but without much hope of success. Fate does not twice provide you with an orphan as pretty as the day, and none of those brazen Chanteilles hussies would be able to take Angèle's place. But at length Madame Londe had made her choice; it was a strange one and might surprise some people, and she hesitated for a long time before making it, even though she had had the idea in her head for some time.

The first thing to do was to test the quality of the bait with which she was going to tempt her customers; it was with this object that little Fernande had been sent to Monsieur Domène, the chemist at Chanteilles. The results obtained were, as we know, most encouraging, and in the presence of this preliminary success Madame Londe had felt her whole life come back; but her joy was short-lived; Monsieur Domène was nearly sixty years of age and the tastes of that age are really too easily satisfied for a sensible woman to draw any general conclusions from them. This reflection renewed her anxiety.

She hesitated to suggest Fernande to her customers. To ask them if they would like to take a little girl out for a walk would appear either ridiculous or terribly suspicious. Some of them were very ill-disposed towards her, like Monsieur Goncelin and certain other ill-humored fellows who might take advantage of such an opportunity to go and spread shocking rumors in the town, or even to denounce her. Besides, how could she rely on a scatterbrain like Fernande? Would she even understand what it was all about?

Several times since the visit to Monsieur Domène, Madame Londe had sent Fernande on errands to one or other of her customers under various pretexts whose futility should have given them a lead, but they did not seem to understand, or perhaps they, too, were afraid of getting into trouble. In vain did Madame Londe dress the little girl becomingly, comb her hair with her own hands, train her to smile sweetly; on one side there was too much innocence beneath a sharp and shrewd exterior, and on the other too much cowardice or indifference.

Altogether a dangerous enterprise which Madame Londe thought it better not to pursue. She would let things take their own course. Some day, perhaps, the idea of taking an interest in Fernande would suggest itself to one of these gentlemen of its own accord; then all Madame Londe would have to do would be to pretend to be stupid and not to notice anything, as had happened when Monsieur Léon had begun to run after Angèle.

But time was slipping by. If she had to wait until Fernande grew up and Angèle recovered her looks, the Restaurant Londe might go bankrupt and then all coöperation between its proprietress and these two girls would be useless. If she were only thirty years younger, or even fifteen; with fifteen years off her age she could manage all right; that would make her just forty-two. How delightful it would be to turn out that brat Fernande and that fool Angèle who let herself be ill-treated and disfigured in broad daylight. All by herself Madame Londe would have the strength to run two, three restaurants like the one that gave her so much trouble now; she recalled many pleasant years when men never looked at her without repressing a sigh, for then she had thick black curls which rioted over her forehead and temples, a cool skin, bright coloring, and firm cheeks; all this still seemed so close to her that she could not believe that so many good things had disappeared, and she sometimes imagined that the present was but a nightmare that would soon come to an end. But her reason soon dispelled this mad hope; the nightmare was true; she was old, ugly, crippled; every step she took wrung a groan and a grimace from her; her teeth were falling into decay; her voice rattled in her throat; her hair came out in handfuls; she had lost her sight; she could not hear properly; in fact, life had done with her.

The sound of chairs being noisily pushed back roused her from these reflections and she shivered; the diners had finished their meal already, perhaps their last meal there. She had been sitting before them for half an hour, her eyes fixed on this group of men which she saw as in a mist, and not once had she noticed what they were doing or what point they had reached in their meal. And suddenly they were getting up to pay their bills and go. She wanted to get up, too, and to wave her arms with the sweeping gestures of a tragic actor, and to shout as though at the end of a drama, in order to banish the melancholy which had been rankling in her heart for weeks. She wanted to live, to be happy. Why was she being heaped with contumely when she had nothing on her conscience? Why could she not have an honorable old age, like other women? It was too unfair. And the little affronts she had to put up with, the humiliations she had to swallow in silence, the anger she had to curb as well as she could, all this leaven of malice seemed to have chosen this moment to shoot up and spread itself. One after the other her customers passed in front of her now and paid her the two francs fifty centimes that dinner cost. They all paid this evening. There were no accounts to look up, no words to exchange; she had nothing to do but to sit still and let the money rattle on the marble and accumulate between the empty vase and the closed book.

The blood rushed to her face in a wave of anger, and she felt it throbbing beneath the skin of her neck behind her ears, as though to incite her to deliver battle and defend herself. Yet she said nothing and did not move; she watched the coins rolling on the desk, without being able to raise her hand or open her lips. She did not even see the sly or scornful faces that succeeded one another before her eyes. Everything was blurred, everything was swallowed up in the gathering darkness in which the gas-jet flickered, and she had the impression that each of these men stopped an hour before her and jeered at her.

They went away; she heard them shout good night to her, but she did not answer.

As the clock above her head struck nine she took her book mechanically and put it away in a drawer. The waiter put out the lights. She rose and left the room with the careful step that old age had taught her. Arrived at the foot of the staircase leading to her room, she put on her glasses and began to grope up the stairs, each of which creaked beneath her large slippers. A gas-jet on the top landing shed a dim light on her head and shoulders and cast on the wall an enormous and grotesque shadow which seemed to be playing some sinister game with her.

She went upstairs without haste, panting a little and taking great care to place her foot firmly on each successive stair. As she reached the first floor and found herself outside Angèle's room she suddenly stopped as though seized with an inspiration, and struck the door panel hard with her closed fist. The answer did not come as quickly as she could have wished. Perhaps Angèle was asleep? She knocked again.

"What is it?" asked a voice.

"Angèle," said Madame Londe, opening the door a little way, "are you there?"

"Of course I am."

"Everything is coming all right, dear," went on the proprietress in a tone of false heartiness. "The gentlemen have decided to take you as you are. To-morrow you can show yourself. Do you understand?"

"Yes, auntie."

"Well, good night," said Madame Londe. "Sleep well, dear."

She shut the door again quietly and continued her way upstairs, her hand clutching the banisters, and bent double as though beneath the weight of some ungodly cross.

Chapter Five

MADAME GROSGEORGE had been waiting in the road for nearly an hour, making up her mind to go away and then not succeeding in doing so, although she had practically abandoned all hope. She was shivering in her beaver coat and her hands in the depths of her muff were numbed. It had snowed all the morning, and the white road seemed to shed a glow into the darkness of the night.

No one had come. She was not in the least surprised, as she had been telling herself from the early hours of the day that it would be pointless to wait in the road, and that a man wanted by the police was not going to risk his liberty, perhaps even his life, to please a woman whom he did not like; for she harbored no illusions about Guéret's feelings toward her, remembering only too well the look of fury which she had several times surprised in his eyes; and she knew that to this fettered soul she represented wealth and all the sins that accompany it. And yet she insisted on taking up her position at the place she had mentioned; it was useless for her reason to tell her that she was wasting her time. What help has reason ever been in the great moments of life?

Besides, another hour spent at home would drive

her mad, mad with boredom, impatience, and disgust. The idea that a certain order of things which she did not accept had assigned to her a place within those walls, among that furniture and those knick-knacks, filled her with a rage that was all the more violent because she realized how vain rebellion was. She could not grow used to it or submit to it. After years of marriage she was still like an animal that cannot resign itself to being caught in a trap and thrusts its frenzied nose between the bars of its cage as though some day they must part miraculously and free it.

She had gone out the day before without any idea of where she was going, walking, running through the country, now downcast and on the verge of tears, now in ecstasy at the thought of some possible happiness, of some marvel that the next day perhaps held in store for her. With the simplicity of a child she placed her entire confidence in the immediate future, even though day by day the future belied its promises of yesterday. She would freely forgive the destiny responsible for her joyless past, her dreary present—indeed what else could she do?—provided that it left her that passionate faith which bequeathed Sunday to Monday, Monday to Tuesday, and so on until the day on which she would be screwed into a black box, she and the extravagances of her poor heart.

She had returned tired and exhausted and had flung herself upon her bed without being able to sleep; her strained nerves refused to relax. The silence of midnight was full of echoes, and the darkness was pierced with great shimmering splotches of light against which her closed eyelids could not protect her. At length she lit her lamp and went and sat near the window, hoping that at any moment the sky would begin to pale behind the trees in the garden; she struggled with herself to put off the moment of consulting her watch, so as to prepare a delicious surprise for herself when she found that it was later than she thought. Then the cold made her move; she got back into the warmth of her bed, put out the lamp, counted two hundred, lit the lamp again, and discovered, with a groan of despair, that she had been wrong by a whole hour and that she still had an infinite amount of time to suffer.

Dawn found her fully dressed, standing at the window with a haggard face and hollow eyes. Nights like this aged her more quickly than the announcement of some great misfortune could have done, but now that she saw the stars receding into the sky and the road gradually emerging from the darkness, she began to recover her courage as though the day were dawning within herself. It seemed to her as though she had traveled for many miles and had come to the end of a difficult stage in her journey. There was still a morning and an afternoon to be got through, but the road was easier and a thousand little distractions would make it seem shorter. Yet it was days like this that made her feel the emptiness of her existence, for when she had given the servants their orders, opened and shut a book and lazily de-

ciphered a page of music, all her resources were
exhausted; she fell back into that appalling boredom that is the damnation of the rich. The hope-
fulness of early morning had vanished. After longing for the light to grow brighter above the tops
of the lime trees, her only wish now was for the night
to come and swallow it up again. What torture it
was to be compelled to follow the slow hours in their
endless journey, when everything within her was
leaping and wanted to run.

The morning dragged on as best it could. Eva
Grosgeorge was several times tempted to go out, but
she knew in what lamentable state she would come
in if she set foot outside the door; she would go too
far and would waste all the strength she needed for
the afternoon, when she would have to curb her impatience and walk slowly up and down the road,
waiting for a man who would never come. For she
was certain that he would not come, and yet she
wanted to have it proved to her that she was right
not to have any hope. Afterward, she might perhaps
find some peace in the thought that even the one
event to which she had looked forward so much
could never occur; that would put an end to the
emotion from which she had suffered since she had
seen Guéret again. Her life, which had been dis-
rupted for a moment and diverted from its ordinary
path, would resume the course it had followed for
thirty years, and it was much better so; anything
was better than this anguish, these heart-beatings,
this alternation of misery and happiness.

She would have been hard put to it to say what there was to hope for from a possible interview with Guéret, and was even careful not to think of it too much, because of a superstitious fear that by anticipating things in her mind she would prevent them from happening. She had also frequently observed that the aspect of the future always changed when it became the present, either because it gave less than it had promised, or because there was always an error in the quality of the happiness anticipated and one only obtained something wretched in place of what one had seen in one's imagination. Was it not wiser to be inwardly silent and to accept tamely whatever boredom or pleasure the hours might bring, without spending tomorrow's boredom or pleasure in advance?

But she could not accept. To accept was to die. It was impossible, for instance, for her to resign herself to the daily ordeal of taking meals with her husband. He was at the bottom of all the contempt and hatred which she felt toward human beings, and the hatred she felt for him had molded her heart and even dominated her senses. Her only passions were those of the mind, and she could never clearly understand those temptations to which her flesh had never been subjected. But at the age of fifty this chastity was bearing fruit and presented her with the horrible gift of a tardy and useless love. This woman had been mishandled by destiny, and now her brain was taking its revenge.

Monsieur Grosgeorge presented to her the spectacle of one of the forms of human greed which she considered to be the most ignoble. Each of his gestures, each intonation of his voice, revived and fostered in her a disgust which increased day by day, his large contented face, his broad frame which no illness ever troubled and which life satiated with pleasures, seemed to her to be instruments employed by fate to mock her, her and her suffering, her and her hunger which mounted to her head and made her dizzy.

When she thought of what her life might have been, when she remembered that shortly after her marriage a young and handsome man had one day cast himself at her feet and that she, as much from alarm as from any scruple, had spurned him with shouts of laughter, she felt herself capable of killing this old man who had stolen her youth and deprived her forever of even the taste for sensuality. And as her memory retraced the details of a scene she would never forget, she asked herself bitterly after twenty years which of the two of them had been more ridiculous, the young man at her feet, or she herself refusing the love that she was now calling out for on the threshold of old age.

Why had life been so unfair to her? Did other women suffer like this? What was the use of giving her riches and beauty, if their only object was to deprive her of happiness? She discovered, at the age of fifty, that after despising and detesting love, it was love she had wanted all her life. If she had known, if anyone had told her, if there had

been an ounce of kindness in her destiny, she might
have been happy, and in any case a much better
woman. She knew exactly what gesture, what look
of her husband's had given her that hardness of
soul; certain words of his had played more havoc
with her than his bestiality which she detested so
much. She had loathed her child, fruit of the violence to which she had been subjected, from the
hour when she first felt him move within her; she
had followed the early years of his youth with her
hatred, taking a pleasure in punishing him that
avenged her for the tortures his birth had made her
suffer, scolding him until he became no better than
a little slave, abject with fear, his heart already
overladen with malice. She was cruel and was quite
aware of it, without, however, being able to experience the compunction which this knowledge of herself might have made another woman feel. There
were too many excuses to justify her in her own
sight; her nature, a barren refractory soil on which
heaven had never shed the blessing of its rain, produced nothing with which poison was not in some
way mingled. The simplest sentiments were warped,
every joy was an object of suspicion, every affection
corrupted at its source. Detached from all worldly
things, not from any asceticism, but because poverty
of mind prevented her from enjoying them, and yet
unable to conceive of any form of happiness in
which the senses did not take part, she wasted her
strength and her life in mediocrity, and tried to find

the peace which refused itself to her by the sacrifice
of herself.

There is a strange satisfaction about touching the
depths of despair. Overwhelming misfortune pro-
duces a kind of security, a haven of peace for the
shipwrecked soul that no longer dares believe. Such
mental distress is the surest shelter and to abandon
oneself to it is to rest. Was not that why she was
walking up and down this road, her limbs frozen,
in spite of the furs that covered her body, impatiently awaiting the hour that should deliver her
from her trouble and make her fate certain?

Now that night had come and that the moment
was approaching, what was the good of the tears
which ran down her cheeks and of the little sigh of
pain which she smothered in her muff? She was
selfish and hard, but at any rate she was brave;
perhaps she was succumbing to the fatigue of her
emotions. In a moment she would go home and go
up to her room; she would take off her coat quite
calmly and make up the fire. Then she would read
or strum on the piano until dinner was announced.
She looked at her watch; it was ten minutes past
seven, nearly a quarter past. Very well. He would
not come now; he was afraid, quite naturally. She
waited two or three minutes more to satisfy her
conscience, and then turned her steps toward the
villa.

Almost immediately she heard the visitors' bell
ring; some one was at the gate and was ringing.

Chapter Six

"You! What are you doing here, Angèle?"

"Heavens! madame, how you frightened me!"

"Whom do you want to see?"

"I came to ask madame for some work."

"Ah! So we have decided to go to work again, have we? Don't hide yourself like that, my girl. You used to be bolder once, I seem to remember."

"Oh no! madame."

"Oh yes! madame. And what sort of work do you want?"

"I don't mind, madame. Some sewing, perhaps."

"So you don't want to go back to the laundry? I suppose that, after having our name in the newspapers, we're not going to stoop to carry washing about the town."

"Madame should have pity."

"Pity! Next you will be talking to me of morals. You! Do you think I didn't know what used to go on here, under my very nose?"

She heard the footman coming to open the gate in answer to the bell, and she called out, sharply:

"Don't trouble about the gate, Jean. Tell your master that I shall be a few minutes late for dinner."

The man's steps retreated. She turned back to Angèle with the sort of eagerness with which a wild beast would have returned to its prey. She seemed to acquire a new lease of energy in the presence of this creature whom Guéret had desired, pursued, beaten. How delicious to vent her own anger on this humiliated woman, to be revenged on her for all that love that had been offered to her!

"I am not going to let anyone else in here, do you understand? I have shut my eyes too long on all the filthy things that go on in my house. And now you will kindly do me the pleasure of taking that shawl away from your face and looking at me properly."

"I cannot, madame."

"You cannot look me in the face? I am not surprised. However, you will either uncover your face or I will go in and give orders that you shall be forbidden the door once for all."

"Will madame please listen to me for a moment first? It was just about that I wanted to speak to her. Madame will understand when she sees me that I cannot show myself any more, and that is why I came to ask Madame . . . "

"Hurry up. What is it you want?"

"I cannot live here any more. I must leave Lorges. It doesn't matter where I go; to Paris, perhaps. I am too unhappy."

"What an idea! Everyone is unhappy. If one had to move every time one was unhappy the railway companies would make a fortune. Take off that shawl and begin to get used to showing yourself in

the street now. At the end of a week you won't
think about it any more."

"I want to ask madame for something impossible."

"Well? Hurry up."

"If madame would lend me a little money."

"Money? What for?"

"To go away with."

"This is an obsession. Just now you told me you
had come to ask me for work. Were you lying?
Whom did you want to see here? Was it me or
Monsieur Grosgeorge? I warn you that you had
better tell the truth."

"Madame would never forgive me."

"So it was Monsieur Grosgeorge you were coming to see. To get money from him, of course. I
knew it. You thought you could wheedle him, as
you used to . . . "

"Oh, madame, I swear . . . "

"So I conclude that something must remain of
that beauty which delighted everyone so much. Let
me see you."

"If I do, may I at least hope that madame will
help me?"

"A bargain? Certainly not! Either you will
obey me immediately and take off that shawl, or
we part at once, in which case I forbid you ever
to ring at this gate again. As for the help you
want, we'll see about that. I promise nothing."

"I am ready to obey madame."

"That's better. Now take off the shawl."

"I am doing so. There!"

"I can't see anything, anything at all. Go under the lamp."

"Dare I ask madame a question . . . Why does she want to see me?"

"I am not used to being interrogated, my girl."

"I am only wondering if madame won't be frightened?"

"Do you take me for a milksop? If my own misfortunes were confined to being hit in the face with a stick I should have no quarrel with life."

"Madame will remember that I always had a high color, and in weather like this the scars show up all the more. The whole of one eyebrow is gone."

"Here we are. Stand there. Now raise your head."

"I implore madame to be kind."

"Don't talk so much, and raise your head. Are you going to obey me, yes or no? I warn you that I cannot bear tears. Come, raise your head and look at the lamp. Right. I can see now. It's not so bad as I thought. People exaggerate so much. No doubt the punishment was administered with a firm hand, but it served you right. After years of filthy debauch you have a debt to pay, my girl. Come, cheer up!"

"Does madame think that the scars will ever go?"

"No."

"No!"

"What's the matter with you? You look as if I'd struck you in the face. Did you hope all that would disappear? Let me give you a piece of good advice: don't hope for anything, ever. Not so long ago I used to be as simple as you, but I'm cured now."

"But madame will understand that I cannot show myself any more in Lorges in this state."

"Why not? Cover your head if you don't want to catch cold. And we can't stop here. I have to go in."

"It wasn't a very big sum I wanted to borrow from madame. A hundred francs at most."

"We won't return to that subject. Is there anything else you wanted to ask me?"

"I should have been so grateful to madame."

I don't need your gratitude, thank you."

"Will madame at least let me ask monsieur?"

"Monsieur? Well, if that doesn't beat anything! I think you must be mad. In the first place, monsieur wouldn't look at you with your face like that. Monsieur is much too callous."

"Monsieur is kind."

"Idiot! Do you think you can please me by saying that? Monsieur has as much heart as that gate. And it is you that have made him like that, you and women like you. Oh, I don't say it is all your fault; he began before you were born. Good night now."

"Madame!"

"Please don't touch me."

"I implore madame to forgive me. I know I have offended madame in the past, but if madame will not consent to help me I shall kill myself."

"That's right. The great refrain of all weaklings. Are you as miserable as all that?"

"Madame has no idea how miserable I am. For months I have thought I should go mad."

"I ask myself what right you have to my pity. Anyway, to prove that I am not so cruel as people think, I promise to think over your case. I will see. Our washing is coming back tomorrow. I will send you word by Fernande."

"Oh madame!"

"No, let go my hand. I told you I didn't want you to touch me. Besides, you mustn't hope too much. Remember my advice."

"Yes, madame."

There was a moment's silence during which Madame Grosgeorge appeared to hesitate; her hand was already on the gate handle when she suddenly asked:

"Oh yes! Why have you never wanted to help the police in their inquiries? You insist on saying that it was not Guéret who attacked you, when several people saw you together on the road. Answer me. If you want me to take an interest in you, you must tell me the truth."

"It was not Monsieur Guéret."

"Then who was it?"

"I don't know. I didn't see him. He hit me from behind and I fainted."

"And the witnesses?"

"The witnesses lie."

"Come now. Think a moment, my girl. You will

be well rewarded if you tell me the truth. Otherwise we part now and you can give up all hope of my pitying you or ever allowing you in my house again. Why didn't you want to denounce your aggressor?"

"Can I rely upon madame not to tell anyone?"

"What do you take me for? Do I look like a person who would betray a secret?"

"Well, then, I didn't denounce him because I was afraid of his vengeance. Even if they had captured him, prisoners sometimes escape. Who knows that he mightn't have come back and cut my throat?"

"Ha! Ha! Ha!"

"Merciful God! Does madame think that so funny?"

"I am laughing at your fear. It doesn't raise you very much in my esteem, but you are just the same as all the others. So it was Guéret?"

"I implore madame not to repeat it!"

"Don't worry about that."

"May I hope that madame will remember me and that Fernande will bring a favorable answer?"

"I will keep my promise."

"Madame is so kind."

"Madame is loyal, neither more nor less. This time, good night."

"Good night, madame."

Chapter Seven

SHE listened to Madame Grosgeorge's step retreating up the garden path and waited for a moment by the gate, as if she thought this hard, cynical woman would reappear in a few seconds with her hands full of banknotes. Then, as a biting north wind was blowing, she tied the corners of the black shawl covering her head beneath her chin and started to walk back to the town.

"I haven't betrayed him," she thought. "Everyone in the place knows, really, and besides, she promised not to say anything."

Actually, although she hated Madame Grosgeorge, she had a reassuring feeling that for all the cold ferocity of her nature she had a contempt for treachery. Yet she congratulated herself on not having told her the whole truth and on having kept to herself the real reasons that prevented her from denouncing her aggressor. Would anyone in the whole world understand her? What did she care if Madame Grosgeorge took her for a coward? This rich, insolent woman might compel her to answer her questions by threatening to withhold help from her, but all her gold could never wrest from her the secret she treasured in her heart. And in spite of her despair the feeling of having baffled her enemy made her pulse beat more quickly.

Of course it was Monsieur Grosgeorge to whom she had wanted to speak; she would have flung herself at his feet and kissed his vile hands. To solve the problem of getting money and escaping, no humiliation seemed to her to be too great. This evening her patience had come to an end. She had lived all her life at Lorges, and now she felt she had not the strength to spend another day there. She counted the hours as if she were on the eve of going on a journey, and fretted about the slowness with which the time passed. It was no use thinking of future plans; the first thing to do was to escape from this place where every stone and every face reminded her of her misfortune. There was nothing she would not do to get away. She would even have promised Madame Londe to resume her former life, she would have crawled on the ground before her, if by doing so she could have got the money she wanted. Her three months of solitude in her room had only lulled her fears; so long as she had lived there, between her bed and her window, like a nun, a ray of hope had remained to her; perhaps not the hope of being entirely cured and of seeing her face regain its former beauty, but at any rate the hope of having exaggerated her disfigurement and of still retaining some of her former attraction. So that, in spite of the tedium of her empty days, she had put off to the last possible moment the time when she should go out. This was the only way in which she could pre-

serve an illusion without which she felt she could not
go on living, and which she could not make up her
mind to submit to the ordeal of a walk in broad daylight; for what her mirror showed her did not reassure her; her mangled flesh had healed up, but the
white scars remained, and even though her features
were the same, all their charm had left them. Beauty
is a marvel which the least thing can destroy and
which should only be admired from a distance; it
disappears in a way as difficult to explain as is its
very presence, and it is always sacrilege for man to
touch it; it had fled from Angèle's face as from a
desecrated spot.

The young woman had long suspected the un-
palatable truth; however often she told herself that
her nose and mouth were the same and that the scars
were not deep, she knew that she hardly recognized
herself. This new face frightened her each time she
caught its anxious and haggard look in the mirror.
Would it frighten other people, too? At first she
thought so, then in the weakness of her heart she
conceived the strange idea that she was mistaken
and that being so much alone had made her take a
distorted view of things. "If one keeps on looking
at oneself, one has no idea of what one looks like,"
she told herself. Of course Madame Londe could
have told her the truth, but how could she ever sum-
mon up courage to ask an enemy to verify the loss
of her beauty? Besides, Madame Londe herself had
no wish to tamper with the ominous black shawl that
hid Angèle's face from her, like the face of her

destiny. How dreadful it would be for her if the harm were irreparable! For a long time now she had preferred to live in doubt. And it was a sign that she had exhausted all the resources of hope when she announced to the young woman that her customers were prepared to accept her as she was.

This announcement had left but a faint impression on Angèle's mind. In the first place, she guessed that it was a lie, and again, little Fernande's attitude when she had shown herself to her—her fear, her silence, her tears—had deprived her of all the remainder of her courage. She had read in the child's eyes the truth of which her mirror had been unable to convince her; she was repulsive; she asked a little girl to kiss her and the little girl shuddered and drew away from her. From now onward she must get used to the thought that she had lost everything. A new life was beginning for her—the life of an ugly girl, so ugly that she frightened love away, for she did not imagine that she could attract a man if she repelled a child. In fact, although she was by no means intelligent, she understood that desire obeys fairly general laws, and that only a degenerate could be attracted by a face on which the fury of an assassin had left such clear and savage marks.

After her first fit of despair she regained some of her calm, months of struggling with herself having strengthened her will-power; the carelessness of youth had given place to a bitter resignation which enabled her to bear the burden of her daily life. She knew herself better now. What she had demanded above all of her solitude was to shelter her from the truth, but when she could bear it no longer she had showed herself to Fernande to find out the worst, and to banish from her heart the last illusions it still harbored. It was one way to freedom; nothing tortures and nothing enslaves so much as the hope of terrestrial happiness, and she realized this after long empty weeks during which each day brought with it the same misery. Standing by the high window of her room, her head swathed in the shawl which never left her, she had learned to humble her pride and to discourage its hopes. The little open space that she once used to look at with such eager eyes no longer excited the least tremor of curiosity in her, and now she seldom even glanced at it; she knew, only too well, the triangle of trees, the uneven cobbles, the rotting wooden seats; this narrow space made her think of a theater in which no drama could ever be produced.

While patching the linen which Madame Londe gave her to mend, she let her mind follow its natural bent. In her soul, devastated by the regret of what it had lost, one joy alone still remained, a strange joy that sometimes came to her and made her tremble with fear, the joy of probing the depths of her humiliation. There was something tempting, something even pleasant sometimes, in the dreadful capriciousness with which fate had treated her and in the suddenness with which disaster had overtaken her. She liked to meditate on the idea of the entire change that had occurred in her life, and to com-

pare the dreariness of her present austere existence
with her former sensual dreams. Then she would be
brought abruptly back to reason, and her misery
would come over her in a wave. Where was she?
What was she dreaming about? How could she think
there could be any good in such an abomination? And
it seemed to her as though the coldness of death descended upon her shoulders and completely en-
shrouded her.

Sometimes, too, quite different thoughts came
pouring into her mind, just as the wind fills a house
when the window flies open. By a freak of her
memory worn out by always dwelling on the same
thoughts, she would suddenly forget that she was
disfigured. This illusion would last but a few seconds. The desire for love possessed her once more,
and her vanity, so long humiliated, lit her eyes up
again, and the illusion of being pretty gave her a
feeling of richness and royalty that lifted her out of
this world and made her sewing fall from her hands.
In these mad moments she saw herself being adored
by a man upon his knees before her.

This man was Guéret. He was as she had seen
him first, shy and ashamed, with a voice which he
tried to soften. Whenever she looked at him he
lowered his eyes, but now and again she surprised a
wild expression on his features, and when he raised
his eyelids she was amazed at the light shining from
his eyes; she could not have said whether gentleness
or ferocity preponderated in his character, she only

knew that she dominated him and that he trembled
before her.

The end of her hallucination would come suddenly.
She would find herself back in her room, staring with
horror at the cloth she was darning, the edge of her
shawl, all that spoke to her of the present and recalled her to her sufferings. These delusive reveries
into which her misery threw her, terrified her, and
she tried to revive her memory of the loathing and
horror that had filled her heart when she saw Guéret's
arm raised above her face. Even before he struck
her she was almost fainting, and she imagined that
the screams issuing from her throat came from some-
one else, from a woman being murdered near her.
She could not conceive of her own life being in danger; death was not for her, it was for that other
woman who screamed, and yet how awful to feel herself nailed to the ground by that man's hand, and
what a dreadful note of fear rang in those incessant
screams! The first blow seared her face from her
left eye to her mouth; the blood trickled down to the
back of her throat; she had lost consciousness and
when she recovered it, a little later, there was a salt
taste on her tongue, but it was the unbearable pain
of her wounds that had brought her back to consciousness; fire seemed to be running over her face.
Blood was streaming from her head and covered her
arms and chest. Her screams attracted a crowd of
spectators, but at first not one of them dared to
touch her, and she had to implore them to take her
home.

These memories tortured her, and she would put her hands to her ears and screw up her eyes as though to shut out of her brain the picture of the anguish she had suffered; but her memory was inexorable and only spared her at one moment in order to crucify her at others, for the wretched girl could only succeed in dismissing this bloody vision by conjuring up the happy moments of her life, and what tears she shed over these journeys into the past!

She remembered one strange night which she had spent in a condition of great happiness. It was after her quarrel with Madame Londe, when she had decided not to return to her room that evening but to go and spend the night with a girl she knew at Chanteilles. So as to give herself all the illusions of running away, she had been careful to tell no one. To escape; to escape from Madame Londe and the restaurant and its customers quarrelling over her! At that moment this had been the only idea in her head. She saw herself, once more, leaning out of a window looking over the Boulevard de la Preste. The night was dark and a light breeze had sprung up; now and then drops of rain fell on her hair and on her bare arms. Behind her the little room in which she had been put was brightly lit; the bed, the table, and the two chairs were not her own and held no memories for her, whereas in her own room everything spoke to her of boredom and oppression. Here she was free; the breeze blowing in her face was not the same one that made the leaves dance in the space in front of the Restaurant Londe. She was happy;

a man loved her; though she did not know where he
was or what he was doing, she was certain that he
was thinking of her and was suffering on her account; she basked in this thought as a flower basks
in the sunlight. True, he was nothing like the ideal
she had conjured up in her dreams, but for all that
it was difficult for her to resist the pleasure of being
loved, and she wanted it to go on and that this man
should never hear of all her love-affairs with other
men. Not that she intended ever to yield to him, but
she was growing accustomed to the rough tenderness
which she found in him, and she understood quite
well that his attitude toward her would change entirely if he discovered what she was trying to hide
from him. She often thought of his gruff, timid
voice, his careful speech, and everything else about
him except his awkward body, his unattractive face,
his heavy hands. When she met him she did not
look at him; she listened to his voice, and unconsciously allowed her thoughts to wander to other
faces seen casually in the highways and byways. But
his voice and the warmth of his fierce, repressed love
gave her a kind of happiness she had never felt before and which was slowly fascinating her. The very
next morning, on her way back to her own room, she
had seen Guéret again in the road, and he had
dragged her past the little wood as far as the bank
of the river whose murmur she sometimes heard in
the restless slumber of her nights. What a price she
was now paying for the short, slight happiness of

her dreams! If she had but known, she thought to herself; but this reflection merely made her angry. You never know when life is about to betray you; it is useless to count on the morrow, or even on the next hour; nothing is certain but death.

This was practically what she said to herself when Fernande left her, refusing her the kiss that would have given her back her peace of mind. What was the use of crying? It would only make her still uglier by making her eyes puffy. And for the twentieth time since morning she studied herself at length in her mirror, moving her head this way and that; then, seized with a sudden fury against herself and against God who allowed such tragedies, she flung the mirror on the tiled floor of the room and crushed it to powder beneath her heel.

What was to be done when unhappiness had reached such a pitch? she asked herself. Around her she saw the furniture and the walls which had witnessed all her misery, and it seemed to her as though this world of wood and stone came to life and spoke to her. Why should she not go away? In the course of the life in which she had desired so many things she had become attached to nothing. Not a single thought or memory had any hold upon her.

So that when Madame Londe had opened her door to tell her that her customers wanted to see her the next day, the young woman had answered yes, so as not to start a fruitless argument, but her plans were quite settled; she would go to Monsieur Grosgeorge and ask him for money and would leave the town as soon as possible. Not for a moment had she any doubt about her success. The stupidity and vanity of the old man were boundless, and she knew by experience how to take advantage of them. Even if she kept her shawl on her head she would contrive to make this man think her pretty. He had swallowed so much humbug already. He would take her refusal to show her face as a piece of coquetry, and besides, he would be so anxious to believe in her beauty that he would not be very difficult to fool. She remembered the desires which her presence alone aroused in him, and the munificence of which he was capable in a moment of impatience. Several times since her misfortune he had tried to see her, and she was sure of the influence she exercised over this poor, idle, sensual creature. After more than three months of absence the mere fact of her going to see him would overjoy him. She would promise him anything in the world provided only that he gave her the money necessary for her flight; lies didn't cost anything; besides, she despised him so utterly and thought him so vile that she did not believe there could be anything disgraceful in tricking him, just as if the old scoundrel's ignominy excused her from being honest herself.

A freak of circumstance had reduced this fine project to nothing. Madame Grosgeorge, that hard, mysterious woman whom she had seen only once or twice and to whom she never gave a thought, had met her on the road and prevented her from seeing her

husband. It was too much like life for Angèle to be
astonished by it. There is nothing hazardous or
mischievous about fate; its treachery, prepared long
in advance, only bears the appearance of chance
because we cannot see its interior workings.

Chapter Eight

A ND in spite of all, she had brought away with her
Madame Grosgeorge's promise to think over
her case. A sorry prize! How much more attractive
had been the otterskin muff in which this woman
kept her hands warm! More than once during the
conversation in the road Angèle had been tempted to
tear the precious fur from her. Perhaps her purse
might have been hidden in it, and in that purse . . .
Oh, why was it always necessary for the rich to be so
hard-hearted? How would the sacrifice of two hundred francs alter the train of affairs at Villa Mon
Idée? Would there be less food? Would the air be
any colder in those rooms in which fires burned from
morning till night? With so much spite and so much
covetousness around them, how did the rich ever succeed in going to sleep?

So she tied the ends of her shawl tightly beneath
her chin and quickened her pace. All that was left
for her to do was to go home and get into bed so as
not to be so cold; her first day out after being confined to the house for months had exhausted her, and
she felt she had no strength left to make plans for
the morrow. Even the desire to struggle was abandoning her; a sort of indifference with regard to
happiness or misery was coming over her. Her head

was heavy. Seated by a fire she would have gone to
sleep at once.

She had been walking along the road for a minute
or two when she heard some one running after her.
With a gesture which had become natural to her she
pulled her shawl across her face and turned round;
but she saw nothing. At far intervals gas-jets shed
a yellow light on the snow, but did not succeed in
dispelling the shadows. She suddenly grew afraid;
the sound had been so close to her that she should
have been able to see the person following her. Her
first thought was to take to her heels; but the silence
was so deep that she asked herself whether she had
not, perhaps, been mistaken. In any case, there was
not much to fear; hardly a hundred yards separated
her from the first houses of the town. But she knew
also, that since the beginning of winter the inhabitants of Lorges never left their houses after sunset.
Would any screams ever induce these cowards to
come to her aid? And her fears, hushed for a
moment, all came back again.

At that moment some one called her name. She
had no time to reply, for almost immediately a man
approached her from the side of the road where he
had been hiding. From his shoulders and especially
from his gait she recognized Guéret and uttered a
cry.

"Hush!" he ordered in a low voice. "I swear to
you that you have nothing to fear."

He was so close to the young woman that she could
almost distinguish his features. A mad terror seized

her and prevented her from making any sign; it seemed to her as if the blood were rushing from every corner in her body toward her heart, whose dull beating pounded against her chest.

"I am risking my life to see you again," he went on. "If I were arrested it would mean prison at least, perhaps worse. Are you still frightened of me? Answer me."

"No," she breathed, drawing back a step.

"I heard something of what you said to Madame Grosgeorge just now. I was hiding near the villa gate. The other day when I was prowling about I saw her. I ran away, but she called after me to come back the next day at seven o'clock. That was this evening. I came, but at the last moment I got suspicious and when she arrived I hid myself. Is it true that you didn't denounce me to the police?"

"Yes."

"Don't tremble so. I swear I won't touch you unless you let me. Angèle, listen to me. You loathe me, don't you?"

She did not dare answer, fearing that he was setting a trap for her. And yet what hatred that voice aroused in her! He had spoken to her like that the day he had taken her down to the river. Why had she been so weak afterward as to hamper the actions of the police by denying that he was her aggressor?

"Will you ever forgive me?" he asked.

She would never forgive him. The shame of having felt even the semblance of love for such a commonplace man made her suffer even more than the loss of her beauty. The only words of love that had ever been spoken to her had been uttered in a voice devoid of youth; she detested that voice.

"Let me go away," she said at last.

"Since you haven't denounced me, it means that you have forgiven me," he urged. "It wasn't only from fear, was it?"

He waited for a moment for the reply that did not come, then he asked, abruptly:

"Why did Madame Grosgeorge take you under the lamp? Why did she want to look at you? Angèle! It isn't possible that you've still got any marks on your face. Is it? Is it?"

She hesitated for a moment, but her vanity was stronger than her bitterness.

"No," she said, "there isn't a trace." And she added at once, moved by something irresistible, "It's the Chanteilles girls who spread that about, out of jealousy."

He seized her hand, as though to thank her.

"How could I have done it? I must have been quite mad. For three days I thought you were dead. Then, when I read the newspaper, I seemed to come to life again. I have done nothing but think of you. My only idea has been to come back here."

As she did not move and did not take away her hand, he suddenly said to her:

"I love you, do you understand? I could have gone abroad, but I preferred to hide in Paris and round about so as not to be too far from you."

She felt his hot breath on her cheek and drew far-

ther back, overcome by the disgust with which this
man inspired her. She dared not free her hand for
fear of unloosing Guéret's rage, but, in spite of
everything, his words of love touched her. He went
on:

"I have reached the point when I don't care about
my liberty any more. Madame Grosgeorge must
have told everyone that she saw me yesterday. Perhaps they are searching for me at this very moment.
And yet you see I'm not afraid of walking about the
place."

"You must go away."

"You want to get rid of me. Have you had many
love-affairs, Angèle? Do you live as you used to
do?"

These questions upset her more than anything he
had said until then. An impulse which she could not
explain came to her; she hated this man, yet she
could not resist the desire to please him.

"No," she said; "that's all done with."

She regretted these words as soon as she had said
them. It seemed to her that the mere fact of replying involved her in a dangerous adventure. Instead
of running away at once, as her instinct had
prompted her to do, she had remained in the road,
talking to this man; she was caught.

"Why do you ask me that?" she asked, sharply.
"Loose my arm and let me go."

She had said the same thing on the highroad by
the Sommeillante; it was as though the same scene
were about to be reënacted, and she was terrified by

the words that came from her lips against her will. Yet he was holding her so firmly by the arm that she did not try to escape.

"What if I found some money?" he resumed, suddenly, without paying any attention to what she said. "Would you consent to follow me?"

She was so astonished that she did not reply at once. Here she was being offered what she had been begging for just now, the means of flight; but fate was granting her the gift in such a way that she could not accept it. To run away with the person she hated most in the world! And what would this man do when he saw her in broad daylight? Nevertheless, she decided, superstitiously, not to reject a resource that might be valuable to her; and as the keystone of her nature was to lie, she argued to herself that it was better to accept Guéret's proposition if she could succeed in getting rid of him in that way.

"Where will you get the money?" she asked.

"What does it matter to you? I tell you I'll have it in three days from now."

His hot fingers were bruising her wrist beneath the sleeve of her blouse; the pressure of this assassin's hand filled her with a terror which made her teeth chatter. She was afraid of arousing Guéret's suspicions by saying yes too hastily, and asked:

"Where could we go?"

"Abroad. I have friends in Belgium. After a few months we would return to France."

He took her in his arms.

"Will you come?"

She stammered, "Yes, if you will let me go now."

"Will you? Will you really come?" he asked in a frenzy of happiness.

"Yes, I will, but leave me now."

He glued his lips to her hands.

"Madame Grosgeorge has promised to help me," he went on. "She is rich. I'll go and see her. Do you know what time she goes out and where she goes?"

She thought, "If he sees her, he is lost. She will betray him."

"In the afternoon," she replied, "usually about three o'clock; I often see her near Chanteilles when I take the washing there. She never used to notice me," she added as though she were talking to herself.

"Does she go on foot?"

"Yes, when it's fine. Otherwise she takes the carriage."

"Alone?"

"Always alone."

"I will meet you here, in two days' time, between the third and fourth lamp from the footbridge. What's the time now?"

"Half past seven."

"All right, then at half past seven. We'll walk to Héricourt, where no one knows us. There we'll take the train."

"Very well."

"Swear to me you'll come."

"Yes, I swear it."

"I shall know where to find you," he said with a laugh which seemed to veil a threat.

"I'll be here. Let me go now."

"Take that shawl off and kiss me, will you?"

"No, no! Look out! There's some one coming."

He released her quickly and leaped to one side, looking about him. She made her escape and a few seconds later ran past the first houses of Lorges.

Chapter Nine

HE HEARD the sound of her steps die down without daring to follow her. No one came along the road; she had tricked him into releasing her, and yet he was certain she would be there in two days' time; fear would bring her there, if love did not. He could not make up his mind to leave this spot, walking first this way and then that, as though his movements were restricted by invisible walls. A hidden force chained him to the piece of ground on which he was going to see her again; she would tread that earth in two days' time as he was treading it now; and with the tip of his toe he scraped at the mud and snow where Angèle's foot had been. It was there, almost in the middle of the road. Three minutes earlier she had been standing there with him and he had let her go.

After a few minutes he went away. The cold came through the threadbare overcoat he was wearing. His numbed hands sought in vain for a little warmth at the bottoms of his pockets; he felt as though he were naked in the rising wind that froze the tears on his face; but his heart was full of joy.

For three and a half days he had lived in complete solitude, hiding in little woods in the surrounding country, and taking his meals in villages where he felt safe. A thick beard covered his cheeks and made him almost unrecognizable; only his shifting eyes and bowed shoulders might have betrayed him if anyone had taken the trouble to notice them, but he counted on the shortness of people's memories. One evening he had even ventured into the streets of Lorges. Certain of meeting no one, and intoxicated by the immunity he enjoyed in the town, he had passed through one street and then another until finally he had arrived at the little open space in front of the Restaurant Londe. It seemed to him as though time had rolled back and that all the anguish and terror of those last months were suddenly reduced to nothing. Perhaps nothing had happened since he had been there; the house and the cobbles seemed the same. If he had really committed a crime, would he risk himself thus in a place where everyone was eager to denounce him? His very imprudence reassured him. From continually living in peril he was growing used to it. And then, the newspapers no longer spoke about him; after the agitation of the first few weeks the police had given up hope of finding him and oblivion was gradually hedging round a crime reduced to the proportions of an occasional news paragraph. It was almost as if the community had given him absolution.

His meeting with Madame Grosgeorge had reawakened him to a sense of danger. Despite his beard and his ragged clothing this woman had recognized him at once. Would she betray him? The question was badly put. He should ask himself,

"Why should she not betray me?"   She had, indeed,
told him that she wished to help him, but what could
she have said better calculated to lead him into a
trap?   What possible reasons could induce her to
come to his help?   The memory of the contemptuous
look he had so often read in her eyes caused him
grave misgivings.   In virtue of what caprice should
this haughty personage become so charitable after
having taken such pleasure in humiliating him?

Meanwhile, it had become necessary to act as
quickly as possible and to see Angèle, since that was
all he had come to do, before the alarm was given.
But how could he see her, and where?   He had waited
for her on the road by which she used to come on her
return from Chanteilles at the end of the day, but
without success; for he did not know that she was no
longer working.   From pure inanition he had followed out Madame Grosgeorge's instructions and
had waited, torn between the fear of falling into a
trap and anxiety not to neglect any possible chance,
but at the very moment when Madame Grosgeorge
was about to appear he had been seized with sudden
panic and hid himself in the shadows, near the gate
of Villa Mon Idée.   From there he saw this woman
he had always feared walk up and down the road,
exhibiting every sign of impatience.   Several times
she passed before him.   What was she thinking
about?   With her head flung back, her quick step
and her way of stopping abruptly to beat her foot
on the ground and look to right and to left, the impression she made on him was exactly the same as

when he had given her son lessons. It showed marvelous harmony between her mind and her actions for an attitude of her body, a way of turning round and of shrugging her shoulders to be able to reveal all the harshness and aridity of her soul! He seemed to hear her biting voice hurling the most insolent phrases in his face. Even when shouting to him: "I don't mean you any harm. Don't be afraid!" her intonation had been that of a mistress scolding a servant. And it was from this woman that he was hoping for an act of kindness. He might just as well go and ask for help at the police station.

Angèle's appearance filled him with a joy which caution forced him to keep within bounds. He was not near enough to the woman to hear all their conversation by the gate, except when they raised their voices, as had happened when Madame Grosgeorge had ordered Angèle to show her face. And although his jealousy was revived by the memory of the note which Monsieur Grosgeorge had read to him one day, he blessed the circumstances which had led Angèle to come back to see the old man.

At present two women knew he was at Lorges; one of them despised him, the other had every reason to fear and hate him, and he must be mad to think that they would keep his secret. An easy vengeance had been put within Angèle's reach; she had only to let the police know where she was to meet him and he would fall into a trap which he had, in some sort, set for himself. Perhaps they were already warned while he was vainly deliberating on the charity he might expect from two women who were both his enemies.

Nevertheless, he did not dream of running away. The question of whether to remain free or to finish his days in prison presented itself to him in many different aspects. If he examined the matter closely it seemed to him idiotic to hesitate for one second between prison and liberty. To avoid being taken he would hide himself for so many days in such a village; one road seemed safer to him than another, and this hour preferable to that one. But at times he seemed to see that the game was being played in quite another manner and that his own plans did not count. The important factor was time, and time is beyond man's control. At the end of a certain number of days or years his destiny would be accomplished. His case was tried and its result known. He was like a playing child who does not heed the passing of time, but whose mother knows the exact moment when she is going to put him to bed and plunge him into the darkness that will send him to sleep.

He remembered that, one evening in Paris, in an alley down which he had dived to shake off a policeman, the idea of giving himself up had occurred to him. Liberty at the cost of hunger, fear, and misery could be as dreadful as prison. Perhaps the place in which he found himself at that moment had put this idea into his head. It was a November evening and, although night was falling, the street lamps were not yet lit. He was cowering among the darkest shadows of the alley, which was a sort of gap in the tall, gloomy mass of buildings that flank one side of the Rue Saint-Lazare. His breath showed like a pale mist in the black fog floating between the walls. Gradually his heartbeats grew steadier, and he began to walk, feeling his way along the wall with his hand. A faint glow showed above the housetops but did not reach as far as the street. His steps faltered like those of a blind man and his legs were still unsteady from having run so much. Near by the continuous rumble of the city was like a great threatening roar, and he could not help thinking of a huge clumsy beast that bellowed as it sought him in the night.

This feeling of an unequal struggle between himself and some vague mysterious form obsessed him at all hours of the day, whenever his eyes met anyone else's or he heard a quicker step than his own behind him in the street; his whole body would suddenly grow hot, and sweat would stick his hat to his forehead. Pursued from street to street by imaginary policemen, he sought out the crowded parts of the city, avoiding deserted squares and long empty avenues; and yet he was terrified of mingling with the crowd. So many newspapers had given his description. It only required a flash of memory for some pedestrian suddenly to remember, on seeing him pass, the description he had read a few weeks before: "Tall, bowed shoulders (he tried vainly to hold himself erect), dark complexion. . . ." No doubt it was unlikely, but even the dullest life is made up of unlikely events. Several times the desire to lose himself in crowds had drawn him to the neighborhood of the big railway stations, and he had found himself swept along in the crush of travelers. His soiled clothing and, above all, the anxiety which his face involuntarily betrayed, quickly drew attention to him; then he would imagine that he had been recognized and that people were pressing round him on purpose, to prevent him from escaping. Why did they look at him like that? Should he force his way through them or wait until an eddy threw him on one side and freed him? He fancied that whichever attitude he adopted would appear suspicious and that his very immobility attracted attention. To his anxiety would be added a terror that gripped him by the throat. It was of no use his telling himself that these men and women did not know him and that they were probably not even thinking of looking for him; the terror of being arrested rose in him like a storm which nothing could quell. In these moments of mental confusion he felt impelled to do the strangest things; to strike his neighbor on the back with all his strength and to make off like an escaping criminal, or else to start shouting and denouncing himself to hasten on the occurrence of an event which he judged to have become inevitable.

He could no longer go out into the street or enter a room without the same question immediately coming to his mind: "Am I going to be arrested here? Is this my last moment of liberty?" He had not stayed two consecutive nights in the same lodging;

he wandered from district to district, obeying the instinct which drove him this way and that, now attracted to and now terrified by certain streets. For weeks, and for no definite reason, he became a prey to a suspicion that kept him away from certain parts of the city and sometimes from the whole of Paris, forcing him to go into the suburbs. Then a period of calm or indifference would bring him back to the capital. Tired of fighting against an enemy whose presence he seemed to feel on all sides of him, he would resolve not to bother any more about the perils that threatened him and to live like other people, like these hundreds of men he passed in the street. Then his reason would take a hand and encourage him in this resolve. After all, he was not such a great criminal. The police are not going to dog your footsteps for months merely because you have violated a girl and killed an old man at a street corner. After a few preliminary inquiries they end by shutting their eyes and directing their attention to malefactors who are worth troubling about.

And then suddenly, in the middle of a meal, fear would grip him again like a recurrent fever, for no reason, perhaps because he had upset the salt and a waiter was looking at him. He had a presentiment of evil. The place was unlucky. A man passing by the restaurant had whistled. He would get up, pay, go out, and run away as fast as he could without looking round. Then a familiar thought would come to reassure him, "I shall not be arrested where I expect it." And by a contradiction of the human brain he found comfort in the mere fact of his anxiety.

In the meantime the memory of Angèle never left him, and made all his efforts to remain free, or even to earn his living, seem futile. At first the horror of his crime had thrown his whole mind into confusion; the disgust of the blood he had shed, of the screams, of that appalling struggle on the banks of the river, that nightmare in which his memory forced him to recognize himself, had occupied him completely. How could he ever have done such a thing and, above all, why had he done it? Not one of the reasons he gave to himself, desire, rage, fear, not one of these explained how for several hours such a complete transformation could have taken place inside him and made his hand an instrument for murder. And even now, after weeks of reflection, he was unable to establish in his consciousness any real connection between the murderer and himself. It seemed to him that if he were arrested he would be expiating another's offense. It was as though he had committed his crime in his sleep.

For this reason he suffered from no remorse; this word, so full of significance for most guilty persons, had no meaning in connection with his own sensations. Should the mind always be held responsible for what the arm does, what the mouth says? Why should there not be moments in which a man's actions are divorced from his volition? Perhaps we sometimes serve forces of which we are ignorant and which take advantage of the disorder into which rage momentarily casts us to substitute themselves for us and to guide our actions. In any case, the thing that struck him most, when he reflected on his crime, was the futility of it. If in attacking the young woman he had even been able to slake his passion and to free himself from it, he would have understood what had urged him to act as he did, for he had been so exhausted and burned up with the violence of his passion, that what he wanted was not love so much as peace for his senses. No one hated the slavery of desire more than did this libertine, and the species of terrified joy which his crime had procured for him had only disgusted him with himself. When it was over he was in exactly the same state he had been in before, more captivated, perhaps, than ever, by the person he had attacked, and in terror of having lost her forever.

This thought dominated everything within him, even the safeguarding of his liberty, for liberty had no meaning to him unless it brought him happiness. A passion that has any strength in it is always somewhat obstinate, for it is a very poor nature that resigns itself to the abandonment of its desires and consents to see imperfections in its idol. He had long ago passed the period of desiring a thing for its beauty; beauty is merely a starting-point. At present his need of the young woman was confused with the very instinct that urged him to live; he would still have desired her if she had been ugly, or even dead.

It was in this state of mind that he had returned

to Lorges, profiting by the fact that the excitement
caused by his crime had begun to die down. The life
he was leading in Paris was becoming intolerable;
besides, to go back to the place where the drama had
unfolded itself was in some sort to force the hand
of destiny, much as the reappearance of the princi-
pal actor on the stage calls for the unraveling of the
plot of a play. It was time to put an end to it all.
Any certainty was preferable to the continual appre-
hensions that tormented him. To know that Angèle
had left, or had ceased to live, was less painful, in
the long run, than to fear it, and on certain days it
seemed to him that it would be a relief to be arrested
at last and thrown into prison, so true is it that there
are moments in which one asks nothing better than
to be deprived of one's liberty.

But now that he was standing in the road where
he had just spoken to Angèle, he felt the imminence
of the end. There was no more time to lose; destiny
was suffering from the violence that was being done
to it, and the last scenes were being played since he,
Guéret, had desired it to be so. It was impossible
for him to go without seeing Angèle again; if it cost
him his life he would be at the appointment he had
made. On the other hand, if she really did intend to
follow him, he would not ask her to go away with
him without money. He had already let the past
well behind him when he had seen her a short while
ago. The game had been a good one to date; it remained to him to risk everything if he did not want
to lose everything.

He stopped. His reflections had carried him beyond the last villas of Lorges. Where did he think of going that evening? With his head thrown back he looked around him as though the wind that whistled in his ears must furnish him with the answer to this question. He clenched his hands in the depths of his pockets and stood quite still for a few seconds. Then he turned and went back the way he had come.

Chapter Ten

Monsieur and Madame Grosgeorge had finished their dinner a good quarter of an hour before, and were ending the evening, as usual, in the little sitting-room on the ground floor. It was a room admirably protected against the inclemencies of the season, but there, as everywhere else in Villa Mon Idée, wealth had lent itself to the most deplorable affectations. Once more a Louis XVI style had been adopted, and from the orange carpet to the peacock-blue hangings covered with white lilies, everything betokened "department store" and an order given to a decorator who was in a hurry. In the restricted space fluted console tables and useless little occasional tables jostled chairs that looked too frail for anyone to dare to sit upon them, but two deep and comfortable armchairs occupied either side of the fireplace, in which four or five logs were burning; in one of these armchairs Madame Grosgeorge was reading a newspaper, in the other her husband sat, doing nothing.

He cast a happy glance over the reproductions of pictures by Fragonard and Boucher that adorned his walls. The hard, uncomfortable light that poured down from a chandelier mercilessly lit up his aged face with its flabby features on which neither lust

308

nor self-indulgence seemed to have left their mark; probably no real passion had ever put fire into those dull eyes or disturbed the serenity of that vacuous forehead. Even the tawdry emotions of venal love were almost as indifferent as they were necessary to him, and not once in his life, perhaps, had he ever desired anything violently, not once had to deny himself anything. The folds that underlined the sagging contour of his cheeks and all the furrows in that mask were not due to anxiety or endeavor, but seemed rather to be the effect of greed and old age. The warmth of the room made him drowsy and he dozed from time to time, as though he were resting after a day's work.

After some considerable time, Madame Grosgeorge folded her paper and stared at the burning logs. When the last one fell to pieces she and her husband would go up to their rooms. It was the signal for which they both waited; that was how their winter evenings came to an end. And while studying the flames she abandoned herself to a thousand reflections. In this room, at the same time ludicrous and sinister, in which everything proclaimed the narrowness of middle-class life, the fire was like a pure strong creature held in respect like a wild beast kept at bay in the depths of its lair with andirons, tongs, and pokers, all ridiculous instruments. Always ready to leap from its prison, to devour the carpet, the furniture, the hated house itself, it had to be watched incessantly and never left alone in the room; the burning fragments it sometimes flung upon the marble had to be driven back and its murderous sparks warded off. She felt that she was like this fire, furious and impotent in its grate, agonizing before things without beauty and cowardly vigilant people also without beauty, whom it could never reach.

Monsieur Grosgeorge came out of his doze abruptly.

"Eh? What?" he said. "Did you say anything?"

"No. You must have been dreaming," she replied in a cold voice in which there was a note of contempt. And she added, "I am going upstairs in a moment."

"Ah? So am I. I'm half asleep already. Give me the shovel and I'll cover up the logs."

He took the copper shovel which his wife silently handed to him and, scooping up the ashes with it, he spread them evenly over the flames to put them out.

"Now the fire-guard."

The metal screen was arranged before the hearth with the same care. Then Monsieur Grosgeorge stretched himself.

"By the way," he said, fumbling in one of the inside pockets of his coat, "I've just received something that may interest you."

"What is it about?"

"It's about your son. He's got a very bad school report, your son has. Listen to this."

He put his glasses on his nose and unfolded a sheet of paper from which he began to read aloud:

"Thiers Grammar-School. Report on André Grosgeorge."

Madame Grosgeorge could not repress a start of impatience on hearing that name.

"Tell me the worst, quickly," she said. "He has been sent away?"

"No, not sent away. But what marks! It's disastrous. Let's see. André Grosgeorge. Conduct, six out of ten. His conduct is average. Application, *nil*. Are you listening?"

"Yes, yes! I'm listening."

"French, one; history, two; geography, two; arithmetic . . . guess what marks he's got for arithmetic."

"How should I know? Zero, I suppose."

"No, worse than that. No marks at all. As there isn't any mark below zero, they haven't known how to translate the frightful incapacity of your son, and they've left it blank. Eh? What do you think of that?"

"I think you had a real brain-wave the day you put him in the hands of those idiots."

"Did you want me to let him stay here, doing nothing?"

"You should have found him a tutor and not sent him to Paris."

"A tutor! After all the troubles we have had over the other?"

"All tutors aren't like that. We were unfortunate, that's all. Besides, I don't want to start another argument on that subject.   Is that all you have to read to me?"

"There are still the vice-principal's remarks!"

"A lot I care for the vice-principal's remarks!"

"A fine mother you are!" said Monsieur Grosgeorge, putting the report in his pocketbook. "Anyone would think the child was not yours."

"Poor child!" she said with a short laugh. "I'm going up now.   Good night."

"Good night," he answered, getting up too.

She had gone a few steps toward the door when she suddenly stopped.

"Did you hear that?" she asked.

"Hear what?"

"Why, the gate bell!   Are you deaf?   There's some one at the gate."

"Some one at the gate?" he repeated.   "At this time of night?"

She crossed the room rapidly, going toward the window.   She drew the curtain, then, immediately changing her mind, came back to the center of the room.

"Why doesn't Marie go and see what it is?" she asked, impatiently.   "She must have heard it.   I wouldn't mind betting the idiot's afraid."

"Why are you so excited," returned her husband, "since I tell you no one rang?"

Without paying any heed to him, Madame Grosgeorge opened the door of the room and shouted across the hall:

"There's some one at the gate, Marie. Hurry up and see who it is."

She shut the door quickly and gave her husband a look of fury.

"Well?" he said.

"Well, my friend? Have you anything to say?"

"No, nothing. But you were looking at me."

She shrugged her shoulders and resumed her place near the fire.

"You don't suppose I was thinking of you, do you?" she asked. "I'm waiting to see who it is."

A sound of steps on the gravel announced that Marie was obeying her mistress's injunctions at last.

Almost immediately the bell rang again. Madame Grosgeorge rose briskly and went to the door.

"I heard it that time," said Monsieur Grosgeorge. "But how excited you are!"

"Go and see who it is. No, don't go," she added at once, in a different voice. "It isn't worth while."

"Are you afraid?"

"Afraid? Are you mad?"

"You don't suppose it's a burglar, do you?" he asked, suddenly seized with alarm.

"Are burglars in the habit of ringing at doors?"

Silence fell; then the sitting-room door opened.

"Madame," said the maid, a little out of breath, "it's a man who says he wants to speak to madame."

"A man? What man?" demanded Monsieur Grosgeorge.

"I don't know, monsieur. I couldn't see him."

"That's all right," said Madame Grosgeorge, taking the gate key from the maid. "I'll go. You can go up to bed, Marie."

"You don't want to go down there," said Monsieur Grosgeorge. "Have the man come in here. Anyway, what does he want?"

"I asked him to come in, but he refused," said Marie.

Without another word Madame Grosgeorge passed between the two of them and went out.

"Do be careful!" cried her husband, making as though to follow her.

But she was already down the front-door steps and halfway to the gate. For some moments her heart had been racing as though at the announcement of some great event, and she did not even feel the cold that attacked her everywhere, penetrating the thin material of her blouse. She knew who was waiting at the garden gate, and she hurried down to him with the desire to arrive as quickly as possible, but afraid at the same time lest the delicious moment through which she was living would be taken away from her too soon. Just as she could not prevent her heart from racing, so she could not prevent it from hoping. This woman who was so hard upon herself and upon others had a superstitious side to her character which impelled her to recognize in the commonplace sound of a copper bell something as mysterious as a summons of destiny. All her cynicism about life did not prevent her from expecting a surprise, if one can connect such con-

tradictory terms, a sudden fit of generosity on the
part of fate which would give her, without warning,
what she refused to beg for.

Now she was running along the muddy path as
though she were hurrying to meet a lover. The
night was dark, but the street lamps cast a sort of
aura all round the gate and she saw his silhouette
beyond the bars, with his wide, slightly bent shoulders and his bowed head. She stopped.

"Is that Madame Grosgeorge?" he asked.

"Yes," she answered. She tried to talk in a less
blunt voice than usual, but without success. The
name this man had just uttered irritated her too
much. "Why weren't you there yesterday evening?"

No answer. She moved a few steps nearer the
gate. She made out Guéret's face.

"I'll tell you why," she went on. "You were
afraid." And yielding suddenly to an impulse in
which there was as much joy as anger, she put out
her hand and placed it roughly on his shoulder,
through the bars. "I am going to open the gate,"
she said. She withdrew her hand at once. "You will
hide behind the bushes and I will come and fetch
you in three-quarters of an hour. Do you understand? Don't be alarmed. I want to help you. If
you need money, you shall have it."

Without a word he came through the gate which
she opened.

"Quick! Hide yourself!" she ordered.

She shut the gate again and, leaning over the

prickwood bushes behind which he had disappeared, she whispered:

"In three-quarters of an hour."

"Well?" asked Monsieur Grosgeorge.

She answered calmly:

"It was only a man begging."

"Begging at nine o'clock at night! I hope you sent him about his business."

"Of course."

They bade each other good night and went up to their rooms. Left alone, Madame Grosgeorge sat upon her bed and waited. She sat quite still, staring unseeingly before her, lost in profound meditation. It seemed to her as though the objects with which she was surrounded took on a new aspect, without her being able to say in what respect this aspect differed from the one they had borne before, and she had a feeling akin to that one experiences on returning home after a very long absence, when the objects one sees during the first hours of one's return take on an air at the same time secret and familiar. It was not unusual for her to feel herself a stranger to this world, but this evening the impression was so powerful and so vivid that she was almost afraid of it, as though an irresistible force were trying to remove her from the earth and from herself.

"What is the matter with me?" she asked herself. "Is this what it is like when one is going to die?"

The sound of footsteps and of closing doors advised her of the movements of her husband and of the servants. All this life going on beside her had so little in common with her own. What abysses separated one soul from another!

She kept quite still and waited until the house was perfectly quiet and all the lights were out, but she felt no impatience; on the contrary, she would have been quite content to prolong this strange hour through which she was living. A kind of torpor came over her. Not a sound came to her. Why didn't she move?

The noise of a clock striking half past nine roused her from the revery into which she was sinking deeper and deeper. She sighed like a woman waking from sleep and rose deliberately. Calmly and firmly she opened her door and shut it again, after blowing out the lamp, and she found herself on the staircase, down which she crept with the wariness and nimbleness of a cat. Then her hand removed the safety chain and turned the key in the front-door lock.

She was outside again, her face whipped by the wind. To avoid making a noise she walked across the big lawn that lay between her and the gate, and soon reached the bushes behind which Guéret was hidden. At her approach he stood up.

"Will you trust me?" she asked, as though she guessed the suspicions that occupied the man's mind.

"Why do you want to help me?"

"That doesn't concern you. Have you decided to come with me?"

"Where do you want to take me?"

"Into the house. You will spend the night there.

I will give you a suit, underclothes, and money. You will go away again tomorrow at half past twelve while everyone is at lunch. With what I give you you will be able to reach the frontier. Think it over."

"And suppose you mean to betray me?"

She walked to the gate and, putting the key in the lock, she opened it.

"Go away," she said.

He stood still without speaking, some yards from where she was.

"What are you waiting for?" she asked. "You had better go if you distrust me."

"I'll stay," he said, after a moment.

Without another word she reclosed the gate and walked straight past him; he followed her.

"As you go upstairs," she whispered to him as they crossed the lawn, "you must keep close to the wall so that the stairs don't creak. When we reach the first story I will take your hand; the landing is a very long one."

"Yes, I remember it."

"There's some furniture there against which you might stumble. If by any mischance that should happen, stay quite still."

They reached the front-door steps and mounted them in silence.

"Think again," she whispered on the threshold. "You can still go away at once if you want to."

They were so close to each other that their arms were touching, and she drew a little away. In spite

of the darkness she could make out the shape of his
shoulders, which towered above her, and of his head,
and she guessed that he was looking at her and that
he too was trying to see her features. A bitterly
cold wind whistled round them.

"I trust you," he said.

They went upstairs. In the silence of the night
she heard his breathing and the noise made by the
stairs, which, in spite of his precautions, groaned
beneath the weight of his huge body. Several times
she stopped, placing a warning hand on Guéret's
shoulder to make him stay still. A clock striking
made them both jump.

When she reached the first story she took him
firmly by the hand and led him step by step among
the sideboards, wooden chests, and armchairs with
which Monsieur Grosgeorge's fancy had encumbered
the landing. She was walking as though in a dream,
both resolute and terrified at the same time, but
filled with a joy which would have upheld her on the
edge of an abyss. Yet she did not dare ask herself
why her heart was so light. Time had at last taught
this obstinate woman that it is often sufficient to examine the cause of happiness to find out how fragile
it is. She knew the value of an illusion. This walk
in the dark appealed to her imagination, and all the
time she was feeling the furniture with her outstretched fingers, she was dreading the moment when
she would have to light the lamp and exchange words
which would come to dispel her intoxication.

In a few minutes they were in the little sitting-room where she had spent so many years of boredom and loneliness. She shut the door and murmured:

"You are above my husband's bedroom. Don't make a noise when you walk. If anyone should ever knock at the door you mustn't answer on any account." She added: "I'm going to light a lamp. Don't move from where you are."

He guessed that she was crossing the room, not by the sound of her footsteps, for she seemed not to tread upon the ground, but from the rustling of her skirt; this sound went from right to left and all around him, a little like the voice of a person looking for some one in the dark and whispering his name. He started when he heard the match strike.

She was a couple of yards from him, her hard, delicate profile bent over the lamp on which she was replacing the shade. In a moment her whole face was bathed in light except her forehead, whose weight seemed to be borne by her large black eyebrows, which were curved like arches. For a few seconds this woman on the very threshold of old age appeared beautiful; it was as though the remaining forces of her life all collected in her to light up her eyes and transfigure her features.

She hesitated for a moment and then suddenly turned to Guéret without looking at him.

"You will sleep there," she said, pointing to the Turkish sofa. "I will get you some bedclothes."

She hesitated again, then walked toward the door, adding, in a voice which seemed to come with difficulty, as though what she was saying went against the grain:

"You've probably had nothing to eat. I'll go and get you something."

This was only a pretext to go away. Without her being able to explain it, she found it impossible to remain in the presence of this man, now that a light was shining in the room.

She went quickly down to the kitchen and placed on a tray a decanter of wine, some bread, and some cold meat. Her hands were shaking; she noticed this and her agitation increased so much that several times she thought she was going to drop the tray on the stairs. On the first landing she had to sit on a wooden chest to recover her breath, which her emotion had cut short. The sound of her breathing terrified her, and the silence of the house seemed to be filled with it as with an immense roaring.

When she reëntered the little sitting-room, Guéret was sitting on the sofa, nodding with weariness, and she was struck by the miserable condition of his clothing. Mud from the highroad incrusted his boots and the lower edges of his trousers, and his overcoat, torn in several places, spoke of long, incessant use.

He rose at once and came toward her:

"Why are you so good to me, Madame Grosgeorge?"

She saw his burning eyes fixed on hers and was not strong enough to return his gaze.

"Don't call me Madame Grosgeorge," she said,

not without a certain roughness. "Take this tray. While you have something to eat, I will go and see about the bedclothes."

Feeling that all this energy was betraying her, she reached the door as best she could and went out; she was in a hurry to get back into the darkness so as to hide her crimson face, and she asked herself if Guéret had noticed her agitation. How could she go back and face that man's curiosity? What would he think?

She clung to the banisters with both hands as she went down to the first story where the linen was; her knees were sagging beneath her. She groped about until she reached the presses containing the sheets and blankets and opened them noiselessly; then she went upstairs again, her arms laden, stumbling at almost every step.

"There," she said, letting the bedclothes fall in the middle of the room.

Her eyes immediately traveled to the tray, but the bread and meat were untouched and the decanter full.

"You haven't eaten anything," she said, with a note of displeasure in her voice.

He shook his head.

"I can't; I'm too worried."

She wanted to say something to reassure him, but the words would not come; the habit of being as severe with herself as she was with other people prevented her from speaking with gentleness. She sighed. For the last few moments she had the strange impression of being lowered by what she did; not that she had done an evil action, but that in this good action, on the contrary, she did not recognize herself. Perhaps for the first time in her life she had an idea of the joy which a generous-minded person experiences in doing good. And sadness returned to her heart like the tide flowing back over the beach.

"I'm going to leave you now," she said. "Tomorrow morning I shall give orders that no one is to come in here until the afternoon. If ever anyone knocks, don't answer. Above all, don't make any noise. I shall come back here at about nine, when everyone has gone down, and then I'll bring you the money and the clothing I promised you."

He seemed to hesitate for a second, then he asked: "Don't you think it would be wiser for me to leave tonight?"

"What do you mean?"

"If you could give me this money you are good enough to promise me, now . . . "

"You don't trust me."

"It isn't that, madame, but in broad daylight I run the risk of being seen."

She could find no reply to this and felt her temper rising. This restored her, in some sort, to herself; this man was resisting her. How dared he?

"You don't trust me," she repeated at last.

"I shouldn't be here if I didn't trust you."

He was breathing heavily, like an animal that is afraid of having fallen into a trap whose mechanism it has not yet understood. His clasped hands gripped each other hard. Doubtless he should not have spoken to Madame Grosgeorge in that tone; she was looking at him in silence, her face in shadow, a sheet of light on the lower part of her skirt, and she was looking at him so sternly that he lowered his eyes and looked at the tip of her little black boot, like a weapon; and in spite of himself he imagined that foot kicking a dog or crushing in a bird's head.

"A short while ago you could have gone," she said, "when I opened the gate. Why did you stay?"

"Please forgive me, madame. I spoke without thinking. I place myself entirely in your hands."

The warmth of the room and his exhaustion obliged him to sit down. She studied him for a moment without speaking, and saw him bend his head and put his two hands over his face as though trying to hide himself.

"You are tired," she said; "you must go to bed." And she added, with an effort: "Don't be afraid of anything. I only wish you well. I swear it."

He raised his eyes to her, but she had already turned her back on him and was leaving the room.

Chapter Eleven

SHE was in her bedroom again, seated before a little writing-desk in which she had opened a drawer. Would three hundred francs be enough for him? That was all she had in ready money. She wished it were twice or three times as much; she would willingly have given five, ten thousand francs to this wretched man, but this wave of generosity on her part did not give her any illusions about herself. She knew quite well that if she had been really good she would immediately have given these three hundred-franc notes to the poor man whom fear was probably preventing from sleeping; she would have added to this sum a suit stolen from her husband, and a warm overcoat, and she would have opened the gate for him after speaking to him and shaking his hand to cheer him and make him feel that he was not alone in the world. Instead of this she was keeping him prisoner in her sitting-room and proposed that he should try to escape the next day in broad daylight, when one glance casually cast from a window would be enough for some one to see him crossing the garden. Why was she acting like this? Just for a whim she was making a human being risk his liberty, probably his life. A little while ago she could think of nothing to answer Guéret when he had asked her to let him go.

She did not want to let him go; she liked to think that she was mistress of this man's fate, and in a sort of way to play the part of destiny. If she wanted him to be free and happy, all she had to do was to go to his room with the money; if, on the other hand, the fancy took her to see him arrested, nothing was simpler than to run to the police station.

These thoughts that came into her mind disturbed her. She had never been given such power, and she was almost afraid of it, as though she dreaded the dreadful words which her lips could pronounce and the gesture her hand was free to make. She had often had the feeling that her happiness depended upon some one else, just as Guéret's happiness depended upon her during the ten or fifteen hours to come; and now she was certain that there was just as much weakness, cruelty, and hesitation in her own will as in that mysterious will that governed her life.

And yet could she, for one second, imagine that she would betray this man? It was not a question of betraying him, but of keeping him near her as long as possible. Tomorrow he would leave forever, she knew that, although she refused to think about it, and she did not want to consider what her life would be after that. Perhaps something unexpected would happen to change the course of her life and to rescue her from the appalling boredom of the long empty days.

Was it the night and the silence that put such

thoughts into her head? She placed the banknotes in an envelope, as though she thought by doing some commonplace act to restore her mind to its proper balance. Since she so ardently desired that Guéret should spend that night beneath the same roof as herself, why did she not go to his room?

This question made her laugh aloud and threw her into a rage. It seemed to her that it was not she who was questioning herself like this, but some other impertinent and malicious person. It was much better to keep to the line of conduct she had chosen and not to let herself slide any farther down the slope of her reflections. And to start with she was going to bed and to sleep.

She undressed slowly, blew out the lamp, and slipped beneath the bedclothes. Through the half-open window a cold wind entered the room and eddied around her. A shiver ran through her; her body had not had time to warm the bed, and her teeth were chattering. Would he be warm enough, up there? Why had she not thought of giving him an eiderdown? Perhaps he would have the sense to move the divan, which was pushed back between two windows. But the noise he would make moving it might wake her husband. Anyway, he would probably sleep with the windows shut. He had looked so worn out when he had let himself fall on the divan! Would he even think of undressing himself?

She turned over, seeking on her left side the sleep that was denied her upon the right, for she wanted to sleep, but the darkness was peopled with pictures which she could not get rid of. In spite of herself, something compelled her to live over again every minute of the hour that had just passed, just as an actor at rehearsals is made to repeat a scene in which he has acted badly. Indeed, she slightly modified the actions which she was performing again in her mind, and the thing she would have liked to do replaced the memory of what she actually had done. For instance, she brought Guéret an eiderdown and helped him to move the divan.

After struggling with herself for some time she finally abandoned herself to this game her brain suggested to her. Now she was smiling at the man and speaking gently to him. What wave of tenderness made him take her hand? He was bowed in an attitude full of submission and gratitude, and she, overjoyed at doing a good action, was calling his attention to a tray charged with delicious dishes. But all he took was a glass of wine which he drank at a draught.

In the wine which she had seen him drink with such eagerness she had been careful to empty a powder which would send him to sleep at once. Send Guéret to sleep? What would she gain by making him sleep? She sat up in bed; her bedclothes made her too hot; her hands and feet were quite damp. She must get up, light the lamp, and shut the window, since she could not sleep and yet could not prevent herself from dreaming.

After a short hesitation she threw off the bedclothes and ran to shut the window. The cold caught

her legs and her chest and she shivered. Her hands
shook and she had some trouble in finding the
matches and striking a light. When at last the lamp
was burning again and she saw in the room around
her the familiar furniture, the windows, the curtains, all the things that spoke to her of her life and
recalled her to herself, she was seized with shame at
the memory of the thoughts that had come to her,
and she flushed.

Ten o'clock struck. She had a long night before
her, like a road that had to be followed laboriously
in order to reach the dawn. When, during the first
moments of the day, the sky paled behind the trees
in the garden and a little of its light slipped in
through the slits in the shutters, she would feel
calmer and braver, it seemed to her. What she found
hard to bear was the inaction to which night condemned her. During the day she could wander
about the surrounding country, and even in the house
a thousand little things occurred to distract her—
orders to be given to the servants, and their work to
be supervised. She remembered that next morning
the laundry would send her washing back; there
would be the bill to pay. With what money would
she pay it if she gave her three-hundred-franc banknotes to Guéret. If she asked Monsieur Grosgeorge
for it he would want an explanation. Bah! She
would tell little Fernande that she would pay the bill
next week.

Nor had she forgotten, and this brought it all
back to her, that she had promised Angèle to give

Fernande a message for her. What a lot of bothers all at once! This girl wanted money, too, but between Angèle and Guéret there was no question of Madame Grosgeorge hesitating for a second.

Now that she was alone with herself and was searching her own heart, that strange heart which life had balked of all happiness, she understood what it was that she so disliked about Angèle. She had felt a secret joy when she had seen, by the light of the gas, her wretched face and the scars on that tortured flesh. Fate was avenging her at last, and Angèle's beauty could no longer harm her.

She rose from her bed, upon which she had been sitting, and crossed the room. She must really have been out of her mind to have imagined such things! As soon as she stopped moving for an instant her imagination got to work again. She took a few more steps, hesitatingly, anxiously, as though she feared that something disagreeable were about to happen, and then suddenly she clasped her hands to her bosom. By some dim labyrinth she had been led to see the truth—what she imagined to be the truth; she loathed Angèle as a woman loathes her rival; she was preventing Guéret from going away because she had fastened upon him as her prey, and she would have liked to put him to sleep, to pour that narcotic into his wine, to do all the things which she had seen vaguely a little while ago in her dreams. For months she had refused to understand what was taking place in her mind, because she was afraid, as she had always been afraid of life; if she had not been afraid she would not have been so harsh toward other people, but her natural distrust had made her see enemies in everyone that came near her and even in herself. Although she was nearly fifty, she still thought that passions could be got rid of by refusing to think about them, in the same way that a judge has a criminal flung into gaol and then goes and dines. And now she was floundering in this horrible morass! She was imprisoning in her house a man whom she would have to release in a few hours' time. How would she live afterward?

The bluntness of this question she asked herself made her a little calmer. Her life would not change; no doubt the days would be the same as the days had always been: the hours of meals would be the same, everything would go on in the same way, which would thenceforth be inevitable. And she would suffer as she had suffered before, possibly more. Perhaps, on the contrary, old age would bring her peace. But it was not a question of that; it was a question of what she was going to do immediately. The hour she was living now was not like the others; it was an exceptional hour which stood out among years of boredom and it had to be realized and taken advantage of. At this moment she was the object of an act of grace on the part of her destiny, which was offering her something, and she was unable to accept it. What did she hope to gain by forcing Guéret to pass the night in the villa? She had stopped halfway through a scheme which she did not admit to herself, and she had no doubt counted upon something extraordinary happening, just as if the fact of being able to hide a man in her sitting-room were not more extraordinary than anything else that could happen.

The idea came to her of going to this man, giving him his money, and sending him away, as she had been tempted to do at the very beginning. His presence in the house made her too unhappy. He himself had asked to go. She would take him back to the gate, she would bid him farewell, and in her despair she would at least have the consolation of thinking that he owed her the means of leaving the country.

She could not do it; this woman was a mass of timidity and weakness beneath a veneer of self-possession and strength of mind, and she suddenly felt weary, weary of life and of this perpetual struggle in her heart. A quarter past ten struck. He must be sleeping soundly now. How could she go and wake him up and tell him to go away? She ought to have told him that before; then was the time to speak and act. It was too late now; the moment had passed.

She opened the window again, blew out the lamp, and got back into bed. If she could not sleep, she could at least remain still with her eyes closed and perhaps sleep would come then, deceived by her attitude. In this way she tried to kill the hours whose coming she had longed for so desperately. A terrible load weighed upon her chest and prevented her from breathing, and she felt as though she had reached the point at which she could not bear to suffer any more and was going to die. The darkness was full of mutterings. She had an illusion that the ground-floor clock kept striking without stopping. The blood was racing through her veins and the icy blast whipped her face without cooling it. She had to get up again and shut the window. And dawn found her asleep at last in her bed, near the lamp which, this time, she had not had the courage to put out.

Chapter Twelve

WRAPPED in her quilted dressing-gown, she sat up in bed and watched the housemaid light the fire. Little flames were beginning to lick the logs and there was a faint smell of wood smoke in the air.

"What is it like outside?" asked Madame Grosgeorge.

"It's colder than yesterday, madame."

"Has the fire been lit in the dining-room?"

"Yes, madame, half an hour ago."

"Very well, I'll go down there in a minute. While I am gone, you will do this room."

"Won't madame breakfast in bed?"

"No. Go and tell Marie to bring it into the dining-room." She got up and crossed the room. "By the way," she said, as she passed into her dressing-room, "don't do my sitting-room this morning."

"Madame?"

The maid had turned toward her mistress in surprise.

"What's the matter? Don't you understand? And when you've done my room you can go out; you can have the morning off. You can do the other rooms this afternoon."

She shut herself in her dressing-room and sat down

before the dressing-table. Two long strands of gray hair framed her temples; as a rule she hid them in her masses of black hair as soon as she awoke, so as not to see them when she looked in the mirror, but this morning she found a bitter satisfaction in seeing them there; they made her look at least five or six years older, and yet it seemed to her that these strands which aged her so much lent an unusual softness to her face. She sighed and reflected that this softness was no doubt the effect of the discouragement which she saw in the depths of her eyes. Until her death she would have to wake in the morning and take life up where she had left it the night before; she would not be given a single day's grace. Night and the strange dreams which it sometimes brought merely accentuated the monotony of her waking hours. Five minutes earlier she had still been sleeping, wrapped in dreams which she could no longer remember, and she had the impression of returning from a far-away country, in which sorrow was unknown, to a hostile one whose paths were rugged and sorrowful.

She combed her hair, bathed her face with rosewater, and went down to the dining-room. Although it was nearly eight o'clock, her husband, whom she heard moving about on the first floor, was not yet down. She blessed this circumstance. In her present state of mind a conversation with Monsieur Grosgeorge was inconceivable. She was exhausted by suffering in the way that fever exhausts a sick person. She had only just enough strength left to carry through the plan she had formed; and she was frightened lest people or things should add difficulties to the task which she felt was already too heavy for her.

After drinking her coffee she went back to her room, which had been tidied, and dressed quickly. A full quarter of an hour passed before she heard Monsieur Grosgeorge go down in his turn with that calm heavy step which, it seemed to her at that moment, she detested more than anything else in the world. Her heart was beating violently; she dreaded the moment when she would have to act, and she knew it to be close at hand. She carefully made sure that the maid was in the kitchen and then made her way toward her sitting-room.

When she reached the door she knocked, forgetting that she had instructed Guéret on no account to answer a call of this kind, but she immediately put the key in the lock and opened the door.

At first she could distinguish nothing, taken by surprise by the gloom, then she suddenly saw Guéret standing in the middle of the room.

"I am going to open the shutters," she said in a low voice. "Don't go near the window. You might be seen from the garden."

She spoke rapidly, as though to hide the agitation that was mastering her, and crossed the room to open the shutters. Guéret had taken a few steps toward the door and was looking at Madame Grosgeorge in silence.

"I've given orders that no one is to come in here

this morning," she added, turning toward him. "You really have nothing at all to fear."

She herself was shaking with emotion and had to sit down; all the blood had left her cheeks and she dropped her eyes, unable to bear the look this man fixed upon her.

"Sit down," she said. . . . "No, not near the window. There." And she pointed to an armchair not far from where she herself was sitting. He crossed the room with the hesitating step of a blind man, then, standing before her, he suddenly asked her:

"Can you swear that you are in the same mood as last night, madame?"

The hoarseness of his voice made her start, but she mastered her agitation and said, without moving:

"You are still afraid. If I had wanted to have you arrested I should have sent for the police last night."

She heard him gasp, and out of the corner of her eye she saw him put his hands to his chest like some one who finds it difficult to breathe. She remained still, fully occupied by the effort not to betray her agitation. In a moment, when she felt calmer, she would get up and leave this man until the time came for him to go.

"Forgive me," he said at last. "You don't know what a night I spent."

"Why? Didn't you sleep?"

"I woke a little before eleven and I couldn't get to sleep again. I was wakened by the sound of steps."

"You must have been dreaming."

"For a long time I thought there really was some one on the landing, and even two, three people coming upstairs. And it seemed to me that people were knocking at the door every minute, all through the night."

"How childish! You ought to have reasoned with yourself and forced yourself to sleep."

"I was in a fever."

She remembered how she herself had spent the night and the memory of her own sufferings moved her to pity for those of this man. Something prevented her from leaving him as she had intended. He went on:

"When one always lives alone and in hiding, as I have done for months, one becomes subject to all sorts of fears. Thus I could have sworn that men were walking up and down outside my window, in the garden. I asked myself whether, by any chance, one of the servants had not heard me come in last night and whether the house wasn't surrounded."

She interrupted him, in a voice which had regained its firmness. It seemed to her that this man's weakness avenged her, in some way, for her own lack of courage and her tears the night before.

"Aren't you ashamed of telling me all this?" she asked him. "What are you driving at? I certainly can't prevent you from trembling if you are afraid."

"I want to go away, madame. I have been afraid; yes, I am still afraid. But I want to go. Even if you don't want to give me that money . . . "

Her only answer was to take from her belt the envelope she had prepared. The state of anxiety in which she saw Guéret brought him down in her estimation and she congratulated herself for not having betrayed anything of the feelings she had toward him.

"Here you are," she said, holding the money out to him. And she added to herself, "Coward!"

He looked at her without taking the envelope and asked her in a steadier voice:

"Why are you doing this?"

"That is my business. Come, take this money."

He obeyed, and put the envelope in his pocket; then, as though regretfully, he lowered the inquiring gaze he had been fixing on her and muttered, "Thank you."

"It's no use thinking of going yet," she said, sitting down again. "You must wait until half-past twelve."

"Very well, madame."

"I will leave you as soon as my husband goes out, for if by any chance he took it into his head to come here . . . "

"What would you do?"

"Don't be alarmed. I shouldn't open the door, but at least I should be here to answer him. By the way, if anyone ever knocks while you are alone in this room, you mustn't answer, on any account."

"Very well, madame."

She rose, and passing in front of him without looking at him, placed herself at the window.

"Why doesn't he go out?" she muttered. "The weather's fine enough."

Her impatience to get it all over made her crumple with her fingers the velvet curtain near which she was standing. She guessed that Guéret was following her with his eyes and was not missing one of her actions. For years to come she would remember each of these minutes—the dead garden, the frozen mud on the paths, the warmth of the room, and the labored breathing of the man who was afraid.

"What did you do in Paris?" she asked him, without moving. "What did you live on?"

"I had a little money with me the day I ran away."

She wanted to ask where the money came from, but in a sudden fit of modesty she was silent. Her vanity counseled her to feign indifference and to keep to herself all the questions she was burning to put to this man, but the fear of seeing an hour pass, such as life would never offer her again, clutched at her heart. Did it show strength of character or merely stupidity to stay like this, without moving, by the window? Anyway, what did she care whether she was strong or weak? She was suffering. If she had left the room a few minutes earlier she would have avoided the awful temptation of talking to Guéret. At present what she wanted most was to see him go. At half-past twelve it would all be over; she would find peace again in despair, but so long as he was there she could not breathe. A little while ago she had despised him and had exulted over the cowardice

she had discovered in him, because she thought that
this cowardice widened the distance between them;
but now she no longer knew how she stood. To remain in the same room with Guéret seemed intolerable to her, but, on the other hand, she was sure that
she would not leave it unless she were compelled to
do so. The reason she had given Guéret for staying
was nothing but a lame excuse; actually, her husband had just passed through the garden to go out,
and she had said nothing about it; she even hoped
that Guéret would not hear the gate open and shut
behind Monsieur Grosgeorge, and if he did hear it,
she decided to tell him that it was not her husband,
but one of the servants.

"You had a little money," she repeated to distract
his attention from the footsteps on the gravel.

She turned toward him and, thinking she was asking him a question, he bent his head.

"A little more than a hundred francs," he said.
"When that had gone I sold my watch and a ring."

"You were never tempted to steal?" she asked him,
abruptly.

"No."

Monsieur Grosgeorge, having reached the end of
the garden, opened the gate and went out.

"You killed a man. Why shouldn't you have
stolen, too?"

She said this with a violence that she could not
control, and crossed the room to where Guéret stood.
He certainly had not heard the gate, and thought

that Monsieur Grosgeorge was still in the villa, so she could remain there.

"Answer me," she said, embarrassed by his look of confusion.

He shook his head.

"I haven't stolen," he answered. "I swear to you I have never stolen."

"What do I care?" she thought to herself in dismay. "He is going away." And, passing abruptly from one attitude to another, she looked him straight in the face and forced him to drop his eyes.

"Why did you do what you did?" she asked. "Why did you kill that man?"

Again she thought: "What do I care if he killed him? That isn't what I want to know." She heard her own stern and steady voice and was surprised at the calmness with which she spoke, while a feeling of giddiness compelled her to grip the corner of the table.

"I didn't kill that man," he stammered, his face ashen.

"That girl, then," she went on. "You aren't going to tell me that you didn't nearly kill her?"

She saw him wince as though she had struck him, but he made no reply. She had never before noticed the lines beneath his eyes and at their corners, and the strange tawny color of his eyes themselves. It seemed to her as though she had never looked at his features until that moment, and she asked herself how she had the strength to stand there in front of him, asking him questions.

"Why do you put all these questions to me?" he asked her at last with a sigh.

She repeated to herself: "Yes, why do I?" but went on, nevertheless:

"That girl Angèle . . . you made her suffer, didn't you? By the river. I heard about it." In that snug little room she had the impression that the silence was trying to stifle the sound of her words, for her voice was dead, almost indistinct. Guéret's look told her that he guessed her uneasiness, and shame sent the color to her face; she could have screamed.

"Yes," she went on, "I heard about it; it was in all the papers. What had you against her, that you ill-treated her like that? You might have killed her. Why did you hate her?"

He shook his head.

"I didn't hate her."

She felt a sudden rage come over her and struck the back of the armchair with her hand.

"You didn't hate her? Why do you lie to me? Why are you afraid of me? I'm not a magistrate. Tell me the truth!"

"I've told you the truth. I was angry with her, but I didn't hate her; quite the contrary. I would have liked . . . "

He stopped suddenly and pressed his hand against his chest. She drew back a little and put up her hand as though to prevent him from speaking. She was suddenly afraid of what he was going to say and

regretted her questions, but she had goaded him too
far.

"Unless one can hate a person one worships," he
resumed.

She interrupted him at once:

"It isn't possible," she faltered. "It's either one
thing or the other."

"I was jealous. I knew that everyone gave her
money," he went on, raising his voice, for during the
last few moments he seemed to have cast aside all
caution. "I had none, and she scoffed at me. One
day I took some money my wife had saved and I told
myself that I would give it to Angèle; and then I
saw Angèle that morning and I thought I should go
mad. And I struck her and struck her . . . "

"Yes. That's enough. I didn't ask you . . . "

She had clasped her hands and stood quite still.

"No one will ever know how much I suffered because of that woman," he said. "I kept away from
her as long as I could. At the end of two months
I had to come back here."

At first she did not understand, then the meaning
of his last sentence slowly dawned upon her and she
thought it impossible that she could have heard
rightly. Her ice-cold hands gripped each other
harder, as though she sought support in their clasp.

"You came back here because of her?"

"Yes. I told you . . . "

Something seemed to choke her.

"I thought it was to ask me to help you," she
said with an effort.

She immediately regretted this remark, which seemed ridiculous to her, but if she had not spoken she would have burst into tears. He saw her confusion.

"I never dared to rely upon your generosity so much," he said in a changed voice that was almost servile.

She put up her hand again to warn him not to add anything, and walked toward the door with the stiff slow step of an automaton. She kept her eyes before her as she passed him and he felt an impulse to throw himself at her feet to implore her to let him go, but he was afraid of arousing her anger by showing her that he distrusted her. A sudden awful suspicion came to him: this woman was betraying him.

"Madame . . . "

She reached the door and, turning toward him, looked straight at him; in her ashen face her eyes seemed to be dead, and he had the impression that she was blind.

"I ought to tell you," she said in a strangled voice, "I've seen Angèle. She hates you."

He started.

"She hates you," she repeated with a sort of outburst. "She is afraid of you. Yes, you terrify her, appall her !"

"It isn't true," he muttered. "I know . . . "

She shook her head convulsively in a gesture of negation and left the room. He heard the key turn in the lock.

Chapter Thirteen

SHE crossed the landing as though she were walking in her sleep, and sat down on a wooden chest occupying the space between two doors. A deep silence reigned throughout the house. The cook was probably at market and she remembered that she had let the housemaid go out. Through the glass skylight which lit the staircase a familiar light poured down, as familiar as all this furniture and all those stairs in the winter morning, the shadow thrown by the chairs on the walls and the reflection from the copper curtain rods on the red carpet. And in the painful revery in which she was plunged, it seemed to her as though all these things around her formed a world which she had been on the point of leaving and which now dragged her back. A little while ago, in that man's presence, everything had seemed changed; her sitting-room was altered in an inexplicable manner, and for the past half-hour she had the feeling that she was not in her own home, in spite of being surrounded by the furniture which she had seen every day for thirty years. This feeling was a familiar one to her. At certain moments of great stress or merely of great boredom, the idea that she was a stranger to this world came to her with such force that for the space of some minutes terrestrial

346

matters abruptly lost all importance for her. She had felt that for an instant as she stood by the window, and then Guéret's words had brought her back to herself. Now she was back once more in the stream of life.

"How can one suffer so much without dying?" she thought. She could not think of Guéret without a mortal shame sending the blood rushing to her face, for she was certain she had made herself ridiculous in this man's eyes, and that was what hurt her most. What fit of insanity on her part had made her think that he had come back to ask her help? Passion alone could have induced him to launch himself upon such a perilous venture as this journey to Lorges, but this passion was not for her. She had no part in the overpowering love that drew this man to a woman; she did not count in this tale of a middle-aged woman who was mixing herself up in what did not concern her. And he? What did he think? She suddenly hated him for the thoughts he might be harboring. What if he were going to imagine that she was in love with him? And yet was it not the truth? She hid her face in her hands. Certain phrases and certain words which she spoke to herself and which expressed her love seemed to her to be intolerably ridiculous, as soon as she admitted the existence of that love which was rending her bowels. She dreaded the precise terms which would have to be used to describe the state of her mind, and preferred, without particularizing, to relegate her passion into the chaos of unadmitted things. But at

present it was no longer possible for her to escape
from the realities of her life; at the very moment
when she was seated on this wooden chest, on this
landing, her destiny was being fulfilled, and she
knew it; and she kept repeating to herself with an
appalling fear lest behind the door of her sitting-
room Guéret would guess her thoughts: "I am in
love with that man, and he loves another woman."

She dared not look at the door she had just shut.
Provided always that he did not suspect anything,
what a blessing it was that she had not brought him
into her room the night before, as she had thought
for a moment of doing! Rather than survive the
atrocious humiliation of a rebuff, she would have
blown her brains out; and the thought of her own
death brought the tears which her recent violent
emotion had been unable to bring. Then suddenly
she heard her name called by a childish voice, and
mopping her eyes she rose and went downstairs. Fernande was waiting for her on the ground floor, a
large washing-basket at her feet. Madame Grosgeorge had forgotten she was coming. Was it possible that in moments of grief as great as this there
were such things as washing-lists to check? It was
so like life to compel us, disdainful of our wounds,
to examine shirts and handkerchiefs while our hearts
bled. She thought of asking the housemaid to count
the washing, but remembered she had given her a
holiday. After all, it would keep her from thinking
if she attended to the washing, and this abominable
morning would be shortened by a few minutes.

"Good morning, madame."

"Good morning, child. Bring your basket near the table. Have you got the book?"

How innocent she looked standing there with her legs reddened by the cold, her chapped hands, and a wretched black shawl whose ends were pinned over her chest!

"Here it is, madame."

"Presently you can go into the kitchen and ask for a cup of hot coffee. You must be cold with your legs bare like that. And what is that shawl you are wearing? Your mother ought to buy you a jumper and some woolen gloves."

Why did she feel this sudden need of tenderness? She had seen this little girl a dozen times without ever bothering about her clothes, and now she felt a vague desire to kiss her red cheeks and to warm her hands in her own. Her knees felt weak and she had to sit down.

"I shan't count the washing today, Fernande. You can tell Madame Brod that if there's anything missing we will mark it in the book next week. Ask the cook for the washing to go back."

"Very well, madame. There is a letter for you in the book."

"A letter! From whom?"

She found the letter among the pages of the book and read:

"*I implore madame to remember that she promised to help me. If madame will be kind enough to tell me what she will do for me, I will be grateful to her for the rest of my life. Madame has only to send a line by Fernande.—Angèle.*"

Angèle! Madame Grosgeorge let the note fall to the ground and mentally repeated this name she hated. What hidden intention lurks behind the coincidences of life? When she came to think of it, it was not surprising that she should have received this note, but, in Madame Grosgeorge's present state of mind Angèle's name seemed to come on purpose to revive her grief. She did nothing for a moment; then she tore out a blank sheet and seized the pencil attached to the washing-book.

"Give this to Angèle," she said in a hard, choking voice.

Yet she did not write. She was gazing at the little girl.

"That's her shawl you are wearing," she said, suddenly. "I recognize it."

"Yes, madame, Angèle lent it to me."

"I wonder if he suspects that she is disfigured," she thought. "I'll go and tell him."

She swept the idea from her with a violent movement with her hand. No, she would not go and tell him. She was not going to fight over this man with a street-walker. Whatever she may have thought when she was alone, now that another human being stood there looking at her, she felt all her pride come back, and all her contempt for the world, for it seemed to her that through the eyes of this child the world was looking at her and judging her conduct. At present she was ashamed of herself. What right had she to disdain humanity? Was she not as weak as other people? Anyone who had seen her the night before, and had pried into her heart while she was dreaming of narcotics and a hundred impossible things, would probably not have recognized the cold, arrogant creature she was now. And for all her pride, it was she who had been scorned, not that girl of whom she was so contemptuous.

"What is the matter, madame? Don't you feel well?"

But Madame Grosgeorge waved the child aside as she came toward her. The blood left her face and hands and the dull beatings of her heart seemed to fill her chest. If a vital organ could have broken inside her, death would have been very acceptable to her at that moment, but life persisted in that body which was being gradually destroyed by the misery of her soul. God alone knows how much is needed to kill a human being.

"Tell . . . Angèle . . . "

Rage seized her at the thought of the dreadful blows fate had dealt her. Other women were happy, but she would never be happy; if it were true that a human being is put into the world to enjoy life, then she might just as well not have been born. Her mind suddenly became filled with an insane spite against everybody, and for the space of several seconds she was obsessed with a desire to hit this child whose face almost touched her hands. It would avenge her to hurt some one in her turn and to create suffering, for the load she was bearing was too heavy for her. Her life was a failure, once for all, and it would be better for her to give it up. Every feeling of this self-tortured woman was vitiated from its origin, and even love assumed the guise of hatred. She hated the man whom chance had delivered into her hands as much as she hated the woman he coveted. She could no longer resist the temptation of placing the fate of the one into the hands of the other, and with the same feeling with which she would have committed suicide, she scrawled on the blank sheet the following words:

"Guéret is hiding here. Go and inform the police."

"Leave your basket here," she said to the little girl, between her teeth, "and take this note to Angèle. Run quickly. It's very important."

Chapter Fourteen

Madame Londe had been sitting by the stove in the dining-room for over an hour, knitting a black woolen shawl and talking to herself all the time, but it would have required a very keen ear to catch what she said, for her lips merely emitted a confused jumble of words. In order, probably, to avoid being seen by curious passers-by, she had placed her wicker armchair between the stove and her desk, and this desire to shun the gaze of the outside world was explained by the fact that she was wearing her spectacles; for, in this old woman on the brink of the grave, certain little vanities persisted whose futility had something sinister about them; if vanity obeys the desire to please, whom could Madame Londe, with all the disabilities of her fifty-seven years, hope to please? Dressed in black, enormous, her back hunched up, she might have been talking to the fire whose murmur answered her own; from time to time her head nodded in that gesture of negation with which old people seemed to answer "No!" to the beckoning of the tomb. Then her hands rested gently on her knees and the shawl slid to the ground; but the sound of the bone knitting-needles rattling on the tiles roused her from her brief doze and she looked round her in bewilderment, settled her spectacles more firmly on her large dejected nose, and bent down with a groan, groping with one hand until she retrieved her shawl.

Suddenly the restaurant door opened and Fernande ran across the long room. She had not seen Madame Londe, and was going straight on when the proprietress stopped her by saying:

"Where are you going, dear?"

The child gave a little scream of fright.

"I didn't know you were there, Madame Londe."

"In the first place, call me 'auntie.' In the second, you seem in a great hurry and I ask you where you are going? Will you answer? Why have you come back so early? Where is your basket?"

"I left it at Madame Grosgeorge's."

"You left your basket at Madame Grosgeorge's? Are you mad, eh? Come, what's the matter? Come here and talk to me."

She caught her by the hand and made her come.

"Let me go, Madame Londe!"

"Madame Londe is going to box your ears if you don't call her 'auntie.' Now, don't cry. There's something up. What is it, eh?"

She was now holding the child between her knees and gripped her elbows firmly.

"Why do you come running back here after leaving your basket at Madame Grosgeorge's?"

"Madame Grosgeorge gave me a message for Angèle."

"Ah! What message?"

"I don't know."

"Do you want your ears boxed?"

"It's written on a piece of paper."

"Then give me the piece of paper."

"Madame Grosgeorge won't be pleased. She said it was for Angèle."

"I'll be responsible for that. Where is it?"

The child took the piece of paper from under her black pinafore and gave it to Madame Londe.

"Go and sit over there," she told Fernande, letting her go. She pointed to a chair some distance from the desk.

When the child had thus been got rid of, Madame Londe put her spectacles on again and puckered her forehead over the unfolded piece of paper, for Madame Grosgeorge's writing was bad and resembled the record of a seismograph. After a few moments she made out the first words and uttered an exclamation.

"It's impossible," she remarked, shifting in her chair.

A new lease of life made the blood race through her veins. The man who was the cause of so much trouble, who terrorized the town and brought ruin on her restaurant, had been delivered into her hands by the justice of Heaven.

She did not even think of reading the last part of the note which she held gripped in the palm of her hand, and for several seconds her emotion prevented her from doing anything. One thought alone filled

her—to make haste. And yet she did not move.
Something riveted her to her armchair, while within
her all her aged strength was gathering together for
the bound that would launch her into the street. She
waited, her lips parted, then suddenly a shout burst
from them:

"Fernande! My hat!"

No reply.

"Where is she? Heavens! Never mind, I'll go
without a hat, without . . . "

And as though suddenly cast loose she hoisted herself on to her legs by a prodigious muscular effort
and cast her eyes around her, as she stood up, like
a person seized with a fit of giddiness. Under the
influence of joy and surprise her eyesight seemed to
give out altogether. She sighed deeply.

"Never mind!" she repeated.

She was, no doubt, looking for some garment with
which to cover her shoulders, for the cold was intense,
and this "Never mind!" which she had solemnly uttered possessed the heroic quality of certain words
uttered by soldiers before battle. She might have
gone upstairs to her room to get a cloak or a wrap,
but she preferred to sacrifice her comfort, even to
risk pneumonia in the street, so as to be able to do
her dreadful duty more quickly.

As she pushed back her armchair and moved
toward the door, she disturbed a rat which the cold
had driven out of its native cellar and which was
trying to get a little rest and warmth almost beneath

the petticoats of the old woman, who was quite oblivious of its presence.

In the meantime Fernande had gone up to Angèle's room. In spite of the lateness of the hour, the young woman was still in bed, lying with her face toward the wall and the bedclothes over her ears; she was dozing when the child pushed the door open.

"Angèle!" called Fernande in a low voice. "Get up!"

"Is that Fernande? Why are you back so soon?"

"I've got something very important to tell you. You must get up and dress at once."

"But I can't. I haven't slept a wink all night. I'm feeling ill. What's the matter?"

"Madame Grosgeorge gave me a message for you; she gave me a note; but Madame Londe took it away from me a moment ago."

"What was in the note? Tell me."

"I read it on the way here. Madame Grosgeorge had written: *Guéret is hiding here. Go and inform the police.*"

Angèle sat up in bed and cried:

"Madame Londe saw the note? What did she say?"

"As I was coming upstairs I heard her calling me; she wanted her hat."

"To go to the police station! You must stop her, Fernande! Run after her, call her! O God!"

"She's gone. I've just heard the door shut. You must get up and run to Madame Grosgeorge's."

"I shall never have time to dress. The police station is only a few yards away. Run to the villa and ask to see Guéret."

"Madame Grosgeorge wouldn't let me."

"What room is he in?"

"I don't know."

"Call him from the garden. Tell him to escape. Run quickly, Fernande!"

Chapter Fifteen

WHEN Guéret found himself shut into Madame Grosgeorge's bedroom, his first thought was to find some means of escaping from that prison, because for the last few moments he had been certain that he was being betrayed and that before an hour, or even a quarter of an hour, perhaps, had elapsed, the police would enter the villa and arrest him. The thing that he dreaded more than death was about to occur; he would be put into handcuffs, he would be taken to the police station, and from there, after a few days, to the county gaol. He had played and lost; he had risked all and lost all, first his liberty and then Angèle. The ledger account of his happiness on this earth was closed; all that remained to him was a few stifling years in a narrow cell, or the agony of a convict's life.

At the risk of being seen he opened the window and looked out. He was more than twenty-five feet from the ground. To scramble down the wall was impossible, as the stonework offered no hold at all; to jump was suicide.

The door, whose handle he turned until its shank twisted, withstood every effort of his powerful hands. He then endeavored to unscrew the lock with his pen-knife, but both blades broke before he had moved one of the four screws. This setback increased his anxiety, and, obsessed with the idea that he must at all costs unscrew the lock to open the door, he searched all through the room for some object with which to accomplish this design. A little pair of scissors which he found in the drawer of a writing-desk soon snapped in his clumsy fingers. Time, skill, and calm would have been necessary to move the little steel heads that he was merely vainly irritating.

Abruptly he abandoned his project and ran back to the window, which he opened again. As he leaned out, the icy wind dried the sweat on his forehead and revived his energy. Perhaps by gripping the window-sill with his hands and letting his body hang down the wall he would diminish the distance between himself and the ground so much that he would be able to drop; he was tall. With his arms raised he was well over seven feet; but how could he let himself drop nearly twenty feet? He would have to let himself fall back, and the fall would break his back. Had he not been afraid of death he would have accepted the chance of safety that was offered to him, but at that moment fear had the upper hand.

He drew back from the window without closing it, as though there were something reassuring in the contact of the air coming freely into the room. Outside, quite close to him, the trees were waving at the will of the wind, and the far-off sound of traffic on the road came to the prisoner's ears. People were going where they wanted to, in absolute indifference. His anguish interested no one. For several seconds he felt crushed by the feeling of complete solitude. An intense longing seized him to be in a crowd of people and to mix with the humanity which he was compelled to shun.

Standing in the center of the room, he looked carefully round him. The door was locked, and the window opened only on death. Nothing remained but the chimney. He had read stories of escapes in which men got away by reaching the roof through the chimney, but what might be possible in towns where the houses touched one another seemed impracticable in the present circumstances; he would not be much better off walking about at a height of forty feet from the ground, when he was afraid of twenty-five. Twenty-five feet. Why, acrobats hurled themselves farther than that through space.

He sat down and reflected. Perhaps the most precious moments of his life were speeding by, and he did nothing but sit there biting his nails while a woman plotted to have him arrested. A little while ago he had seen a servant go out. Where was she going? It was not the cook, whom he knew by sight, as he did everyone else in that house; it must have been the housemaid, who had spoken to him at the garden gate the evening before. A dozen details suddenly recurred to his mind. In the darkness the woman could not have recognized his face, but how had he known who it was? By her voice. Who would say whether she hadn't recognized him by his? He clasped his hands together in anguish; they were bitterly cold. At that moment the garden gate opened and shut, but he did not hear it; the mere fact of dwelling upon the danger that threatened him seemed to estrange him from the outer world. All the dreaminess and irresolution of his character outweighed, at that moment, the need of action which usually accompanies great terror; but terror gripped him again almost immediately, the terror of being shut up forever in a real prison, with no open window and a door that could not be broken down.

He ran to the door again and seized the handle roughly between his hands as though to tear out the whole lock with one mighty pull. It seemed to him impossible that this little combination of iron was enough to keep a man of his strength captive, and, in his rage, after struggling for some minutes, he hurled his shoulder against the panel.

The strain made him gasp and he stopped, bent almost double, his back against the wall, gazing around him in impotent rage. The sight of the room excited him to such a pitch of hatred that the idea of setting the curtains alight crossed his mind, but he dismissed it; it would be childish to vent his spite on the inanimate world; and his thoughts switched off to Madame Grosgeorge. What reason had she to betray him? Why had her voice been so bitter and her face so pale when she spoke to him of Angèle? Perhaps she was insane and had a mania for harming people and making them suffer; she had amused herself by exciting false hopes in him, only

to give him up to the police afterward. He ought
to have guessed the instincts that possessed her the
day he had seen her strike her son with such passionate calm.

The thought struck him again that he might
break the door down, and he tried to smash a panel
by hurling his shoulder against it, but it was stoutly
built and he made no impression upon it.

He felt that if he remained another quarter of an
hour in this room he would jump out of the window,
not so much in order to escape, as to put a definite
end to his sufferings. From where he stood the
ground seemed quite close, but this was only an illusion: as soon as he approached the window and
leaned out there was a twenty-five-foot drop to defy
him to escape without killing himself.

However, in order to assure himself once more
that all chance of escape in that quarter was impossible, he walked toward the window and stopped halfway. Some one had just gone out; it was Fernande
going on her errand; he could see her running along
the highroad toward the town, and at first he did
not recognize her; then he remembered that he had
seen her one day when she was leaving the
laundry with Angèle. This memory drew a groan
of misery from him. If he had only realized then
that happiness consisted in freedom.

He turned back to the door and drummed on the
panel with his fists. Almost at once he heard some
one coming rapidly upstairs, and backed quickly
into the room.

The key turned in the lock and Madame Gros-george came in. He was about to dash forward and escape, but her appearance took him by surprise and he hesitated; she was so pale and her eyes were so cold and steely that she seemed like a dead woman whose eyes they had forgotten to close.

"I have come to ask you something," she muttered without looking at him.

"What?"

She reached out behind her and shut the door.

"You said that you came back to Lorges because of Angèle. Do you believe that she loves you?"

He hesitated for a moment.

"Yes, I believe it."

"Your fate is being decided at this moment. Look what's happening in the garden."

He ran over to the window and leaned out. She seized the opportunity to double-lock the door, and before he could have prevented her she crossed the room and threw the key out of the window. A cry broke from him.

"What have you done?"

"You see what I've done. I've thrown the key of this door out of the window. Toward midday my husband will come in. I will call him and he will bring me back the key and open the door. So that he shall not see you, you will hide in the dressing-room, and while we are at lunch you will go away."

"Why did you throw the key out of the window?"

She turned her eyes toward him.

"Angèle knows that you are here. You have no

cause for anxiety since you say that she loves you. But if the police do come to arrest you, it is she who will have informed them. Then you will have proof that she detests you."

He stood quite still, looking at Madame Grosgeorge, while he tried to read in her drawn features the full meaning of the words he had just heard.

"If they arrest me . . . " he said, roughly. "But, madame, it's impossible. You're not going to betray me."

"Who said I was? If anyone betrays you, it will be Angèle."

"How does she know I am here?"

"I sent word to her."

"Why?"

"That doesn't concern you."

"Madame, let me go. Call some one to bring you the key."

"So you are afraid this woman will betray you? I thought she loved you so much?"

"I want to leave this room. If you don't call I'll break the door down."

"Then I shall scream and have you arrested. There are two men in the house, the gardener and the footman. And, anyway, I'm not afraid. You can try the door if you like; it's pretty solid."

He stamped on the floor and shouted:

"And suppose I killed you? Suppose I strangled you."

Her shoulders moved as though a shudder passed

through her, but she did not take her eyes from this man suddenly drunk with fury.

"I'm not afraid of you," she said, sitting down, for her knees had grown weak. "Do you think I would have come here if I had been afraid of you?"

"Be careful, madame. I swear that if they come to arrest me I will kill you first."

"We'll see about that. I'm not afraid of death."

She spoke so calmly that he was amazed, and perhaps in this hour of anxiety that would have been unbearable to any other woman, she felt more at peace than she had ever felt before. After a few seconds, during which she seemed to be making an effort to gather her strength together, she rose and crossed the room to a writing-desk in one corner of the room and sat down at it. He followed her with his eyes and saw her open one of the drawers.

"What are you doing?" he asked.

"I am looking for a pen to write a letter with," she answered, shutting the drawer.

"To whom?"

"To the first person who finds it."

He came behind her and placed his hand on the back of her chair.

"You are going to lean out of the window and call a servant," he said, menacingly. "This door must be open in five minutes. Get up."

"No."

"I warn you that your life is in danger."

"A lot better off you'll be when you've killed me," she said, without moving. "Dead, I can do nothing for you. Alive, I can order the door to be opened, if I choose to."

"Have mercy on me, madame. I implore you to call some one."

"Let me write my letter."

"But what have I done to you? Why do you hate me?"

She made no reply.

"Why do you hate me?" he asked again.

"That is my business."

"If I've offended you it has been unintentional. Why have you shut me in here?"

"I tell you to let me write."

"Don't you know that my life is in danger, if I am taken?"

She made no reply. He threw himself at her feet:

"I beg of you, madame. Think of the remorse you will have later if I'm ever condemned to death. You don't want to see me on the gallows . . . "

Her face was so expressionless that he doubted if his words had even been heard, and leaping up he cried:

"I ought to have known that you would betray me. You wouldn't turn a hair if your own son's head was being cut off. You are not a woman, you are a monster, and you have only come here to laugh at my agony. You hate me, but your hatred is nothing compared to the hatred I feel for you at this moment. Do you understand me? I hope that you never have another hour of peace upon this earth, and that one day you may suffer as I am suffering now."

Still she did not move. He looked at her for a moment, half tempted to raise his hand against her, but he did not dare; there was too much power in her immobility. Then in a fury he hurled himself at the door, in an effort to break it down.

Madame Grosgeorge seemed to have waited for this moment to reopen the drawer and to take from it, not a pen, but a little steel and mother-of-pearl revolver which she slipped into her belt, close to her watch, which was fastened round her neck by a long chain.

A voice calling from the garden made them both start. It was Fernande, and she was calling to Guéret. He ran to the window. Madame Grosgeorge got up.

"Run away quickly!" repeated Fernande. "The police know you are here. They are coming to arrest you."

In his agony he turned back to Madame Grosgeorge.

"You see, she didn't love you, after all," she said simply.

He saw her move to the other end of the room, as though walking in her sleep, and he leaned out of the window again.

"The key!" he cried to the child. "Pick up the key and bring it to me. It's there, in the pathway. Look for it, on . . . "

He heard a report behind him. At first he did not understand, and for the space of a second he stared at the child who was speeding out of the garden; then he leaped back into the room as though a hand had seized him by the collar.

Madame Grosgeorge was kneeling on the carpet, bent double, and with her arm folded beneath her. In the groans that came from her lips he caught the words: "Finish me off. I don't want to live any more."

Chapter Sixteen

"WHAT are they saying, Fernande? They're all talking at once. I'm going out on the landing for a moment to listen. Give me my petticoat."

The child placed her hand on Angèle's arm.

"Do be quiet," she begged. "Madame Londe is only telling the same story over again. It's cold on the stairs and you are soaking in perspiration. Cover yourself up, Angèle."

But the young woman resisted Fernande's efforts to compel her to lie down; she was sitting up in bed, almost naked, heedless of the icy temperature of the room.

"If you don't want me to get up," she went on, eagerly, "go downstairs and open the door of the restaurant a little, so that I can hear what they are saying."

"Will you cover yourself up?"

In order to make the child obey her more quickly, Angèle let herself fall back on the bed, and gathered the bedclothes over her chest; but as soon as Fernande had left the room she threw them off again, gasping with fever. Sweat was running down her limbs, and suddenly, irritated by the moisture which stuck her nightdress to her flesh, Angèle seized a handkerchief and rubbed her neck, shoulders, and body with it.

After a moment she heard Fernande, who had reached the bottom of the staircase, cautiously open the dining-room door and, in the way water comes through the sluices of a lock-gate, the sound of shrill voices flowed up toward the young woman.

"I shall never believe that he didn't want to kill her," Madame Couze was saying.

"But she would have said so," retorted Madame Koppé, the draper.

"Of course she would," said Madame Londe, whose *rôle* always seemed to be to calm Madame Couze's fears and to prevent her from spreading panic. "Do you imagine she would have been afraid to say to the police: 'This man has just shot me in the body,' since he was arrested, anyhow . . . ?"

"Then," resumed the Grosgeorges' cook, obstinately, "why doesn't she say that she wanted to kill herself?"

"She doesn't want to admit it," replied Madame Londe, to whom the question was addressed and who was clearly embarrassed by it.

There was a very short silence which indicated the respect with which the restaurant proprietress's explanation was received. However, Madame Couze returned to the attack.

"And why doesn't she want to?" she asked.

"Yes, why?" repeated Madame Pellatane, the butcher's wife, an insolent woman whom Madame

Londe only tolerated because she always owed her money.

"I happen to know why," said the proprietress.

She hesitated long enough to invent something in her poor old head, tired out by the excitement of the day.

"The man," she said at last, struck by a sudden inspiration, "made an attempt on Madame Grosgeorge's honor."

A shrill laugh greeted this remark, and it was obvious that neither Madame Couze nor Madame Pellatane believed in this interpretation of the drama; but Madame Londe's irritated voice rose again at once.

"What are you laughing about?" she asked. "I know what I'm talking about. See how he behaved toward Angèle."

When she heard these words, Angèle seized the child's hand in her own.

"Why are they talking about me?" she asked. "What are they saying, Fernande?"

"I don't know. Would you like me to go and shut the door now?"

"Yes. No. I want to hear a little more. They talk so loud it's difficult to understand."

It was, indeed, very difficult to understand, as the ladies had all begun to talk again at the same time; they were not talking of Angèle now, but of Madame Grosgeorge's condition.

"I tell you she will recover," shouted Madame Koppé to the cook.

"With a bullet in the body? Ha-ha!"

"The bullet is being taken out," cried Madame Londe in exasperation, as if it was herself that Madame Couze was sending into the next world. "You're only talking nonsense. If things don't turn out as badly as possible at once, you are always furious."

Madame Couze was sitting near the door which Fernande had opened, and her only reply was to sneeze violently.

"There is a draught here," she groaned. "I've caught a cold."

"Be careful," said Madame Londe, ferociously, only too glad to instill fear into the heart of this craven woman. "One begins by sneezing, and at the end of the week one goes to church feet foremost."

Some one got up and shut the door.

"Fernande," asked Angèle, "why can't I hear any more?"

"Why, they've shut the door! Madame Couze sneezed because there was a draught. Didn't you hear what she said?"

Angèle did not answer. Her thoughts, sharpened by her fever, were wandering off into other channels. Night had fallen an hour before, and the only light in the room came from the street lamps outside, and that so faintly that one could only just make out the bedclothes.

"Fernande," said the young woman, suddenly, "leave me alone now. I want to go to sleep."

This was not true; she could not sleep, there was

too much roaring in her ears, there were too many stars in the darkness, for sleep to be able to close her eyes, but she wanted to be alone so that she could get up and dress. The idea that had slowly been maturing in her brain ever since nightfall had at last taken such a hold on it that it had overpowered her will. A strange existence began for her, an existence which partook neither of the state of wakefulness nor of that of dreams, but seemed to borrow certain qualities from each, confusing them. Everything in the universe she had known changed its meaning; the impossible became true and time no longer exercised its tyranny over human actions.

She was alone now, and searched gropingly for her clothes, which she slowly put on. The hour was at hand. She must not linger any more, but must take advantage of this short moment of liberty to leave her room and the house and reach the road. She would go through the kitchen, and if anyone saw her and questioned her she would say that she was quite well and that the camomile tea she had been made to drink a little while before had cured her. This and many other things she repeated to herself as she stumbled among the furniture in her room, like a woman who has been drinking and cannot find the door.

This awful weakness which compelled her to lean against the wall astonished her all the more because she now felt a great need of activity, whereas a little while ago she had felt quite worn out, and even to breathe had demanded an effort on her part. She would have liked to run, to jump down the stairs two steps at a time, as she used to do as a child.

There was no one in the kitchen but a waiter, who was reading a newspaper and smoking; he looked at her and made as if to rise, but she passed by him quickly, sickened by the smell and the heat of the kitchen, and went out.

As she closed the door behind her she almost fell on the doorstep; the icy blast struck her in the face and seemed to enter her through her parted lips; she gasped, dizzily thrusting out her hands as though to seize something to support her.

She wandered from one side of the deserted streets to the other with a tottering step that led her on and on until she reached the highroad. This was where she was making for, obeying that mysterious command which had been dinning in her brain for the last few hours. If happiness existed anywhere, she must seek it on that road and not in the town she had left forever. After months of anguish she was happy at last. She was going away; she would never see Madame Londe again, nor her odious customers who made her suffer. Some one was waiting for her on the highroad; some one had promised to wait. The night was so dark that it could not be far from seven o'clock, and she had been told seven o'clock, between the fourth and fifth street lamps, counting from the footbridge. She was there.

The milkman brought her back in his cart. She had almost been trampled on by his horse, for she was lying motionless on the ground when he found her. Madame Londe's first care was to put her to bed and to light a little log fire in her room. It was the first time a fire had ever been lit in that room, but it did not really matter whether Madame Londe took all this trouble or not.

It did not matter whether it was light or dark in the room and whether the heart of man was hard or charitable. The world was fading away like an evil dream; all that remained of life was the pain which still racked her body, but even that became fainter as the last bonds snapped. In the extreme confusion in which all earthly things appeared to this woman, the sound of human words reached her faintly, but she no longer understood what they meant. Her eyes were already fixed on the vision which the dead contemplate for all eternity.

THE END.

THE HOUSE OF HARPER

NEW YORK
Publishers of BOOKS and of
HARPER'S MAGAZINE
Established 1817

The Harper Prize Novel Contest

IT was in 1922 that Harper & Brothers inaugurated their Prize Novel Contest, a competition in which motion picture, dramatic and serial rights, which frequently have so much bearing on other contests, play no part. It is the conviction of the judges and of Harper's that this freedom from influences that tend to standardize and too greatly hamper an author's individuality in developing a novel is responsible in large measure for the selection of four Harper Prize Novels of such distinguished literary quality. The public and the booksellers alike have come to look upon the Harper Prize as a badge of unusual quality, a guarantee amply sustained in the case of each of the Harper Prize Novels by the literary critics of the country and by sales running to the hundred thousand mark and beyond.

The Harper Prize Novel for 1929-30 is THE DARK JOURNEY, by Julian Green, whose earlier novel, THE CLOSED GARDEN, won the Femina-Bookman Prize in Europe for the most distinguished novel of the year, was crowned by the French Academy, and was selected by the Book-of-the-Month Club for May, 1928. This new novel is a dramatic story of life in a French provincial town, a work of such distinction that it has drawn from Arnold Bennett the comment: "The author is developing, and 'The Dark Journey' is his best yet. The originality of the author's mind is more freely disengaged in this book than in previous ones. And the sombre power of the tragedy is simply tremendous. Mr. Green is assuredly of the lineage of great novelists."

THE GRANDMOTHERS, by Glenway Wescott, the 1927-28 Prize winner, placed Mr. Wescott's name in the forefront of younger American writers.

The Harper Prize Novel Contest

Anne Parrish won the Prize in 1925-26 with THE PERENNIAL BACHELOR, a novel which was hailed by critics and readers alike.

THE ABLE MCLAUGHLINS, by Margaret Wilson, won not only the first Harper Prize Novel Contest, but the Pulitzer Prize as well, setting a high mark for all succeeding Prize Novels.

The prestige of the Harper Prize is obviously justly deserved. The judges have been writers and critics of international distinction; they cast their votes without knowing who the authors are (all names are removed from manuscripts until after the Prize is awarded); and they reach their decision without consultation among themselves or with the publishers.

The judges of the present Contest were CARL VAN DOREN, author of "The American Novel"; ELLEN GLASGOW, author of "Barren Ground," etc., and GRANT OVERTON, formerly fiction editor of "Collier's" and author of "The Women Who Make Our Novels" and "The Philosophy of Fiction."

Judges in the previous Contests have included JOHN ERSKINE, author of "Galahad," "The Private Life of Helen of Troy," *Professor of English Literature, Columbia University;* HENRY SEIDEL CANBY, Editor of "The Saturday Review of Literature"; JESSE LYNCH WILLIAMS, former President, Authors' League of America, author of "Why Marry," etc.; and STUART P. SHERMAN, late Editor of "Books," and former *Professor of English Literature, University of Illinois.*

The next Harper Prize Novel Contest will be announced in 1930. Information as to terms will be sent by the publishers on request.